HAW]

by

Amanda Lawless

Copyright © 2013 by Amanda Lawless

Acknowledgements

I'd like to take a brief moment to thank the readers out there. It's only because of all of you that we authors are able to do what we love for a living. This story is dedicated to all the dreamers and doers who make this world a wonderful place. Always follow your heart and never give up hope.

I hope you enjoy Ellie and Trent's story as much as I loved writing it.

Special Thanks

Editor: Ashlee Whitting

Copy Editor: Connie Evans

Beta Readers: Barbara Rahway, Jessica Kline, Kelly Allsop

Formatting: Carl Jenks

Table of Contents

Chapter One

Ellie

"Is that really necessary?" I ask, nodding at the recording device that's resting on the table among the coffee cups and condiments.

The eager young reporter looks at me through his thick lenses, instantly apologetic. "I'm so sorry Miss Sims," he says, snatching up the device, "I didn't mean to make you at all uncomfortable, I—"

"It's OK," I say with a reassuring smile, "I was just asking. You really don't need to be nervous around me, Teddy."

"You...know who I am?" he asks, his eyes bugging wide.

"Of course," I tell him, leaning my elbows on the oilcloth tabletop, "Your brother Gary was in my year at Barton. You must be a senior now, right?"

"Th-that's right," Teddy says rapturously.

"I was the editor of the *Barton Bugle* when I was a senior too," I say, "I loved it. After jazz band, writing for the school newspaper was probably my favorite part of high school."

"You were the best editor the *Bugle's* ever had," Teddy says eagerly, "Your editorial about gender stereotypes in elective classes is legendary."

"Ah, shucks," I smile, bringing the coffee cup to my lips, "You're too kind."

"Thank you for agreeing to this interview, Miss Sims," Teddy says, leaning back in the well worn booth, "This is quite the exclusive."

"You can call me Ellie, you know. And I'm glad that everyone thinks this is such a big deal. The hometown support is nice, I have to say."

"Well, it is a big deal!" Teddy says, "You were chosen out of millions of up-and-coming bands to play at the Hawk and Dove festival. Haven't you seen the lineup? Some of the most famous musicians in the world will be there this year, and you'll be right there with them."

"Not just me," I correct him, "My partner in crime will be there too."

"Of course," Teddy says, scribbling into his notebook, "Your duo is called Ellie & Mitch—I guess that Mitch is a pretty important component!"

"Very," I laugh, running my fingers through my short blonde bob, "I've got the pipes, but Mitch takes care of most of the music. He's amazing, actually. He plays the guitar, the ukulele, the mandolin, the dulcimer...I could keep going, but we leave for Kansas tomorrow, and it would take me all night to sing his praises."

"And you two met at Barton High, right?" Teddy asks, his slight frame leaning forward to catch my every word.

"That's right," I say.

"And your relationship with Mitch is...?"

"Very dear to me," I say simply. I can see that Teddy is a little let down by my vague answer, but I'd rather not offer up my personal life as gossip fodder for the bored teenagers of my hometown. The little East Coast town of Barton can be rather dull at times, a fact I knew well enough from my own childhood and adolescence.

I'm home again for the summer after wrapping up my second year at the Berklee School of Music in Boston. Mitch is going to Berklee with me, thank god—it would have been tough getting to know a new city without a familiar face close by. Mitch and I have been buddies since we met in High School, and now, with our little band gaining some traction in the music scene, we're pretty much inseparable. Tall, somber Mitch has always carried a torch for me, though we've never spoken about it frankly. If we go our entire lives without addressing that particular elephant in the room, I'll die a happy woman. I love Mitch like a brother, but I don't think that's what he'd be hoping to hear. We work perfectly together as a musical duo, and I don't want anything to ruin that. Especially now that the world is finally starting to notice us.

"You two want some more coffee?" says Vera, the buxom queen of this particular eating establishment. I've known this endlessly cheerful woman my entire life, and being back in her company after a year away at school is a balm for my homesick heart.

"I'd love another cup," I say, offering my mug.

"Me too," Teddy says, clamoring to follow my lead.

"You're a lucky man, Teddy," Vera says as she pours the coffee, "This girl's about to be the most famous person ever to come out of Barton. She'll be too busy posing for *Rolling Stone* to give us the time of day."

"That's just ridiculous. On about three counts!" I exclaim, "First of all, the entire town is making a way bigger deal out of this contest than is reasonable. And even if Mitch and I were about to become overnight celebrities, you know full well that we'd still be back here at Vera's on our days off."

"Maybe you would," Vera says, "But I don't know about Mitchell. He's never been much for community, has he?"

"He's just private," I say, "You can't blame him for not wanting to be the center of attention in this town. You all are wonderfully supportive, but it doesn't exactly add to our 'hipster cool' factor, does it?"

"I don't give a rat's ass about your hippy dippy cool factor," Vera sniffs, "I'm hanging a big old picture of the two of you front and center in this diner whether you like it or not. We're all so proud of you kids, Ellie."

"Thanks Vera," I smile, "I hope you know we appreciate it, even if Mitch can be a little..."

"Stiff?" Teddy suggests, "Withdrawn? Broody?"

"I was going to say quiet," I say, a bit archly, "But thank you, Teddy."

The young man blushes brilliantly and scribbles away at his notebook as Vera laughs and bounces away. It feels a little silly to be giving an exclusive interview to my high school newspaper—it's like I'm playacting at being a musician, rather than actually living it. But I suppose that's how everyone feels right before they have their first big break into the business.

Stop that, I think to myself for the umpteenth time. I can't think of the Hawk and Dove festival as anything but an awesome opportunity for Ellie & Mitch. Sure, we won the New Voices contest, but that doesn't mean we're going to be strolling down Easy Street from here on out. We're still going to have to work our asses off to make it as a band, and it won't do to forget that. Still...I can't help but think that big things are going to happen once we make it to Kansas.

At first, Mitch didn't even want to enter the contest with me. We've been playing music as a duo for a couple of years, and our sound is pretty offbeat. The musicians influencing us are all over the map—from Joni Mitchell to Joanna Newsom, from Johnny Cash to Eddie Vedder, and everything in between. We're as far away from commercial rock and roll as it gets, a fact that Mitch is extremely proud of. He nearly spat when I mentioned playing at the Hawk and Dove Festival, to him it would be selling out.

It took me the better part of a month to convince him otherwise...or at least to convince him to come along with me. I know he'll be happy once we get there, but I'm not exactly looking forward to two days in the car with him griping all the way. I push the thought out of my mind and bring my attention back to Teddy, who I only now realize has been talking for about two minutes.

"Sorry," I say, "Could you start over? I'm a little spacey today."

"Oh," Teddy says, "I was just wondering what you're most excited about, when it comes to the festival. Have you ever been before?"

"Every year since I was sixteen!" I say happily, "Usually with my older sister Kate. But she's got a big girl job now, so this year it's just me and Mitch."

"What keeps bringing you back to the festival, year after year?" Teddy asks.

"I don't even know where to begin," I say, "It's five straight days of nothing but music, art, food, booze...and excellent company. There are no distractions, there's nothing to worry about. The community there is so enthusiastic, and welcoming, not at all what you'd expect. It's probably my favorite place on earth, that little field in Kansas."

"A lot of drugs too, right?" Teddy smiles.

"I plead the fifth," I wink, "But honestly, that's not the main attraction for me. I just love driving down there with the windows open, pitching my tent, and enjoying the atmosphere."

"It's going to be pretty different for you this year, though!" Teddy says.

"That's true," I laugh, "Though I don't think anyone's going to make a big deal out of us. We're playing on the teeny tiny stage they save for the no-namers. Don't get me wrong, I'm so grateful to have been chosen at all, but we're still a pretty new act, you know? Ellie & Mitch is a toddler compared to some of the other bands that will be there."

"Is there anyone you're really excited to see?" Teddy asks.

"Oh, yeah," I say excitedly, "The coolest thing about the festival is how many different kinds of musicians and artists show up. I'm definitely pumped for some of the folk groups and jam bands. That's more my speed than anything else."

"Not so much the headliners?" Teddy asks.

"To be honest, I'm not even sure who they are this year," I say, "Usually they get some famous rapper or classic rock star to show up. That's cool and all, but I'd kind of rather listen to someone who's contributing to the present musical moment, you know?"

"I don't know," Teddy says, "The lineup's really stacked this year. The Exes and Ohs are going to be there, and The Forward Facing. They even managed to get Trent Parker this year."

"Pretty impressive," I admit, "But my heart belongs to the littler guys, I guess."

"Fair enough," Teddy says, "Is there anything else you'd like to say to the readers of the *Barton Bugle*?"

"Jeez, Teddy, I have no idea," I say, popping the last of my fries into my mouth, "It's not like I have anything figured out that's worth passing on to posterity. I'm just making it up as I go along, you know?"

"But that's what's so cool," Teddy presses, "It's not like anyone who's a senior in high school now has a straight shot at an easy life. We're all fighting tooth and nail to get into college, but once you get in, they just spit you out with a bunch of debt and no job opportunities. We're all scared shitless, you know? So to see you doing what you love...it's kind of inspiring, is all. I hope you don't think that's super weird."

"Not at all," I smile, "Thank you, Teddy."

"Thank you for the story," he says, "They're going to give me a gold medal on Monday when I say that I snagged some time with you."

"Anything for the *Bugle*," I say, pulling myself up out of the booth. Teddy follows me out of the restaurant, with Vera wavering feverishly as we leave. There's nothing like coming home to get your ego inflated like a damn hot air balloon. I can't help but worry that all this fuss everyone's making is going to get my hopes up before the festival. To everyone in Barton, Mitch and I are already famous, but to everyone at Hawk and Dove, we're just going to be another pair of hopeful kids.

I drive home in my twenty-year-old sedan, nostalgia pulling insistently on my heartstrings. Even though I'm back home in Barton, I'm still feeling wistful. Even though these are the exact streets I used to drive on, even though nothing has changed about the town itself, I feel like I don't quite belong here anymore. Every time I come home from school, it's like I've outgrown the space I used to take up here when I was younger. I can't ever quite be the person I was when I left. I know that it's normal, that everyone has these growing pains, these bittersweet metamorphoses, but that doesn't make it any easier.

Shaking off the insistent, cloying touch of heartache, I swing into the driveway. Our little Victorian desperately needs a paint job, and there's some clutter on the front porch that always seems to reappear, no matter how many times we clear it. My mom bought this house when Kate was ten and I was six. Before that, we lived in a big old pre-fab suburban monstrosity across town. That was when my dad still lived with us. He was a Wall Street type back then, a real captain of industry. He and my mom met in New York City back in the eighties. She was a waitress, trying to be an actress, and he wandered into her restaurant one night and wouldn't leave until she agreed to go on a date with him.

Their early years together sound like a fairy tale. A grungy fairy tale, but all the same. They shared a little studio on the Lower East Side while he worked up the power chain in his firm. She did weird, awesomely experimental off-off Broadway plays and spent the days exploring the markets of Chinatown. They were happy together, when they were poor. But then Dad started to earn a little money, and decided that he wanted to get married and make an honest woman of Mom. She agreed, not realizing what she was getting herself into. No sooner was the ink dry on the marriage license than Dad moved them out to the suburbs and knocked her up with Kate.

The promotions came rolling in for good old Dad, and by the time I was born, he was bringing home buckets of money. As his bank account grew, so did his penchant for the "finer" things in life. But to him, those finer things were booze, coke, and hookers. He bought an apartment in the city, in which he entertained his vices in excess. For some reason when I was born things only got worse. This fact makes me feel unreasonably guilty.

Soon, his bad habits started catching up with him, and my mom did the only thing she could. One weekend, while he was off paying for love and whole lot of other drugs, she had divorce papers drawn up and made an offer on a house for us girls. Dad didn't even seem to notice that he'd been divorced when he got back. Probably, he was happy to be rid of us. Joint custody was never a question. He sold the house once we were gone and holed up in his New York bachelor pad.

The last we heard, he'd been fired from his big, cushy job. And he definitely wasn't going through any much-needed twelve-step plan, or we would have heard about it. He certainly has a few things to apologize for, not that he necessarily deserves forgiveness.

Mom pokes her head out the front door as I step out of my car. She's got a calico scarf wrapped around her blonde curls, and there are streaks of yellow paint all over her arms. I can't help but grin back at her as I make my way up the front walk.

"What's today's project?" I ask, taking the steps two at a time.

"The kitchen!" she says happily, "I'm making it sunnier."

"I thought you'd be building sets or something," I say, giving her a kiss on the cheek and earning myself a paint splotch in the process.

"Not this time," she says, bounding back toward the kitchen. It was a fair guess, though. Mom's been the drama teacher at Barton Elementary for over a decade. She gets pretty enthusiastic about the yearly musical, and has always been the type to take her work home with her. I can't even count the times I'd come home as a teenager to find a bunch of twelve-year-olds rehearsing *Guys and Dolls* in my bedroom. It wasn't always the most welcome thing in the world, but it's more than a little endearing to look back on, now.

"Is Kate home?" I ask my mom, trailing her into the kitchen.

"She's just about to head out," Mom tells me, snatching up her paint roller. The kitchen is in utter disarray—just the way Mom likes it.

As if on cue, my older sister comes hustling down the stairs. "Do we have anything to eat?" she asks, pulling her hair into a tight knot. Her baby blue scrubs are a little rumpled, and her eyes are still half-full of sleep. As a night nurse, Kate is constantly bouncing back and forth between Full-Throttle energy drinks and coma-like slumber. She's saving up for a place of her own, and the night shifts at the hospital pay a little better. But even so, I can't imagine doing what she does. I know that music is important to people, but this girl literally saves lives every day. She should be the one with the story in the newspaper, not me.

"There's some quinoa in the fridge," Mom says, scrutinizing the wall.

"The perfect portable snack," Kate says, rolling her eyes, "I'll stop somewhere along the way."

"Have a good shift," I tell her.

"You're not leaving until the morning, right?" she asks, wrapping me up in a quick hug.

"That's right," I say, "You know I wouldn't leave without saying goodbye!"

"I don't know," she sniffs, "Now that you're a big, famous musician, who's to say if you still have time for the little people?"

"Not you too," I groan.

"I'm kidding," she grins, making tracks, "I'm just proud of my little sissy-poo!"

"Yeah, yeah," I grumble good-naturedly, "Get lost, weirdo."

Kate lets the front door slam shut behind her, and we hear her second hand car rattle to life and drive off into the distance. As I watch my mom's emphatic, disorganized progress around the room, a powerful stab of sadness shoots through me. In no time, Kate will have enough of a cushion to find a place of her own. And I certainly don't mean to move home once I graduate from Berklee. Thinking of her alone in this house brings stinging tears to my eyes, tears I blink away in a hurry lest she see. The three of us girls are kind of like old war buddies. We survived the utter force of destruction that was my father and made a new life for ourselves in this little nest. It was terrifying, starting over without Dad, but we made it through, stronger for the struggle.

"Whoa!" Mom cries, as I rush forward and wrap my arms around her middle, "What's the deal, kiddo?"

"I'm just going to miss you," I say softly.

"You'll be gone for a week," she says, "I'm sure you'll manage to live without me."

I let out a little laugh and pull away from her, my skin dappled with her yellow paint. I shouldn't worry so much about her—Mom is nothing if not unflappable. I turn on my heel and head up to my old bedroom to pack.

The same old posters that I put up in high school still cling to the cluttered walls of my room. I haven't changed a thing about this space since I went away to college. There's something comforting about knowing that this little shrine to the way my life used to be still exists somewhere in the world. When I'm away in

Boston, stressing out about a vocal performance, or some insane exam, or some one night stand gone stale, I can remember that my poster of Carly Simon is right where I left it. It makes me feel a little better, every time.

I sink down onto my faded quilt and take a deep breath. My every nerve is buzzing in anticipation of this trip. Tomorrow, bright and early, I'll go collect Mitch from his parents' picket-fenced shrine to normalcy. We'll head south, all the way down to Kansas. I've already resolved to stop at as many oddities and pit stops along the way as possible, much to Mitch's inevitable chagrin. I can't help it—I love the bizarre, kitschy nooks of this country. That's half the reason I love trucking down to the festival every year. Every time, the whole thing becomes a little more familiar. I start to recognize other regulars, truck stops, "natural wonders". Only this year, I'll get to be one of the chosen ones. For a few beautiful hours, I'll be the one singing into the heavy summer air, listening to my music float up into the clear, starry sky and out over the country.

Humming happily through a new melody that's been stuck on my mind of late, I rummage under the bed for my luggage. The sudden ringing of my cell phone startles me, and I smack my head roughly against the underbelly of the bed. Yelling out a string of creative curses, I pull myself back into the open and fumble through my purse. Mitch's name is blaring across the screen of my phone. Even his ring tone sounds moody.

"Yes?" I say, answering the call.

"Have you seen it?" he demands angrily.

"Seen what?" I ask, "Mitch, what are you—?"

"Turn on a computer," he growls. I hurry across the room to my desk and tap idly at the keys of my laptop. "Type our band's name into the search engine," he tells me. I do so, and wait for the results to load. The first hit blinks onto my screen, and I feel my jaw drop a full foot.

"Exclusive interview with Ellie & Mitch's front woman, Eleanor Jackson," I read, "What the hell is this? That's a major music blog, isn't it? I haven't given any interviews to them."

"Click through to the article," Mitch demands. I follow his orders and let my eyes travel down to the byline of the piece.

"By Theodore Farmer," I groan, "That twerp Teddy sold me up the river! God, I was doing him such a favor, too! The most exciting thing the *Barton Bugle* ever gets to write about is parking meters and the occasional teacher getting fired for smoking too much weed."

"This isn't funny, Ellie," Mitch says, his voice raking harshly across the line, "He's got you saying all kinds of ridiculous shit in this thing. Did you really say you like the Hawk and Dove fest for the drugs?"

"What?" I cry, "Of course not. Mitch, he's just cashing in on his one degree of separation moment. No one's going to believe any of it. Hell, no one will even read it, probably. No one knows who we are outside of Barton and Berklee."

"Really?" Mitch says dryly, "Maybe it looks like that right now, but I've been checking our website's analytics this afternoon. Our page views have gone through the roof. Our band email is getting flooded. Ellie, this is exactly the kind of attention we don't want."

"I thought all press was good press," I say quietly.

"False," Mitch says, "If things keep up like this, we'll never be respected as real musicians. We'll just be another couple of hipster assholes getting high and mumbling nonsense. You're too good for that, Ellie. We're too good for that."

"I made a mistake, Mitch" I say, "I'm not exactly used to this kind of thing. Ever since we won this contest..."

"We could still back out," he offers.

"No," I say firmly, "We're leaving for Kansas tomorrow. We can stop by Teddy's house and egg it or something."

"Yeah. Maybe he'll write an article about how we're vandals *and* junkies," Mitch sighs, "I'm going to bed. Get some rest, would you?"

"You too," I tell him. The line clicks off, and I toss the phone not-too-gently across the room.

I know I shouldn't give a crap about some dumb high school kid trying to get noticed on the Web, but this whole thing makes my skin crawl. And I hate that Mitch is trying to make me feel reckless and irresponsible over it. I know he's trying to maintain his position of power within our little duo—he's always been the one to make the decisions, to guide our direction. When it comes to our music, he demands control...maybe because he doesn't have any when it comes to our relationship.

With a heavy sigh that feels very appropriate for my teenage bedroom, I begin to toss things into my worn leather suitcase. I summon up the excitement that's been building inside of me as the trip looms ahead. Whatever happens at the festival, our being invited to play is still a huge deal. But suddenly, and not for the first time, I wonder if going along with Mitch is the best thing for me. He's always been my music partner by default, and I love what we do together, but his attitude is dragging me down.

I let my eyes skirt across the room to my guitar case. I only have the most basic knowledge of the instrument—some chords and strumming patterns, no plucking or anything fancy. Mitch is the instrument guy, after all. I unfold my long legs beneath me and ease the case open, taking my starter acoustic out into the open. I settle down onto my quilt, crossing my legs and draping my arms over the body of the guitar. I hold it to me like I might a new lover—tentatively, tenderly.

I arrange my fingers into a simple G chord and strum. The sound reverberates around my little room, and I add another chord to the pattern. I move between them, adding others when the mood strikes. The new melody begins to sing itself through me, weaving through the assortment of chords. With my voice, I can bring new complexity to the impromptu song, offsetting the basic chords. An illicit little shudder runs through me as I let my voice slide all through my range—making music without Mitch feels a little bit like cheating.

My hands fall still, happy with the memory of movement. I can't quite shake the lingering tension of knowing that Mitch is angry with me, but I'm not going to let it ruin my last night at home before we set out. I place my guitar reverently down on my bed and head back toward the kitchen. Mom is still hard at work coating the wall with sunny yellow. I cross to the fridge and pull out a couple of cold beers.

"Why don't you take a break?" I suggest, waving the drinks in front of her.

She smiles, her forehead beaded with sweat. "Good idea," she says, letting her roller fall back into the tray. We trek through the front hallway and step out into the early evening air. A few rusty lawn chairs are arranged around the little deck, and we settle into them in unison. I hand her a beer and clink my bottle against hers.

"To your trip," she suggests, taking a sip.

"Sure," I say, following suit.

"What is it?" Mom asks, her brow furrowing, "You've got your serious face on."

"It's nothing," I tell her, "That dumb kid from the diner gave some information to a music blog, and I guess it's been getting attention. I've been getting attention, I mean. Now Mitch is all pissy, like he wasn't already dragging his feet with this whole thing."

"Mitch isn't excited?" Mom asks.

"Not really," I tell her, "He thinks the festival is a waste of time."

"Is that what you think?" she asks.

"Of course not!" I say.

"Well...I doubt that it's the festival he's upset about," my mom says, "You know he's been waiting for you since you two met. Waiting to be more than friends with you, that is."

"He can keep waiting," I grumble.

"People are going to ask, you know," she says, "You can't wander around with an asterisk between your names and not expect people to ask."

"We're just friends," I insist.

"That's not how it looks when you play together," she tells me, "You look like a couple of kids in love, is what you look like."

"That's just the music," I say.

"It's the music for you, and it's you for him."

"You're nuts," I tell her, and we both know I'm dodging the subject like a fast pitch aimed at my head. Kindly, she lets it drop. Almost.

"That article is just the beginning, Ellie," she says softly, "The more exposure you get, the more money that'll start to flow in. It can be overwhelming, becoming successful all at once. I don't want you getting swept up in all this attention. I don't want you to let it change how you think about yourself."

"It won't," I tell her. But I know it's not really me we're talking about. "I'm not like Dad, you know. I'm not going to turn into some monster once I get a little money. If I get a little money."

"I know it's kind of backwards," she says, "But I sort of hope you'll always be a starving musician. Money does horrible things to people."

"Well, thanks Mom," I say, rolling my eyes, "I'll try and not be very marketable."

"Just scowl at Mitch a lot onstage," she suggests, "That'll throw people off."

"I might not be able to help it, if he keeps up his whining," I tell her.

"I bet things will be OK when you get down there."

"Yeah...I bet."

We lapse into silence, staring out toward the hilly horizon, each wondering what the next week might hold.

Chapter Two

Trent

Something heavy smashes against the rickety door separating the tiny kitchen from the rest of the tour bus. Tipsy cheers rise up from the main cabin—my band mates have started power hour without me, what a bunch of dicks. And I'm stuck back here giving my ten thousandth interview to some first-time music journalist who hasn't gone ten words without saying "um" since she's arrived. At least she's got a nice rack.

"What was that?" squeaks the mousy girl sitting across from me.

I shrug, turning my gaze away from her. "Just the usual," I say, "Probably a bottle of tequila. We have plenty of those to spare."

"Is your band always this...um...destructive?" she asks.

I scoff and turn back to face her. She's practically trembling with nerves. Usually, that kind of thing turns me on—the feigned reluctance, wilting flower thing, but this girl does not wear it well. She actually dressed up in a power suit to come meet me. A power suit.

"My band is a force of nature," I grin, "They're as destructive as they feel like being, whenever they feel like it."

"That must make traveling like this difficult," she ventures.

Another loud crash rings out from beyond the barrier. I smile, silently thanking the guys for their impeccable comedic timing. "You're assuming that we're trying to abide by anyone's rules," I say to the girl. I'm laying on the bad boy thing thick. Reporters don't know what to do with me when I'm not acting like a caricature of a rock and roller. I've long since given up on being up front with these people. Instead, I try and feed them a couple of good lines and get them on their way as quickly as possible. And I can tell that this one is starting to wear thin.

"Um. Mr. Parker," she starts.

"Trent," I say, leaning forward with my best screw-it-all smile, "You can just call me Trent."

"Um. OK, Trent," she says, her eyes widening in her already narrow face. "Why did you decide to play at the Hawk and Dove festival this year? You usually steer clear of things like this, don't you?"

"What kinds of things do you mean?" I ask, giving her a very obvious once-over. I can feel her shiver from three feet away. "You mean commercial pig sties brimming with rich hipster kids with poor taste in music and even worse taste in beer?"

"Sure, yes that." the girl says softly.

"Well, what can I say," I smile, "The money's great." Before she can leap in with a follow up, I hold up my hands and go on, "I'm kidding, of course. Look, any chance to perform is one that the guys and I are going to take. And this whole festival needs a few more hawks and a few less doves, if you ask me."

"Fewer," she mutters.

"What?"

"It's fewer doves, not less," she says, picking her chin up bravely.

"Aha," I say, "Your journalistic balls have finally dropped, I see. Care to ask me a few real questions, now that you've arrived?"

She clears her throat and begins, "You call the Hawk and Dove festival commercial, but compared to your recent behavior with regard to touring and merchandising, they're practically a charity. Wouldn't you say that you've become a commercial commodity yourself, rather than the more independent artist you once were?"

"Coming out swinging I see," I say, nodding with approval, "I like that. As it happens, Lindsay, I'm not—"

"Lucy," she interjects, "My name is Lucy."

"Right," I say, waving away her interruption, "Anyone who says that they're not hoping to make a little cash as a musician is just lying through his teeth. Their teeth? Whatever. My guys and I have hit the jackpot with our popularity. So, yeah, we're playing all the concerts we can, selling all the albums. So there are tee shirts out there with my face on them. So what? I still sleep perfectly sound at night."

"Do you think that you've lost any fans, as you've become more mainstream?" the reporter asks.

"What do you think?" I shoot back.

"I...I think..." she stutters, "Well, yes. I know that some of my friends who were fans during your early years no longer think you represent the core values of rock and roll."

"Oh, please," I groan, "What core values? Rock is not a moral code. It's the negative space of one. It's not a prescriptive movement, it's how you choose to interpret it." Lucy's scribbling down my words like a maniac, and I heave a heavy sigh. "Scratch all that out," I tell her.

"What?" she says, looking baffled, "But that was all brilliant! Why—?"

"Scratch it out," I tell her again. That was all far too heady for the blogosphere. I have to watch myself during these interviews, make sure that I'm staying on message. Jesus...In ten years, I'll have so much experience with bullshit politics, I'll be able to run for president.

The tour bus slows to a crawl in front of a rundown motel. We're dropping off Nancy Drew here and heading on into Kansas tonight. The door separating us from the rest of the bus swings open, and my manager Kelly peers in at us. She's all teeth and pep, just like she always is for the press.

"Here's your stop!" Kelly trills to the reporter.

"Right," Lucy says, standing up awkwardly, "Thank you for speaking with me, Mr. Parker."

"Trent," I remind her again, "For God's sake, just Trent."

She nods quickly and hurries away. I watch her step over broken glass and brimming ashtrays, ignoring the cat calls of my band mates. The engine revs back to life as the little lady makes her way across the parking lot and disappears into the hotel. The second that the revolving door has swallowed Lucy up, Kelly turns to me, her features crumpled into a cynical, bad-tempered scowl.

"What the hell was she wearing?" Kelly asks, "God. Do you think they sent us an intern or something? Remind me not to take any more interviews from them."

"You got it, Boss," I say, watching the hotel disappear behind us.

"Well, how did it go?" Kelly demands, crossing her skinny arms in front of her chest. I let my eyes linger on her fine body, wondering as I always do why Kelly doesn't have any effect on me. By all rights, she should leave me in a puddle every time she walks by. She's tall, lean, with a surgically perfected rack and blonde curls as far as the eye can see. Maybe I just know her too well to be attracted to her. It's a pity...I bet she'd be a good, angry fuck.

"It went fine," I tell her, "The usual. I was hoping to have a little more fun with the girl."

"That girl?" Kelly asks.

"Not that kind of fun," I tell her, "The cat with a mouse kind of fun."

"Well, preserve your energy," Kelly tells me, "We'll be there soon, and then the festivities can really kick off."

"You sound thrilled," I say sarcastically.

"Well, this is a royal waste of our time," she says, exasperated.

We've had this argument many times before.

Kelly had no interest in taking this little field trip down to Kansas, but I held out. Whatever I might have to say in front of the press, I've honestly just been craving a good stretch of days filled with nothing but booze, food, and some excellent bud. We've been touring like lunatics promoting our latest album, and because I'm technically a solo act with a backing band, I end up doing all the press crap myself. But for these seven beautiful days, I don't have to worry about any of that. No interviews, no signings—nothing but a few excellent shows and the clean country air.

I've secretly been looking forward to this for months, though my manager would rake me over the coals if I admitted that I'm dragging us all down to Kansas for the sake of my own peace of mind. Half the time it seems like Kelly's job is making me happy, the other half I just feel like a whipping boy. Anyone who says that being a good ol' fashioned rock star isn't as much of a pain in the ass as any other job is selling you something.

I never thought I'd have the chance to learn that little lesson first hand. Growing up, rock stars were pretty much on par with astronauts and circus clowns—cool guys with jobs that were totally off limits to even dream about. I was raised in a factory town in the Midwest, not exactly a hotbed for creativity. Both of my parents worked long hours, longer than nine to five on most days. So, my big brothers and I were left to entertain ourselves most of the time. For most of us, that meant watching a lot of TV and eating Hostess cakes by the dozen. But for me, it meant saving up my pocket change to buy my first acoustic guitar. I bought it at a pawn shop downtown, it didn't even have all its strings...but it was the most beautiful thing I'd ever laid eyes on.

I used to practice in the shed we kept in our back yard. That was the only place on the property I could find any peace and quiet. With three older brothers around, secrets didn't last for long. I wanted to be good and ready before they heard me play. We were all competitive with each other, and I didn't want any of them getting ideas about picking up the instrument themselves. If I was going to play guitar, I was going to be the best at it. So, I kept practicing and practicing, straight through junior high. When I got to high school, I grabbed some buddies by the scruffs of the neck and forced them to be in a band with me. We signed up for a talent night at a local pub, and I invited my family to come see me play.

A little cringe seizes me as the memory of that night unfolds in my mind's eye. I was fourteen years old, and out of my mind with nerves over playing in front of a whopping ten people. The two kids I'd forced into my band were on the verge of puking, or wetting themselves, or both. We were not what you might call a class act. But when the poor bartender who was forced into emcee duty that night called out our band's name— Raptor Flesh—we trudged onto the stage like good little soldiers.

And as the hazy stage lights hit my face, something snapped into place inside of me. I knew what to do, instinctively. I greeted the crowd, feeling a foreign confidence holding me up. I could feel exactly what the audience needed in order to get excited. I could get a laugh, I could get a moment of silence. I had control. I led our little trio through the one song we'd picked out for the occasion: Nirvana's "Lithium". (We were babies of the eighties, after all). The song moved through me, through my guitar, and out into the smoky dimness of the bar.

We raced through the ending, the other two kids struggling to keep up with me. I knew we hadn't sounded perfect, and I didn't much care. I smiled out into the bar and saw four faces looking up at me in baffled, impressed silence. My mom and four brothers rushed the stage, yelling over each other about how great I'd been. Through their embracing arms, I could see my dad checking his watch. He walked over to our happy group and announced that it was time to head home—he was missing the game already.

My parents never hit me. We were poor, but not destitute. I have all four limbs, all five senses, and a career people dream about, but it's never really felt like enough. From that night on, I've been single-minded, obsessed with my music. I practiced until my fingers bled and calloused, said "no thank you" to college so that I could focus on my next move. I left that tiny town in the middle of the country and moved to LA, along with what felt like half my generation. And that's when it all started to work out.

I was eighteen when I moved to California, fresh out of high school. I had about two thousand dollars to my name, and a good half of it was gone when I rented my first apartment. But I can still remember sitting in that empty apartment, my first night in LA, beaming into the darkness. I don't think I've ever been happier in my life. Part of me thinks that I'd be better off giving all my money away, and throwing myself back into the rat race. But there's no way to rewind the past seven years. No way to quit.

Even if I could take myself out of the spotlight—retire, or whatever—I'd never make it back to that place of happiness that I found alone in a bare apartment in LA at the ripe old age of eighteen. I'll never be able to feel that optimism, or that star struck hope again. I'm only twenty-five, but you see a lot of the world as a musician. You start to realize that people are the same everywhere, that just about anyone you think you can trust will sell you for a hundred bucks and a pack of cigarettes. Sometimes I wish I could even go back further—never play that talent show, never see the blank look on my dad's face afterward. I could work in the factory now, like him. Or tend bar. Or do any number of normal, comfortable things. I've got all the money in the world, and none of it will buy me a moment's peace.

"You OK?" Kelly asks, snapping me back to reality.

"What?" I ask, shaking my head. My father's eyes still linger, just behind mine.

"You look like you're about to start drooling," she shudders, "Did you hear anything I just said to you?"

"Not even one word," I tell her honestly.

"Typical," she sniffs. "Well, if you can bear to be interested for a moment, we're closing in on the festival grounds. Gird your loins, would you?"

She turns on her heel and walks away as I pull myself to standing. Through the window, I can see the festival looming up on the horizon. Giant staggering tents and stages rise up out of the plains like titans. Alone in the back of the bus, I let myself smile a little. Maybe this will actually be what I've been needing for so long.

"Trent!" a chorus of drunken, merry voices cries. My band mates come staggering back toward me, blundering around like rambunctious puppies. The Three Stooges look like refined gentlemen compared to the guys I play with, but I can't help but love them all. Having grown up with three older brothers, the easy friendship of guys is where I'm most comfortable. Ever since I started getting famous, women haven't approached me with the most unbiased of views. Don't get me wrong, I'm not going to pass on banging a hot chick just because her motives boil down to "he's famous", but I'm definitely not going to be friends with someone like that either.

My drummer Rodney is leading the pack, his thick, stocky body is blocking the doorway entirely. Rodger, the bassist, is clamoring behind him, all angles and long limbs. Kenny is jumping up and down like a damned Jack Russell, but his enthusiasm is contagious. Kenny's always been like a kid brother to me, and this is his first big music festival. Hell, it's our first festival as a group, too. We've been playing together for three years, ever since my record label insisted that I do more than just play solo. I was reluctant to bring on new meat at first, but needless to say, the guys have grown on me.

"Hello, Kansas!" hollers Rodney, grabbing my by the arm and pulling me into the main cabin, "Who knew the corn states could be so awesome?"

"I thought we'd never get here," Rodger moans, "Why didn't we just take the jet?"

"I wanted us to have the road trip experience!" I say, shoving him roughly, "We're getting too pansy assed, lately. It's been bottle service and private jets for our entire tour. Let's get a little dirty out there, don't be a bitch."

"What, did you bring a tent Bear Grylls?" Rodney asks, rolling his eyes.

"I did," I tell him.

The guys stare at me like I'm a lunatic.

"What? We have a fuckin tour bus, and you bring a tent?" Rodger asks.

"I told you, I want to experience the festival," I tell him, "Take a breather, you know?"

"He just doesn't want us around to scope out all the festival ass he's going to be getting," Kenny laughs.

"Sure," I say, trying to placate them, "Whatever. I'm going be enjoying myself, roughing it like a real man, while all you assholes sit around in the air conditioning like a bunch of—"

"Watch it!" Rodney says, "You don't want to be down a band when it's time for you to play, do you?"

"I don't indeed," I say, "I also don't want to be anywhere near sober. So let's drink."

The guys rally around the nearest bottle of whiskey, and I pour out four generous shots. We raise our glasses to each other and slug back the booze. I close my eyes, savoring the burn at the back of my throat. Now this is the right way to kick off a vacation. I'm about to pour us a second round when Kelly barges back into the cabin.

"Save it," she says shortly, "We need to make sure that camp is set up. I have plainclothes security guards circling the perimeter."

"Kelly, no need to call in the secret service," I say, "Would you try and ease up, a little? Change into something more...casual."

Our manager glances down at her impeccable skinny jeans and flowing white top. I've never seen this girl in anything but three inch heels. She's a few years older than I am, and she's singlehandedly responsible for finding me in LA. One night, after I finished an acoustic set at some hole in the wall bar, she approached me out of nowhere. She was just setting out as an independent manager, and wanted to take me on as one of her first clients. I agreed, thinking that it would go nowhere. But after a couple of years being in the right place at the right time, her connections and my following paid off. The way she tells it, I owe my success completely to her. I personally wouldn't go that far, but Kelly will never let me forget that she discovered me. And it's finders keepers for her.

"Let's get a move on," she chirps, beckoning for us to follow her out into the early evening air.

I step out of the tour bus and take a deep breath. Green plains stretch out for miles all around us. We're parked in the talent campsite, the whole place is a maze of tricked out busses and RVs. The five of us move around the bus, and take in the view of the festival from afar. The event is splayed out across the field like it's always belonged there. It looks like a little city that's cropped up out of the ground. I can see people milling and seething all over, tens of thousands of people.

There's one big stage in the middle of everything, rising up into the dusky sky. This is the epicenter of the entire event, where the big names play. We're playing there ourselves, along with some wrinkled classic rocker and a hip hop dude who's always making an ass out of himself in the media. Smaller stages are spread out in ripples around the main playing space, and even tinier spaces are tucked into corners and crevices all around. Hundreds of acts play every year at this festival, even if it's only on a tiny little stage that only three people end up coming to. Spread out between all the vast and various playing spaces are food trucks, people selling handmade clothes and crafts, the works. The festival's like a marketplace, a music hall, and a rave all wrapped into one.

"Would you look at all that mud?" Kelly says in my ear.

"That would be what you notice first," I say, rolling my eyes, "Why don't you try and enjoy it here, Kel? You're stuck here for five days, whether you like it or not."

"You know that I'd do anything for you Trent," she tells me, her eyes hardening, "Even if it means rolling around in the dirt all day so that you can feel like you're reconnecting with the people, or whatever the hell you call this."

"You're a doll," I tell her, breezing past.

I rush back into the bus and gather all my old camping stuff up into my arms. I haul it down onto the grass next to our tour bus as my band mates shower me with snarky remarks. There certainly aren't many tents going up in our little campsite, but what the hell do I care? Those elitist assholes don't know what they're missing. I'm glad that there aren't any photographers allowed up here, however. The last thing I want making the rounds is a picture of me acting like a boy scout. It would be terrible for business.

Finally, when I've got the tent up, I unroll a thick blanket and drape it from a pole above the entrance. I stand back and check out my work, pleased with the result. There are a few celebrity types looking at me strangely from inside their fancy busses, but I couldn't care less. I'm going to do this the old fashioned way, and they call all just kiss my—

"Hey," says a mopey voice from behind me. I peer over my shoulder and see a lanky guy, no older than twenty by my guess, glaring at me like this is the gunfight at the OK Corral. I've never seen the kid before in my life, and for a second I'm worried he's some kind of deranged fan who wandered up from the general campsite. But he's got a badge that tells me he's with one of the acts. From the looks of him, he probably plays the jaw harp in some eighteen person jam band that sings exclusively about the rays of the sun or some bullshit.

"What's up?" I ask him, "You're not looking for an autograph or something, are you?"

"Not on your life," the kid says, rolling his eyes dramatically, "I make a point of not listening to commercial drivel like the stuff you put out."

"You're too kind," I sneer, "I'm sure I've got nothing on whatever emo, navel-gazing mumblecore genius you have going on. Please tell me your band has a synth?"

"We—No—" he splutters. I love picking on pretentious little shits like him.

"Spit it out, junior," I tell him, "I still have about half a bottle of whiskey to put away before this night kicks into gear."

"You need to get your stuff out of here," he spits.

I gaze around at my modest little camp and pull an exaggerated pout. "But I just got here, Boss. How come I have to leave?"

"Could you be more obnoxious?" he asks, appalled.

"I think you've seen pretty good evidence that I could be, yes."

"God, you're even more of an asshole in real life than I could have—"

"Mitch!" a soft, lovely female voice calls out.

I peer around the lanky twerp and see a long-legged girl stepping out of a beat-up sedan that's parked up on the grass. She winces as she straightens out her lean body—I bet she's been stuck in that jalopy all day long, trekking to Kansas. She swipes her short blonde hair away from her forehead, revealing a pair of big, wide set eyes and an adorable button nose. Her full lips are pulled into a scowl as she approaches the kid who's been hell bent on pissing me off as thoroughly as possible.

"What are you doing?" she demands, squaring off against the punk.

"Don't worry about it. Why didn't you wait in the car like I asked?" the boy hisses.

I fold my arms, watching the lover's spat unfold. I'd be lying if I said it wasn't a little enjoyable.

"Don't tell me to wait in the freakin' car. This isn't a family road trip," the girl snaps.

"You're right," the guy says, "It's a freak show, is what it is. We should really just get back in the car, turn around, and—"

"Enough of that," she says, lowering her voice, "I swear, if you don't stop with the paternalistic, macho, elitist—"

"Do you guys want me to leave?" I ask, "I'd say you could borrow my tent, but I'd like to break it in myself. You understand."

The girl opens her mouth to reply, but as her wide eyes focus on me, the words fall right out of her mouth and into the air. I smile, not without a bit of sadness, as recognition sweeps over her face. It was nice, watching her move across the grassy plain without self-consciousness. People tend to close themselves off around me, become versions of themselves. It's always such a pity.

But as I keep my eyes trained on her face, the moment passes. Her body shakes off its knowledge of my celebrity, right before my eyes. There's no shift, there's no facade that goes up. She smiles at me as herself—now I'm the one that's speechless.

"You're Trent Parker," she says simply, taking a step toward me.

"That's right," I say, offering my hand. She stops short, and I realize what an awkward gesture it is to offer a handshake at a music festival. But she's a good sport about it. She places her hand in mine and shakes firmly. She's strong, but pretending to be a little stronger than she really is. Compensating, just a little. My skin smarts as she takes her hand back—the contact was too brief. A sudden, hot longing for her stabs me between the ribs. I've always been a sucker for stubborn girls.

"I'm Ellie," she says, "This is Mitch."

Mitch glares at me, not too pleased about having Ellie take over the proceedings. Whatever they are, anyway. I wave cheerfully, infuriatingly, at Mitch—his cheeks light up with every shade of red you can imagine.

"Can I help you two with something?" I ask, "You need a mediator?"

"What? Oh, no," Ellie laughs. Her laugh is rough, clumsy, not at all the practiced little trill I'm so used to hearing in LA. There's something genuine about her—not wholesome, certainly not naive, but kind of unpracticed. She must be new to the music scene. No one stays this interesting for long in our business.

"Are you looking for your campsite?" I ask. "I don't really know my way around."

"That's the, uh, thing," she says, grinning sheepishly, "You're sort of...in our spot."

I look around at my tent and gear, the little kingdom I've set up for myself. Ellie points at a numbered marker in the ground, a feature of the landscape I just now notice.

"Oh," I say, disappointed, "Sorry about that."

"It's OK," she says, "We don't have a lot of stuff. We could probably share."

"Isn't that your bus?" Mitch asks flatly, "Do you really need an entire extra site? Consumerist bullshit—"

"Would you stop it?" Ellie hisses.

"It's fine," I laugh, "I don't know who I was kidding, setting all this up. You guys just go ahead and set up. I'll get everything cleared away."

Out of the corner of my eye I see Ellie shoot Mitch a look. He stalks on back to the car to get their things. She watches me quietly as I start to break down my stuff. I can feel myself performing for her, turning all my best angles her way, tensing the muscles in my arms more than necessary. I know I'm preening, but I can't stop myself. She's not the type of girl I usually pursue, but she's the kind that never fails to catch my eye.

"Sorry about that," she says, "He's just annoyed that we're here in the first place."

"So's my manager, if it makes you feel better," I tell her. "So, are you two a band or something?"

"Yeah," she says, "Ellie & Mitch."

"That's your band's name?" I ask.

"Sure," she says, a little defiantly. I like her more every minute.

"I can't say I've heard of you," I tell her honestly.

"No one has," she shrugs, "We won the New Voices contest is all."

"Aha," I say, "Well, congratulations."

"Thanks," she says, grinning, "I've heard a thing or two about you, you know."

"Do tell?" I smile, straightening up, "What's your first impression, now that you've met me in the flesh?"

She looks at me long and hard. "Maybe, if it develops into a lasting impression, I'll share it with you."

Mitch yells something from the car, and Ellie rolls her eyes at me. I laugh as she stalks back toward the sedan to help her partner unpack. I watch the sway of her hips, her easy gait, the way her short haircut bounces behind her as she moves...

I may not have ever heard her music, but I'm a fan already.

Chapter Three

Ellie

I'm pulled up from a deep slumber by the oppressive, heavy heat. I brush the sweaty hair away from my face and force my eyes open. The walls of our little tent are glowing dimly.

The first day of the festival has hardly begun, and already it's sweltering. I try to roll off my quickly-deflating air mattress, but something is anchoring me. As I glance down, I see a thin but firm arm wrapped protectively around my belly. I glance over my shoulder and stifle a sigh. Mitch must have rolled over in the middle of the night and made me his little spoon without me noticing.

I let my eyes linger on Mitch's sleeping face—he looks downright cherubic. His signature scowl must be slumbering, too, since for once it doesn't seem to be occupying his features. Mitch has always been a handsome guy, in the rakish, brooding way that some girls go nuts for. He's had the misunderstood musician thing down pat since before I met him. His parents raised him rather...unconventionally.

While the rest of us were watching cartoons and going to soccer practice, Mitch was reading Shakespeare and eating baby bok choy. His house didn't get cable, and he had to beg his parents to install a computer when he started high school—and even then, he could only use it for typing up homework assignments.

Mitch's rebellious stage was rough. He was angry with his parents for raising him the way they did. He felt like an outsider, and he blamed them completely. When I met him, he was just reemerging from a good few years of destructive behavior and deep depression. And the thing that finally brought him back out into the world? Music, of course. Making music saved Mitch's life, he'll tell you.

My heart smarts as I feel his arms close tighter around me. Mitch can be a royal pain in the ass sometimes, but I can never hold it against him. Beneath his above-it-all exterior, there's still a lonely little kid who just wants to be noticed for a minute. He'd kill me for saying it, but he acts a whole lot tougher than he really is. I want our time here at the festival to be good, and amiable, and maybe a little bit fun. I can be patient with his grumpiness; I'm used to it by now. Maybe he'll even have a good time, if he can stand to let himself.

Delicately, I maneuver my way out from under Mitch's arm. He sleeps on, looking peaceful and serene. I wish the rest of the world could see him the way I do. To most people, Mitch comes across as a temperamental artist. But to me, Mitch is a wonderful friend. He's helped me work through so much of my own baggage, just by helping me express my angers and fears and joys through music. Even though he can be a pain in the ass, he's still a good guy at the end of the day.

As quietly as I can, I unzip the door of the tent. Cool air rushes into the tiny, enclosed space, and I step eagerly out into the morning. Though our makeshift dwelling is as hot as an oven, the air outside is clear and delicious. I fill my lungs with the fresh coolness of it, savoring the smell of the morning. All around us, giant tour busses and RVs stand silently—like big metal cows sleeping for the night. I look out from atop our hill, down across the sprawling festival below.

Here and there, tiny patches of movement catch my eye. I wonder if the people still wandering around the huge general campsite have even gone to bed yet? I'm not used to the up-all-night, raging type of musical atmosphere. Ellie & Mitch fans tend to be bookish, nerdy, and academic. We're more likely to get stoned in someone's backyard and talk about the cosmos than snort coke off toilet seats, or whatever it is that famous musicians do. I can handle myself just fine around more adamant drinkers and druggies, and have always been just fine at Hawk and Dove. I just hope that doesn't change, now that I'm going to be performing.

A sudden familiar smell catches me off guard. Someone else must be awake in this little city on a hill. I turn around and notice a thin ribbon of steam rising from a tent across the site. As I reroute towards the fine smell of good coffee, I see that it's a craft service tent. I remember someone telling me that our food and drink would be complementary while we were at the festival, but I never dreamed that they'd be able to accommodate my early bird ways so well!

I'm sure that my eyes are as big as saucers as I approach the lofty food tent. A couple of industrious souls are setting out fresh trays of pastries, bagels, and toast. I spot a brigade of waffle irons, bowls of fresh fruit, and a whole array of cereals and goodies. There even looks to be an omelet station off in the corner. This is certainly a far cry from the way I'm used to eating during the festival. In years past, I've spent five days munching on Pop Tarts and peanuts, exclusively. This will be a welcome change of pace, I must say.

"Would you like something?" asks one of the people setting up.

"A coffee would be fantastic," I tell her. She nods and starts to turn, before a voice from over my shoulder stops her.

"Make that two, would you?" croons a rich baritone.

I look over my shoulder and swallow hard. Trent Parker is standing three feet away from me, looking sleep-rumpled and terribly sexy. All six feet of him are perfectly balanced, from his scruffy brown curls to his worn out sneakers. He looks strong but not bulky. His muscles look natural and fine, not bulbous and gym-manufactured. His jaw line is like a straight razor's edge, though it's covered in dark stubble. His full lips are curled into a subtle half-smile, and his vibrant green eyes are smiling, too.

I had a hell of a time yesterday trying to keep my cool when we met. I'm no super fan, but running into someone so famous had been a little disorienting. It didn't help that he is even more attractive in real life than he is in any picture. There's this charming, open quality about him in real life that doesn't seem to come across in print or on the web. He's got quite the bad boy reputation, Mr. Parker. And while I'm not one to get intimidated easily, I can't say that I'm not a tiny bit star struck. He's a wonderful musician, after all. And above anything else, I find talent to be incredibly sexy. I give him my best, *it's-cool-we're-totally-equals-right?* smile.

"You're up early," I say, keeping it light.

"I don't sleep much," he shrugs, slipping his hands into his back pockets. God, what I wouldn't give to be those hands right about now. "What's your excuse?"

"I'm an early bird," I tell him, "Always have been. I've been waking up at five in the morning for as long as I can remember. It certainly wasn't welcome come Christmas morning, I can tell you that much."

He laughs easily. "I can imagine. Your boyfriend must not be too happy about it either."

I can feel my brow furrow. "My...? Oh, you mean Mitch?"

"Yeah," Trent says, "That squirrelly kid who yelled at me yesterday."

"He's not squirrelly," I say, "And he's just my band mate. Well, not just. He's my friend too, obviously. But he's not...We're not..."

"Together?" Trent suggests.

"Right," I say quickly. Why am I babbling in front of this person? I try to redeem myself as we wait for our coffee to brew. "This is your first time playing at the festival, right?" I ask.

"It is," he tells me, "Just like you."

"But I've at least been here before," I say with a grin, "If you need someone to show you the ropes..."

"You're too kind," he laughs, "But I think we'll be OK. My band mates and I are very adaptable."

"I've heard you described otherwise," I tell him.

"Oh?" he says, "What have you heard?"

"Well," I say, turning toward him, "I've heard you guys tend to not give a damn about who or what gets broken when you roll into town. I've heard that the only thing harder than your heads are the parties that you throw."

"You can't leave a 'harder' joke open like that," he warns.

"Forget it," I say, "I'm sure you're all perfectly lovely in real life."

"Well, I wouldn't go that far," Trent laughs, "But we're not terrible guys, once you get to know us. At least not to each other."

"How about to women?" I ask.

"Is that something else you've heard about us?" he asks, looking at me intently.

"I mean...Yeah," I say, sorry to have started in on this weird critical kick, "Your reputations precede you, is all."

"It's one of the perks of the gig," he says sarcastically.

I'm about to press him further when two steaming cups of coffee materialize in front of us. I grab mine eagerly, breathing in the dark, roasted aroma.

"It's the good stuff," I moan.

"Should I give you and the coffee a little privacy?" Trent laughs.

"Maybe," I kid, "I tend to get carried away."

"Is that so?" he asks. I feel his eyes lingering on me, and I feel suddenly exposed before him. And much to my surprise...I kind of like it. Is Trent Parker, international rock star and bad boy of every girl's dreams, actually hitting on me right now? Maybe I haven't actually woken up yet this morning, maybe—

"Ow!" I yelp, as hot coffee singes the tip of my tongue. Clearly, I'm awake after all. And clumsy as ever. Trent winces kindly on my behalf while I wag my tongue around like an idiot, trying to cool it off. I've never been good at the whole sexy vixen thing, but this has got to be a new sort of low.

"Hope that won't interfere with your singing," Trent says. I can see that he's trying hard not to laugh at me.

"Our first little show is tonight," I tell him, "So if I show up with a bandage on my tongue, you'll know why."

"You're playing tonight?" he asks, "You must be excited."

"There will probably only be three people at our stage," I tell him, "But still. It is exciting. We've never really played anywhere besides campus and hometown bars."

"I started out in bars too," he tells me, "It's nothing to feel embarrassed about."

"Thanks," I smile, "I'll take your word for it, that's for sure."

We wander away from the food tent together, our steps falling in line with each other's. I'm certainly in no hurry to scamper away, and it doesn't seem like he is either. If someone had told me a year ago that I'd be strolling around the Hawk and Dove talent campsite with Trent Parker, I would have had them committed. I feel like I've snatched someone else's body, that the authorities are going to arrive any minute and arrest me for impersonating a successful musician. So, before the clock strikes midnight and my VIP pass turns back into a pumpkin or whatever, I'm going to enjoy myself as best I can.

"So, Ellie," Trent says coming to a stop on the crest of the hill, "How do you usually spend these early morning hours?"

"It depends," I tell him, "I'll run or do yoga every once in a while. Mostly I just sit with myself. Or write, if I'm in the mood."

"Ah. You're the writer of the duo, huh?" he asks.

"That I am," I tell him, "Do you write your own stuff?"

He looks genuinely offended that I asked. "Of course," he says, "What did you think?"

"I don't know," I try to backpedal, "A lot of musicians don't write their own songs, necessarily."

"A lot of pop stars don't write their own songs," he corrects me, "I'm not Kelly fuckin' Clarkson."

"I didn't—"

"I've been writing my own songs since I was fifteen," he says hotly, "And I still do. Just because I'm successful, doesn't mean I'm selling out. So—"

"OK, OK!" I say, cutting him off, "Take a breath, would you? It was an honest question. And in the future, I prefer to not have people jumping down my throat before the sun is even up. Or really ever, quite frankly."

He stares at me for a long moment, and the anger drains rapidly from his face. In its place is utter embarrassment, and, if I'm not mistaken, a little bit of wonder. Clearly, Mr. Parker is not used to people speaking honestly with him.

"Sorry about that," he says gruffly, "Haven't had my full cup of coffee yet, is all."

"It's cool, I'm with ya on that," I say.

"It's not," he insists, "But it's nice of you to say so."

"I'm not *nice*," I tell him, "Not really. But I try to be kind, when I can be. And understanding."

"I think being kind is a lot more important than being nice," he says, looking at me with a steady, unwavering gaze. Those bright green eyes of his are shining, even in the dim light of the morning.

I take a sip of coffee so he won't notice how tongue tied he's making me. I'm not usually one to get tripped up talking to boys. But then again, Trent Parker isn't some boy—he's a man, through and through. Before I can stop them, my eyes skirt down across the panes of his chest, his tapered waist...It's like he's become my new center of gravity, I can't help but feel drawn to him.

It must be the rock star thing, I reason. I'm just not used to being around famous people yet. I drag my eyes back up to his and force a big, goofy smile across my face.

"Well," I say, "I'm going to head back and try to wake Mitch up. I want to get a little practice in before the day kicks into gear."

"Right," Trent says, "Good deal. I'll see you around, Ellie. It was nice having someone to wake up with."

I stifle a little sigh, thinking about what it would be like to really wake up to Trent Parker. "Yeah, you too," I blurt nonsensically, "I mean, see you later. Have a nice day."

I turn and hurry away from him, my cheeks burning. So much for playing it cool. He probably thinks I'm a drooling groupie, rather than a fellow musician. Well, so be it. I don't need him to like me...though I certainly wouldn't mind it if he did.

The tent is far too hot for productive thought, so I make myself comfortable on the trunk of my sedan. I sip my coffee as the sun peeks over the horizon, sending ribbons of yellow and orange spinning through the clouds. There's nothing like a Hawk and Dove sunrise. Nothing. Memories of all the years past start to well up and swirl in my mind.

I feel a stinging pang of nostalgia, thinking of coming here with Kate. We'd set up camp among the masses, always with a handmade flag hanging over our site so we could find it at the end of the night. There aren't any showers in the main part of the festival, so by the end of five days we would be absolutely caked in mud. That first shower after a fest was ecstasy.

Suddenly, I find myself wishing that I were back down the hill instead of up here among the stars. There are bathrooms and showers and probably saunas set up here. I know I shouldn't be complaining, and I know how lucky I am to be here, but I'm feeling that same longing that comes over me in Barton when I visit from school. I feel like I've outgrown the pocket of air that I left behind here. Surely I haven't changed that much, just because I happened to win some kind of contest? I'm sure that once we get down into the thick of things,

I'll feel better. No one's going to know who I am, or care that much about our little band. It will be just like old times—dirty, boozy, and full of great music.

At least, that's what I'm going to keep telling myself, anyway.

Little by little, the festival begins to wake up and greet the day. Watching from up here is amazing—it's like the whole festival is one big, shaggy animal with a million little eyes. I see people crawling out of their stuffy tents and rubbing the sleep out of their eyes, techies and stage hands swarming all over the stages, setting up for the day. Even behind me, in the talent camp, people are finally starting to show their faces. I feel my heartbeat pick up as I spot celebrity after celebrity. Huge names and minor stars alike line up for their breakfasts, looking a little bored. I can't believe I'm up here with them.

A flash of gold catches my eye from around the corner of Trent's tour bus. We're next door neighbors, after all, just a stone's throw away. I peer over the roof of my car and catch a glimpse of a gorgeous, impeccably dressed woman stepping out of the bus. Her blonde waves are artfully tousled, and her careful "natural" makeup is flawless. Trent follows close behind her, and I feel my heart tighten in my chest. I shouldn't be surprised that he's traveling with someone, of course, but I can't help but feel a little let down.

There's a rustling inside my tent, and I watch as Mitch stumbles through the unzipped flap, panting. His hair is matted with sweat, and his cheeks are bright red. I stifle a smile, trying not to notice how silly he looks. Mitch is not a guy who likes to be giggled at. He looks over at me with a dazed sort of annoyance.

"It's, like, a thousand degrees in there!" he gasps.

"Fahrenheit or Celsius?" I ask primly.

"Pick one!" he grumbles.

"You've got plenty of time to beautify yourself," I tell him, "We're not playing until this afternoon, remember?"

"How could I forget?" he sighs.

"You *are* going to try to sound good, right?" I ask.

"Of course," he says, looking around for the source of my coffee. His eyes fall upon the craft services tent, and I watch his eyebrow arch critically. "Naturally..." he sighs.

I follow his gaze toward the beautiful blonde from next door and see that she's resting her manicured hand protectively on the small of Trent's back. My blood runs red hot for a split second, but I shake the feeling as fast as I can. What is the matter with me? It's not like he's mine. I can't possibly be jealous of some woman I've never met for being with a man I could never have.

"Shouldn't be surprised that the asshole's walking around wearing women as accessories," Mitch grumbles.

"It's one woman," I correct him, "And you just don't like him because he's famous."

"I don't like him, and he happens to be famous," Mitch insists, "The dislike is purely for him, not just the idea of fame. Though that's disgusting too."

I roll my eyes and ignore him. I try not to indulge him when he gets all preachy like this, it only encourages bad behavior.

"Why don't you get yourself ready so that we can practice?" I say.

"OK, Mom," he mutters, stalking off toward the glamorous shower station.

I watch him walk away, weaving through famous musicians without so much as a second glance. He's a strange, wonderful creature, this partner of mine. I just hope that he can hide his disdain in front of our tiny little audience today.

The morning passes in a bustle of motion and excitement. As the sun creeps higher in the sky, my fingers begin to tremble unaccountably. I hardly ever get nervous before I perform, and we're sure to have a pretty small turnout. They're basically humoring us by letting us play at the festival at all, and I'm perfectly aware of it. Still, as small as it is, it's still a dream come true for me to be among the performers, here. I feel like I'm joining some elite club, even if it's only as a junior member. I'm practically bouncing by the time we have to start heading down the hill. Mitch can see right through my barely collected exterior. He shakes his head at me as we gather our things.

"Would you calm down?" he says, "This is not the defining moment of our lives."

"Just let me enjoy it, sourpuss," I say, socking him lightly on the arm.

"If I must," he sighs.

We sling our various instruments over our shoulders and begin our trek down into the heart of the festival. Out of the corner of my eye, I see Trent leaning against his tour bus, watching me go. There are three scruffy men and the same gorgeous woman clustered around him, but I can swear that he's looking right at me. I turn away quickly, certain that I'm imagining things.

Mitch and I walk down the hill together in our usual performance attire. Mitch is wearing gray wool slacks, red suspenders, and a square brown tie. I once suggested that he add a fedora to his look, and he didn't speak to me for a week. For my part, I've got my favorite vintage dress on. It's a beautiful sea foam number from the sixties with a big, billowing skirt. My hair is combed and tucked behind my ears, and my face is scrubbed clean but for a streak of red lipstick. If not for the array of instruments, we could very well be dressed for a picnic, but a very stylish one.

We make our way through the densely packed crowd, and something doesn't feel quite right. We're dressed rather differently than the average festival-goer, but there are costumes of every sort all around us. As we pass, eyes linger on us, conversations fall away into silence. I can hear excited chatter spring up around us, words whispered behind hands flit by my ears.

"*That's Ellie & Mitch,*" I hear someone whisper. Mitch and I trade a baffled glance—do people actually know who we are? Since when?

As we continue, the crowd seems to part for us. People are staring unabashedly as we pass, staring after us like we're the last specimens of an endangered species. This doesn't make any sense...how is it possible that we're being recognized? We're the least popular act in the entire lineup. Sure, we have tiny groups of admirers in Barton and at Berklee, but we're far from home, and still people are acting all funny as we go by. What gives? Maybe they're just impressed by the instruments. Maybe it's all just a fluke or something.

We skirt around a large, unmoving group as we come up to our tiny stage. As a festival organizer waves us over excitedly, it clicks. That large, unmoving crowd is standing in front of our stage. They're here to see us! But how...?

"You must be Ellie!" the organizer squeals, shaking my hand vigorously. She's a couple years older than us, and very perky. "And you must be Mitch!"

"That's right," Mitch answers, frowning as the woman pumps his hand.

"I'm Pearl, your stage manager," she says, smiling a big, toothy grin. "You about ready to go?"

"Pearl..." I say, "Who are all those people out there?"

"Why, your fans of course!" she exclaims.

"But...we don't have any fans," I say, mystified, "Do they all have the right stage? Maybe they're trying to find someone else's show?"

"Nope!" Pearl says, "They're all here for you! It was such good timing, that article coming out when it did. You two went a little viral, didn't you?"

"What article?" I say, "Teddy's article?"

"I suppose!" Pearl says.

"Mitch, what was in that article, besides a falsely quoted endorsement for drugs?"

Mitch shrugs. "I don't know, I didn't read the whole thing."

"Let's just get set up," I say, lugging our instruments toward the stage.

"Don't be silly!" Pearl says, as two men appear to take our stuff off our hands, "We've got stage hands to do that kind of thing."

I watch, amazed, as the men take our instruments out onto the stage for us. Mitch and I have been a total DIY operation for as long as we've been playing together. This whole being-pampered thing is totally foreign. I can't tell whether I'm excited or uncomfortable all of sudden, though I have a pretty good idea which way Teddy is leaning.

With mounting anxiety, I look out into the jostling crowd. I feel eyes all over me, eyes of people that I've never met before. I suppose this is what famous musicians feel like all the time, but I'm not a famous musician. I'm just Eleanor Jackson from Barton. I'm not anyone special.

I feel like I've led these people on, somehow. That they must be mistaken. I let out a gasp as I see a very tall figure saunter up in the back of the crowd. Trent's decided to come watch the show. He's got big old aviator sunglasses on, but I can tell it's him. That blonde is still hanging onto his arm, too. Perfect. He catches me looking at him and gives a little wave. I avert my eyes quickly, pretending that I wasn't staring. Mitch raises an eyebrow at me when he sees the source of my caginess.

"Don't tell me you're getting all swoony over that asshole?" he asks, not very kindly.

"I don't get swoony," I tell him angrily, "I'm just a little confused. And a little nervous."

"You don't need to be nervous," Mitch says, taking my hands in his, "This is just like every other show we've ever played."

"Not exactly," I laugh.

"Well, try to think of it that way," he urges, "You've got nothing to worry about. Your voice is beautiful. These people obviously think so, or they wouldn't have come."

"Maybe they just like your suspenders," I suggest.

"Well...they are excellent suspenders," Mitch admits, cracking the rare joke.

"Are you guys ready for me to introduce you?" Pearl asks excitedly, "We like to do a little Q and A before a new act takes the stage. Is that OK?"

"Sure," Mitch says, "Whatever."

"Super!" chirps Pearl. She dashes through the curtain, a pretty arbitrary divider since both the backstage and audience are open air. We watch her tap the mic and address the audience.

"Hello everyone!" Pearl says, her voice amplified in the afternoon air, "It's my pleasure to introduce a brand new act to you today. You've probably been reading all about them the last couple of days, as their most recent song, 'Patch Me Up', has been all over the Web. Please give a big Hawk and Dove welcome to the adorable and magnificent duo, Ellie & Mitch!"

"Adorable?" Mitch hisses.

I grab onto his hand and drag him through the curtain. A huge wave of applause washes over us as we step out onto the modest stage. For a moment, I'm caught like a deer in headlights, totally frozen before this unexpected wash of praise. I look over and see that even Mitch is startled by the attention. We're used to playing in tiny little bars and dorm rooms. This is another animal completely. I don't think I could have fully imagined the sensation of walking out before a big group of people who are actually gathered to listen to me...it's absolutely wonderful. And terrifying.

"We're so glad you two could be here!" Pearl says.

Mitch and I take our places before our microphones. My fingers tighten around his—I'm too nervous to let go. I lean into the mic, smiling. "We're glad to be here!" I say brightly.

"I hear that you're a veteran of the festival yourself, Ellie," Pearl says.

"Oh yeah," I say, "Big time."

A cheer goes up in the crowd as Pearl goes on. "Well, you two have become quite the internet darlings over the past week or so. That interview you gave, Ellie, gave such a wonderful account of the way you two met, fell in love, and started making this excellent music together."

"I—What?" I splutter.

"Everyone here loves to see a couple on love making music. It always adds so much to the sound, don't you two agree?"

I feel Mitch's fingers leave mine as the heavy weight of his arm settles across my shoulders. I look up at him, utterly bewildered, and see a big, silly grin spread all across his face. He pulls me tightly against him and plants a kiss on the top of my head.

"You're absolutely right Pearl," he says into his microphone, "You can absolutely tell the difference. It's a pretty new thing for us. In fact, this interview is really the first time I've been able to know Ellie's heart about us. So, if we're a little giddy, you all know why."

The audience lets out a collective "aww," grabbing at each other gleefully. I look out over the crowd, utterly tongue tied. What is Mitch doing? What the hell did Teddy write in that article?

My eyes lock with two vibrant greens orbs, staring up at me from the back of the audience. Trent Parker's mouth has straightened into a firm, unreadable line. He doesn't look pleased, and that makes two of us.

Chapter Four

Trent

I cross my arms firmly over my chest as Ellie and her lanky beau take their places onstage. A scorching, acidic anger starts to rise inside of me as I watch that nerdy try-hard asshole beam at her. It's completely, utterly irrational that I'm mad at some snot nosed kid for having the audacity to like the same charming, adorable, intelligent girl who's happened to catch my eye...but I've never been an extremely rational person.

As Mitch settles onto a stool, cradling a stupid little ukulele, all I can do is fantasize about storming the stage and smashing it over his head.

"Why did you want to see these two play?" Kelly asks, sounding bored.

"They're our next door neighbors," I tell her, digging my fingers into the skin of my arms. "I thought it would be nice to come out and support them. They're pretty new at this, apparently."

"Seems like they've got a nice little following," Kelly remarks, looking around at the boisterous crowd clamoring for a better look at the stage.

"Yeah," I mutter through my teeth.

"What's the matter with you?" Kelly asks, narrowing her eyes at me, "You were the one who wanted to schlep down here for amateur hour. I'd rather be enjoying a vodka rocks in the bus, if I may be frank."

"You always are," I say, "That's why I keep you around."

"Not because I'm singlehandedly managing your entire career?" Kelly asks, threading her arm casually through mine.

"That too," I allow, keeping my eyes trained on the stage. Trained on Ellie, if I'm being honest.

She's been nervous all day, but there's a new element to her anxiety, now. I watch her take her place before the standing mic, smoothing down the front of her old-school dress. She tucks her hair behind her ear with a quick, aggravated motion. As she lifts her eyes, I can see it clearly—she's *pissed.*

A little bubble of hope rises through my unaccountable anger. Maybe Ellie isn't too thrilled with Mitch's little romantic spitball. I have to give her credit, she's keeping her annoyance hidden pretty well. Just not well enough for an old pro like me. I've been crafting this persona of mine long enough to see through just about anyone else's guise. Ellie's playing the cool, collected songstress, but I can practically see her cracking open right in front of my eyes.

The weirdest thing is, I now feel responsible somehow. Not that I had anything to do with what's bothering her, but I feel like I should be here to comfort her. I don't even mind feeling like I should stay and offer what support I can. I want to be here.

Ellie's eyes flit upwards and catch mine for half a moment, and I see that our fleeting connection steadies her at little. I try to smile at her encouragingly. If I can do anything at all to help her through this performance, I'm glad to. I remember well enough what it was like to get up in front of a crowd for the first time, after all. I guess I'm just feeling a little sentimental. Or something.

Ellie looks over her shoulder at Mitch and nods her head, ever so subtly. He takes a deep breath and curls his long form forward over the instrument. His fingers begin to pick artfully, sending a high, clear melody spinning up into the sky. Even I have to admit, the kid has skills on that dinky little thing.

A hush falls over the crowd as he weaves through a sunny but sad tune, clearing the way for Ellie's voice. I watch her long-lashed eyes flutter closed for half a heartbeat. Her chest rises beneath the fine fabric of her dress, and a shot of longing courses through me. Finally, she parts her lips and begins to sing, holding her hands peacefully at her sides.

The sound that comes of out her isn't at all what I expect. Most of these singer/songwriter types have the exact same voice, that throaty, overly embellished wail that's so popular these days. But Ellie doesn't adorn her voice with any stylistic trappings. Her tone is clear as a bell—smooth, full, and unlike anything I've ever heard before. I'm so blown away by the quality of her voice that for a minute, I forget to listen to what she's saying. But her words make their way to me, at last.

After four lonesome days of beaches and boats
I bumped into my shadow, and traded hellos,
She took one look at me, and wouldn't you know—
Set me free from this sorrow, and sent me on
home...

I watch her, transfixed. It's like her soul is streaming unfiltered through her lyrics. Word upon word tumbles from her mouth, twisting through the air like the wispy smoke of a just-extinguished cigarette. The girl is good, but I can tell just by watching that being "good" is of little interest to her. She's not singing to impress anyone, or to be the most interesting girl at the party, or even because she can. She's singing because she has to.

"Wow..." I mutter, my gaze steady on Ellie's curvy figure, swaying before the rapturous crowd.

"She's good," Kelly says begrudgingly.

She catches me gaping at the girl onstage. I snap my jaw shut and nod, but there's no getting anything past my manager.

"She's not really your type, is she Trent?"

"Yeah, well," I sigh, "My type sucks, don't you think?"

"Usually, yes," Kelly says, "But right now I'd advise you to stick to familiar waters, my friend. Don't go getting all misty eyed over some Joan Baez wannabe. As your manager and dear friend, I have to warn you that chasing after this little girl would be...problematic."

I scowl at her. "If you had your way, I'd be trapped in a recording studio dungeon with a chamber pot and a pack of cigarettes, cranking out an album a week and never having any fun."

"Guilty as charged," Kelly smiles, "I'll be back at the tour bus. Try not to be too long, would you?"

"Yeah, yeah," I murmur, as Ellie lingers perfectly on the last note of her opening number, "Get out of here, you dirty buzz kill."

"Love you too," Kelly says, rolling her eyes. She stalks away, managing (miraculously) to walk gracefully through the mud in her signature, towering heels. I turn my attention back to the stage and see Ellie, beaming out into the crowd. She looks—and I've never been caught dead using this word before in my life—*radiant*.

"Thank you all so much," she says, picking the microphone up off its stand and walking to the edge of the stage. "I can't tell you how amazing it is to be playing here tonight. I've been coming to Hawk and Dove for years, as a fan. My big sister and I used to drive down from up east every summer and spend a few days rolling around in the dirt. No pun about 'rolling', I promise."

The audience lets out a collective laugh. They absolutely love her, and I can hardly blame them. She has this wonderful unpolished quality about her. You can tell she's never been media trained, never stared down a sea of paparazzi flash bulbs, never negotiated a record deal or given into temptation and taken some groupie up on a good offer. She's so real, it almost hurts to look at her for long.

I wonder if I was ever that genuine and unpracticed. I feel like I've been putting on an act since I was fifteen years old, but what about before that?

Mitch picks up his guitar, one of the several instruments lined up onstage, and looks expectantly at Ellie. Her body tenses just noticeably as they trade a few words. When it's just her and the music, she looks like she's on cloud nine. But every time Mitch butts in...I'm probably just imagining things. I know it would be wise to back off and let her have this experience without subjecting her to my company.

God knows, my side is not the easiest place to spend time. In the five or so years I've been a successful musician, I've had plenty of one night flings, but never a girlfriend that stuck around longer than a week. I don't blame any of them for picking up and moving on. I wouldn't want to get sucked into a world of no privacy and jet setting if I had another option...At least, not if I wasn't at the center of it.

Not that I'm necessarily such a self-absorbed person, it's just that music has always meant more to me than anything else. As long as I have my music and my career, what do I need other people for?

Ellie lets out a long, moaning wail, soaring into a second number. The beat is fierce and ruthless, and she's practically spitting out the lyrics now. I watch her pace across the stage, more than a little turned on by her powerful, take-no-prisoners attitude. The words ring out like a battle cry across the late afternoon sky:

Plowshare baby, won't you till the ground
We've been digging our heels into for decades,
now?
Give it a shot, kid, and make us proud—
But don't you make a sound...

I wonder where these lyrics come from inside of her? It is just her engaging persona that's leaving me hungry for answers, or is it the girl herself? She's definitely a performer, no doubt about that, but I don't think it's her act I'm falling for.

"Snap out of it," I utter to myself, running my fingers through my hair. She'd probably be completely turned-off if I tried to woo her away from Howdy Doody up there. That little introduction they gave made it pretty clear that she's not even on the market. And the last thing I need to do is get myself tangled up in a little tabloid kerfuffle. As public as my life is, I do my best not to play directly into the hands of the media moguls. I like to be in control of what they get from me. It's better that way.

"We've got one more for you today," Ellie says over the uproarious cheering of the crowd, "But we've got another performance later on in the festival. We hope to see you there!"

"And one more thing," Mitch cuts in, grabbing Ellie's mic out of her hands, "I just want to say, in front of all you, how much of an honor it is to play with this beautiful woman. Ellie, I'm so glad you convinced me to come down here. And...well..."

"Mitch," Ellie whispers urgently, "What—"

But her words are cut off as Mitch pulls her against him ungracefully, kissing her full on her surprised mouth. The audience loses its mind, and a deep, roiling revulsion churns in my stomach.

I watch Ellie push Mitch away roughly. Her face is pulled into a furious scowl. What the hell is going on up there? Who does that punk think he is? I'm just about to charge through the crowd and pull her away when she gets a hold of herself, and covers up her annoyance and outrage with a congenial smile. Her lips are pulled into a contented grin, but her eyes are very clearly saying, "We'll talk about this later." As I watch, I'm sure that I see her gaze flick toward me for just an instant.

I turn away from the stage, shaking my head. There's no way I'm sticking around here to see that pimply little dweeb suck face with someone as talented and gorgeous as Ellie. She's way out of his league, and he's totally taking advantage of the opportunity. I can't stand guys like that.

A laugh escapes my throat as the full hypocrisy of my criticisms slaps me in the face. Who am I to talk? It's not like any woman in the course of my romantic life has ever liked me for any reason other than my celebrity status.

Before I was famous, or before I was even good, the fact that I played guitar was the only thing I had going for me. I guess I'm pretty good looking, but plenty of guys have that going for them. For me, the music was always the thing that sealed the deal. How could I blame this Mitch kid for trying to play the same game?

It's not the same with Ellie though, she's not like the rest of the groupies and hanger's-on. The women I've always pursued haven't been interesting, or at all interested in talking about anything besides how much money I have. They've all been gorgeous, without question—tits out to here and legs that go on for miles. But we've always been on the same page. They know I only want one thing from them, and I know they only want one thing from me.

I get a good lay, they get to tell their friends they slept with a rock star. It's a win-win. Or something. But I'd never think of pulling something like that on Ellie. I'm sure it wouldn't work, for one thing. But more importantly, she deserves better.

Where is this shit coming from? I quiz myself as I trudge back up the hill to the talent campsite. I don't even know the girl. Not really, anyway. We've had one and half conversations, and not even very deep ones at that. She seems like an interesting, complex person, but for all I know that could just be an act. Yet here I am, speculating about what she does and does not deserve?

Who she does and does not deserve? I need to snap out of this. It's none of my business.

My tour bus is practically rocking on its hinges as I approach. The guys must be pre-gaming hard for the first night out of the festival. They've only got bunk beds in the bus, as the tiny little master bedroom at the back is mine, but that's never stopped them from carting women back after an evening full of debaucheries. Looks like tonight's headed in that direction for sure.

I take the bus steps two at a time and find the guys sprawled across the main cabin of the tour bus. Rodney has a bottle of tequila in one hand and a bottle of rum in the other, and a dozen emptied shot glasses stand on the little table. Rodger appears to be dancing with himself, as he's been known to do when he's on his way to getting hammered, and Kenny is playing air guitar along with the Rolling Stones album they're currently blasting. I can't help but grin as I take in the sight of them.

"You assholes started without me?" I yell over the music.

"Trent!" Kenny cries happily, "Now the party can really start!"

"Where'd you go, man?" Rodney asks, promptly pouring me a shot.

"Just checking out some of the other acts," I say vaguely.

"Kelly said you were listening to some little indie duo," Rodger said, "What gives, man? Since when are you into anything acoustic?"

"Whatever," I say, trying to avoid to subject, "Don't be a dick about it."

"What an eloquent comeback," Rodger laughs.

"You need to start drinking," Rodney says, handing me the shot, "We've each got about a half-bottle head start on you."

"Duly noted," I say, and slug back the rum. That first drink of the night always feels a little like coming home. I'm just about to settle in to get nice and wasted when Kelly comes blustering out of the back of the bus.

"You idiot!" she yells, slapping me on the arm.

"What did I do?" I ask, pouting theatrically.

"I just read the little blog that your mousy friend wrote for us," Kelly snarls at me.

"What's wrong with it?" I ask quizzically, "I did the usual song and dance for her."

"Really?" Kelly demands, pulling her smart phone out of her pocket. "Did you happen to say, 'Rock is not a moral code. It's the negative space of one. It's not a prescriptive movement, it's how you choose to interpret it'?"

"That...sounds familiar," I admit.

"What in the world were you thinking, acting all philosophical?" Kelly cries.

"I told her to scratch it out. I told her it was off the record!" I yell back.

"She's a blogger, you idiot! Not a real freakin' journalist," Kelly says, exasperated.

"So I've got one smart line out there to counteract the usual, macho bullshit you have me spouting," I say, "So what? I think that my image will survive unscathed."

"Is that so?" Kelly says, shoving her phone in my face, "Because your little friend seems to have penned a wistful little think piece about how you feel trapped by fame, how the real, genuine Trent Parker is being squashed by the pressures of celebrity. She's painting you as a sensitive, intelligent bed-wetter who really just wants to sit on his front porch and sing love songs into the goddamn sunset."

"Is that so terrible?" I ask.

Kelly's face hardens. "It is if you've created your image by being a crude, rule-breaking bad boy. Which you have."

"You have," I correct her viciously.

"That's right," she snaps, "And if you're so exhausted by being a successful musician, you can always pick up and get the hell out of here. I'm not going to pull you kicking and screaming through the rest of your career, Trent. Either nut up, or shut up."

She storms away into the depths of the tour bus before I can get in another word. The guys have fallen silent, each trying very hard to avoid my gaze. I grab the bottle of rum from Rodney and take a long gulp. Furious, I tuck the bottle under my arm and march out of the bus, into the darkening night. Red, boiling rage is popping and seething behind my eyes. How dare that woman try to dictate how I go about presenting myself in the world? It's not like she was going anywhere fast without me to bring her along on the ride to stardom. Sure, she's the one who "found" me back in LA, but I'm the reason she has a career at all. I'm her meal ticket. Her show pony. And I'm fucking sick of it.

I lean against the front grill of the tour bus and take another long, satisfying pull of booze. This is not the first time in recent memory that Kelly has driven me to drink. Honestly, I think she does it on purpose sometimes, just to keep my image edgy enough for her own liking. I thank my lucky stars that photographers are banned from our camp site—I'm putting on quite the show for them right now.

I close my eyes and let the myriad sounds of the busy festival float up the hill to me, hoping that they might calm me down. But the nearby sound of shouting voices drowns out the happy murmur from down below in Normal People Land. I peek around the front of the bus, toward the source of the shrieking argument.

Ellie and Mitch's tent is illuminated from the inside by an electric lantern. I can see their shadows moving around in the enclosed space, darting and pacing in aggravation. Ellie's shadow sticks its finger into Mitch's thin chest, and I hear her muffled voice lobbing angry accusations his way. I know I shouldn't look, I know I should keep to myself and enjoy my bottle in peace...but I can't help it. My voyeuristic side is intrigued. I only wish I had some popcorn, is all.

The tent's zipper is torn open, and Ellie lunges out into the open air. Her face is flushed and furious, and her eyes are positively sparking with the need to fight. Her long fingers are balled up into fists, and I half expect her to start swinging. I know she's mad, and I know I shouldn't be thinking this way...but her passion is more than a little sexy.

Mitch climbs out after her, his face set in a grim mask. He doesn't look like he's taking his scolding passively, that's for sure. Neither of them seem keen on cooling down anytime soon, either. Ellie whips around to face Mitch across the tiny patch of grass between them.

"How could you do that to me, Mitch?" she demands.

"I didn't realize that expressing my affection for you would be received as a freakin' war crime," Mitch shoots back. "I thought you said in that interview—"

"I didn't say anything to anyone about wanting to be more than friends with you," Ellie says, "I don't want to be anything but your friend, Mitch. Not ever."

"But the article—"

"The article was made up!" she shouts, "You know that kid just took everything out of context and threw it against the wall so that he'd have something to write about! Sure, I told him you were a wonderful musician and that I love playing with you. And that's the truth!"

"Is that really all you feel for me?" Mitch asks plaintively.

"You're one of my best friends Mitch," Ellie says, "If that's not enough for you, then..."

"What?" he asks.

"Maybe we shouldn't have come here together," she says softly, turning away from him.

"That's what I've been saying this whole time," Mitch says angrily.

"It's not my fault you can't separate the music from whatever pipe dream you've been harboring. You really think I could feel anything for your scrawny, privileged, elitist—"

Mitch raises his hand into the air, winding up to slap her. Before I can second guess the impulse, I fling my body at him and tackle the kid forcefully to the ground. I cock my fist back, holding the bottle of rum, ready to break it over his fucking face, but hold myself back.

He's nothing more than a pile of twigs crumpled up on the ground—it wouldn't be anywhere close to a fair fight. He's looking up at me with impotent rage surging behind his eyes, and as much as I want to teach his punk ass a lesson, I know I have to be the bigger man. The last thing I need right now is a lawsuit.

"What the fuck do you think you're doing?" I growl.

"Where did you come from, asshole?" he cries, scurrying away from me.

I try my best to swallow my anger. I don't know how to explain the feeling that crashed over me the second he raised his hand to Ellie, but I want to kill him right now.

"You have no right," I tell him. "Maybe that's how they do things in whatever redneck hellhole you were raised in, but it's not OK. You need to apologize and get the fuck out of here."

"Fuck you, man!" Mitch yells, pulling himself onto his feet.

"Apologize," I say again, setting down my bottle and balling my hands into fists. Mitch's face drains of color as I approach. I'm just about to really get in his face when I feel a hand on my shoulder.

"Don't," Ellie says from behind me, her voice thick with tears.

The fact that she's upset only makes me want to pound the kid even more, but I stand still. This is her fight, not mine. That doesn't mean I'm not going to stand here and make sure this asshole doesn't try any bullshit. But I'll let her take the lead.

"I never thought you were the kind of girl to let a man fight her battles for her," Mitch says, trying his best to hurt her more.

"I never thought you were the kind of man who would dare try to hit me," she says back, "But for the record, Mitch, I could snap those twiggy arms of yours between my teeth. Next time, I won't hold back."

"There's not going to be a next time," he says quietly.

"You're damned right," Ellie spits.

"We're through," Mitch goes on, brushing off his jeans.

"What?" Ellie says, "What do you mean, through?"

"You don't think I want to play with you, after all this?" he scoffs.

"Oh, come on," she says, taking a step forward, "You can't handle one little fight?"

"This is more than one little fight, Eleanor!" Mitch says, "This whole time, I've been waiting for you to turn around and notice..."

"Notice what?" she asks.

"That you...love me, too," he finishes, pathetically.

Ellie stares at him, her mouth hanging open prettily. I suddenly wish that I were a mile away from this scene. I pick up my booze and take a drink, trying not to visibly show how thrilled I am to see this kid's heart getting shattered.

"Mitch," Ellie says, "If you can't be happy just being my friend, my partner...If the only reason you're hanging around is in hopes of scoring with me...then, yeah. You should really go."

"Is that what you want?" he asks.

"She said get the hell out of here," I can't resist saying.

Mitch glares at me in the gathering darkness. His angry eyes flit back and forth between Ellie and I, suspicion seething from his every pore. To his credit, Mitch doesn't voice his jealous thoughts. He doesn't say anything. Without a word, he turns on his heel and stalks away from us, his narrow shoulders up high around his ears. Ellie and I stand side-by-side, watching him disappear down the hill, losing himself among the gathering crowds.

"He'll be back," I tell her.

"Yeah," she says sadly.

"That doesn't mean you have to let him back in," I say.

"I know," she says, turning to look at me, "I wish I could. But...I think that's it. We're through, me and him. Jesus...we've only played one real show."

I offer her my bottle. "You need a drink," I tell her.

She laughs hollowly and accepts the offer. I watch her bring the bottle to her lips like an old pro. God, to be the mouth of that bottle at this very moment...*Stop it!* I chide myself silently. *Don't be that guy, Trent.* I shove my hands into my pockets, trying to keep Ellie from noticing my growing erection.

"Thanks for stepping in," she says, "I really would have been able to take him, but I'm glad I didn't have to."

"Has that happened before?" I ask cautiously.

"Never," she breathes, "I have no idea what got into him..."

"He really loves you, I guess, and he can't deal with it," I say.

"No," Ellie sighs, "You can't love someone and act that way. Mitch doesn't even know me. He can't possibly love me like he thinks he does."

"I don't know how you can write music like that together and not know each other," I say honestly.

"Well," Ellie says, "We divvy it up. He takes the music. I take the words. I mean, took..."

"You're damned good at the words," I tell her, resting a palm against my bus.

"Oh yeah," she says with a little smile, "You were there..."

"I was curious," I tell her. "I wanted to hear what you sounded like."

"So?" she says, leaning her tanned shoulder against the bus, not a foot away from my hand, "What did you think?"

"Honestly?" I ask.

"Honestly."

I level my gaze at her. "You're unbelievable," I say, "You're absolutely amazing."

"Really?" she asks, her eyes growing wide.

"Really," I say, "Trust me, I'm not one for sugar coating, either. You've really got something, Ellie. Or do you prefer Eleanor?"

"It's just Ellie," she says with a happy laugh. I'm glad to distract her from Mitch's bullshit for a minute, if I can.

"Let me guess," I say, "Your parents were Beatles fans?"

She grins at me in her comfortable, unpracticed way. "That's right. My name is Eleanor Rigby Jackson. A mouthful, right? But how did you know?"

"Oh please," I say, "You can tell from a mile off that you were named after that song."

"What do you mean?" she asks.

"There's a...sadness about you," I say slowly.

"...Oh," she replies, her smile falling.

"Not like, a morose thing," I tell her quickly, "It's more complicated than that. It's not like you're a sad person...at least, that's not how it seems. It just looks like you're longing for something. I don't know. I'm probably just a rambling drunk."

"I don't think so," she says softly. She's looking up at me like she's just recognized her own face in the mirror.

I hand her the bottle and let her take a long, long swig. For a little while, we don't say anything. We simply listen to the rollicking sounds of the festival below, safe from our little pocket of quiet.

"You're awfully nice for a womanizing asshole," she finally says with a wicked little smirk.

"Aha," I say, "The truth comes out. Is that what you really think of me?"

"Of course it is," she says, "And that's the way you want it, right?"

"I..."

"That's what you show the world, anyway," she says, her eyes trained on mine. "What I'm wondering...is whether or not that has anything to do with who you really are."

"And what do you think?" I ask her. My voice has dropped low with something that feels like desire...only even more urgent.

"I...Can't tell yet," she says. There's a tell tale blush rising in her cheeks.

"Well," I say, swallowing down my sudden lust, "I guess you'll just have to get to know me a little better, won't you?"

"I guess I will," she says, taking a step away from me. "Look...I'd better go find Mitch. Just to make sure he's OK and to figure out logistics."

"Sure," I say, "I should get back to my band, too."

"So long, Trent. Thank you," she says, turning from me.

It takes every ounce of self control not to grab her by the hips and push her up against the tour bus. But I know that can't be the way it happens. I realize something strange, something I've not felt in a long while. It's not just that I want this girl...I actually like her.

Since when is *that* allowed?

Chapter Five

Ellie

It took me half the night to find Mitch among the throbbing sea of people down the hill. When I finally stumbled upon my wayward band mate last night, he was as drunk as I'd ever seen him, sitting on a tree stump with a clown-like frown on his face.

It was quite the struggle, getting him back up to the tent to sleep it off. Especially now that people have a vague notion of who we are. Ever try smiling and nodding to excited almost-fans while hauling an entire human being up a marked incline? Not exactly my idea of a good time.

I hardly slept, though Mitch passed out cold. Now, in the early morning glow, I look over at my music partner and try to muster up the compassion to forgive him. Mitch has always been temperamental, but yesterday was out of control.

I don't know what horrified me more—the kiss, or the near-slap. Both were presumptuous, uncalled for, and abhorrent to me. I keep trying to think of reasons why I should accept an apology and move on, but none of those reasons stand up. Mitch's behavior yesterday was inexcusable...but we still have a show to play.

Leaving my slumbering partner to his boozy dreams, I creep out into the gathering daylight. I peer earnestly at the tour bus beside our meager little camp, but it doesn't look like Trent is awake yet.

Thank god he was around last night. Not because I wouldn't have been able to handle Mitch on my own, but because he made me feel so much better about the whole messed up situation. Somehow, I don't have to explain anything to Trent. He just understands what I'm going through, without any coaching. It feels like he understands me. But how can that be possible when he doesn't even know me?

I fetch myself something to eat from the blessed food tent and wait for Mitch to roll out of bed. Down the hill, the festival is waking up for another day of music and fun. Even though it's happening right there, I feel like I'm a thousand miles away.

I wish I was just experiencing the festival as I always have—as an audience member. I always had this crazy notion that getting to do the thing I always wanted—playing music—would be some kind of special treat. My mistake.

A loud groan from within the tent alerts me that Mitch has finally awoken from his slumber. I peek into the tent and see my partner staggering toward me, bleary-eyed.

"Ellie..." he croaks, pulling himself out of the tent.

"You look like hell," I tell him, "How much did you drink last night?"

"Not that much..." he says, squinting into the sunlight, "It was more the weed that got me."

"Excellent," I say, crossing my arms over my chest.

"I don't feel very well," he mutters.

"Neither do I," I say, "But not because I can't handle my booze. Mitch, everything that happened yesterday...It was unforgivable."

"I know," he whispers, looking miserable, "And I'm sorry, Ellie."

"Fine, but that's really not enough," I tell him, "How am I supposed to play with you when I can't even trust you?"

"You can trust me, Ellie," he insists, grabbing onto me for support.

"God," I say, wrinkling my nose, "You're a mess. Why don't you lie down in the back seat of the car and sober up a little? Take the day off. It's not like we're playing tonight."

"OK..." he says, staggering toward the car.

I help him inside the sedan, which is less likely to cook him than the tent, and hurry to fetch him some water. Though I resent having to take care of someone who's been nothing but horrible to me for the last twelve hours, *someone* has to make sure he doesn't keel over and croak. I suppose I owe him that much, at least—basic human decency.

As I'm hurrying back again from the food tent, I see a figure stepping down from the tour bus next door.

Trent's long, perfectly balanced form straightens up as he waves to me. I smile back, and meet him half way.

He's wearing dark jeans that hug his muscular legs just enough and a plain white v neck. How in the world can he be so effortlessly handsome? I don't even bother glancing down at the ratty shorts and tee shirt ensemble I threw on before bed last night. He probably thinks I look like a ten year old at her best friend's slumber party...though he's nice enough not to show it. In fact, the only thing I can see in his face is a hint of concern, and a fair bit of interest.

"How's it going?" he asks, glancing toward the pair of feet hanging from the open door of the car.

"Well, I found him," I sigh.

"That's not what I asked," Trent says.

"We'll be OK," I say, more to try and convince myself than anything, "He just needs to sober up."

"What he needs is a swift kick in the ass," Trent grumbles.

"Maybe that, too," I admit.

"You're not going to play nurse all day, are you?" Trent asks.

"Hell no," I say, "He gets provisions now, then he's on his own."

"Good," Trent smiles. I notice the subtle little dimples in his cheeks that appear when he smiles at me. My knees actually start to tremble a little—I thought that only happened in movies.

"I'd better..." I say, a bit breathless.

"Sure," Trent says, "Go ahead. But when you're done wiping up Mitch's spittle, get ready and come on over to the bus. I'd love to hang out with you today, now that you're down a companion."

"OK," I grin, "Sure. I'll just...I'll be right there."

We part ways for the moment, and my heart starts hurling itself against my ribcage. Am I nervous...or am I excited? Or am I about to be sick...no time to ponder the question.

I hurry back into the tent and rummage through my suitcase. I've got all my performance outfits folded neatly, but can I really wear a vintage romper onto a tour bus? I'm afraid I might be tossed out if I do. Why didn't I pack any normal clothes, like a sane person would do?

The best I can manage is a flowing, Carole King style top and a thick leather belt. It's still retro as hell, but maybe the rock and roll guys won't give me too much trouble about it.

As I step back out into the sunshine, I hear a low groan emanating from the sedan. With a sigh, I turn and see Mitch struggling to sit up. He's bleary eyed and red in the face, a look he's not wearing very well. Feeling anxious to start the day off right with Trent, I bustle back over to Mitch with more than a little bit of annoyance in my tone.

"Are you OK?" I ask, "If you're going to be sick, do it in the grass, not the car."

"I'm OK..." Mitch moans, "But I'm...Where are you going?"

"Just...down to the festival," I say shortly.

"What for?" Mitch asks.

"What do you mean what for?" I laugh, "What else does one do at a music festival but go to the music festival?"

"You're not going to stay with me?" Mitch says miserably.

That's it. I'm done. I plant my hands on my hips and level a sharp glare at my partner.

"Mitch," I begin, "It's not my fault that you got plastered last night and don't know how to take care of yourself. I'm your songwriter, not your mother. And even if I was your mother, I would have disowned you after the way you treated me last night. So go back to bed and try to grow a sense of decency during your beauty sleep."

He stares at me blankly as I turn and stride away from him. I round the tour bus, feeling more empowered than I have in years. This is exactly what Mitch and I need in our professional relationship.

Since we started playing together, he's always been in the seat of power. But from now on, I'm not going to take his shit. We're going to be equals in all things. And why not? After all, he needs me as much as I need him.

He's got all the instrumental talent, sure, but I've got the voice. Without me, he's just another gangly kid with a ukulele. And without him, I'm just another untraditionally cute songstress with too many vintage dresses. We've got a great act together, and I certainly don't want to jeopardize that, but Mitch has to start meeting me halfway.

Maybe now that he's got his stupid profession of love out of the way, we can start working together as partners. As adults, god willing.

I stop in front of the tour bus door, suddenly feeling very small. I stall for time, smoothing down my hippie top, tucking my tangled bob back behind my ears. Why the hell am I so nervous? It's not like I have anything to prove to Trent or his band mates. Our sounds are on opposite sides of the spectrum, not to mention our levels of fame and images. I can relax. I need to relax.

With a cheerful (but not too cheerful) smile, I lift my hand and rap solidly on the door. With a hydraulic hiss, it slides open.

My mouth falls open as the tall, stunning woman I'd seen hanging around with Trent earlier steps into the doorway. She's got an entire foot on me, though her three-inch heels certainly give her an advantage. There doesn't seem to be an ounce of fat of her entire body, and what she lacks in body fat she makes up for in voluminous blonde curls and a staggering bust. She's the quintessential center fold, right down to her skinny jeans and low-cut pink tank top. *This* is the sort of woman that Trent's used to hanging around with? What the hell is he doing bothering with me?

"Oh," the gorgeous woman says, crossing her arms over her massive chest, "You're that alternative girl."

Her voice is low, sultry, and absolutely deadly. I wince at her description of me—it takes a particular kind of bitch to turn the word "alternative" into an insult, but she's managed it just fine. I draw myself up to my full height, trying to remind myself that "real women have curves", or whatever. It's hard to gain any sort of ground in the presence of someone like her, artificial confidence or not.

"Hi," I say bravely, "I'm Ellie. I don't think we've been properly introduced."

"I don't see why we would have been," she drawls. It doesn't appear that she's in any hurry to let me inside.

"Sorry," I venture, "I didn't catch your name?"

"That's because I didn't offer it," she sneers.

"Um..."

"I'm Kelly," she finally allows, holding out a perfectly manicured hand, "I'm Trent's manager."

"Oh!" I exclaim, shaking her hand vigorously as a wave of relief washes over me, "His manager!"

"That's what I said," she sighs, snatching her fingers away. "Is there something you needed help with? I don't think that Trent is signing autographs right now."

"Uh, no," I say, "I mean, I'm here to see Trent, but not for...He invited me."

"He...what?" she asks, her eyes flinty.

"He invited me over...to hang out, I guess?" I say.

"Why would he do that?" she demands.

"You should probably ask him," I tell her. I'm just about through playing the two card to her queen. All this status nonsense is giving me a headache. "Is he here?"

"I don't answer questions about Trent's whereabouts," she sniffs.

"Look," I say, planting a palm on the tour bus, "I don't know what you've got stuck up your—"

"Ellie!" Trent shouts from within the bus. I watch him bound to where Kelly and I are locked in the staring contest from hell. He's beaming ear to ear, oblivious to the awkward standoff he's just interrupted. "I see you two have met?" he smiles.

"Oh, yes," I say, grinning widely at the stony woman blocking my way. "Kelly and I are very well acquainted, now."

"Brilliant," Trent says.

"You didn't run any social obligations by me, Trent," the manager snaps, "What have I told you about adding items to your schedule without consulting me?"

"Oh, calm down," Trent says, waving away her concerns, "Can we suspend the schedule bullshit while we're here, please? We're in the middle of a field in Kansas, for god's sake. I think we can afford to be a little more causal than usual."

"It's the principle of the thing," Kelly insists through gritted teeth.

"Kelly," Trent says, "Rodger's got enough valium hidden under the passenger seat to sedate a herd of bull elephants. Why don't you make with the popping?"

He reaches for my hand and helps me onto the bus, pulling me past Kelly's livid, quivering form. I get the sense that she's the last person in the world I should want to cross...but crossing her feels so damn good.

I look around in awe as we step into the main cabin of the bus. It's like a hotel suite on wheels! Big, comfy chairs stand against the wide windows, bunks hang down the corridor on either side, and there are even some more secluded rooms in the back. I can only imagine the insane parties this little cockpit has been witness to...how many women have come and gone from that back room.

But best not to dwell on the specifics.

"This place is amazing, Trent!" I exclaim.

"Yeah it is," he agrees, heading to the fridge. He pulls out a couple of ice cold beers and hands one to me.

I take the bottle tentatively. "It is noon yet?" I ask.

"Just barely," he smiles, cracking open the bottle. I shrug and join him. This is what Hawk and Dove is all about, after all—a suspension of real world rules, a total break from responsibility and decorum. A time to do whatever you want with whoever you want. I let my eyes graze down Trent's body as he tosses the bottle caps into the trash. The thick denim of his jeans pulls taunt against his firm, shapely ass, and I can scarcely rip my eyes away.

Luckily, the sound of bounding footsteps upsets my reverie. I turn to see three men leap onto the bus, followed by stone cold Kelly. They're falling all over each other like puppies, and I can't help but find them a little endearing.

They're all three grown men, but I can tell by their disorganized energy that they're little boys at heart. Most of the male musicians that I know are overgrown boys, come to think of it.

"Trent, you've got to come down to the festival!" pants the tallest and skinniest of the bunch. "This girl group called Baby Doll Disaster is playing, and they're smokin'—"

"Who's this?" asks the thick set one, taking a curious step toward me.

"I'm Eleanor," I tell him. I'd like them all to know that I'm perfectly capable of introducing myself.

"Oh," says the youngest-looking of the three. "Are we...uh...interrupting?"

"What?" I say, looking back at Trent.

"Not at all!" he exclaims, a little too loudly, "Ellie is camping right there next to us. She's one of the other acts! I wanted to show her around the bus."

"That's usually a euphemism," Kelly tells me in a sickly sweet voice.

"Noted," I mumble.

"What band are you with?" asks the thick man, "I'm Rodney, by the way."

"Hi Rodney," I say, "I'm with...Well, we're not really a band, per se."

"Sure you are," Trent says, "And you're great, too."

"We're called Ellie & Mitch," I explain to the others, "We won the New Voices contest. So, you know, they're kind of humoring us by letting us play."

"Don't sell yourself short," says the tallest man, "I mean, thousands of people enter that contest every year, right? It's an honor to be chosen!"

"It is," I say, "And we're grateful, absolutely. But I mean...you know. We're not like, professional musicians or anything. I mean, no one knows our names or anything."

"No one knows our names either," the youngest of the bunch says, "We're just Trent Parker's band, after all."

"Hey, hey," Trent says, frowning, "None of that. I floated the idea of changing our name years ago."

"Yeah, but Kelly wouldn't let us," grumbles Rodney.

"Because it was a stupid idea," Kelly snaps, rolling her eyes, "I swear, if you lot were left to brand yourselves, you'd be playing kids' birthday parties in Saskatchewan."

"Beautiful place, I've heard," Trent smiles.

"I like your outfit," says the tall guy, "Very Janis Joplin."

"I'll take that as a compliment," I smile.

"Stop trying to sweep Ellie off her feet, Rodger," Trent says, "She's out of your league."

"I was just being friendly," Rodger pouts.

"Where's the other half of your group?" asks the young guy.

"Passed out in the car," I shrug, "He had a rough night."

"What a lightweight!" Rodney snorts.

"We're off to take in the festivities," Trent announces, placing his hand on the small of my back.

It takes a herculean effort to stifle a shudder of pleasure as his fingers graze my skin through the thin fabric of my top.

"You do remember that we have a show this evening, right?" Kelly asks primly.

"Yes, Captain," Trent says, leading me back through the cabin, "Don't get your panties in a twist, OK?"

"See you later," says Rodney.

"Nice to meet you, Ellie!" calls Rodger.

I wave at the guys as we step off the bus and into the blazing hot sun. "They seem nice," I say to Trent.

"They're just on their best behavior for a particularly pretty girl," he says. I hope my suntanned cheeks hide my blush well enough.

"So, where are we headed?" I ask, eager to change the subject.

"Well, where do you want to go?" Trent asks, gesturing toward the festival with a wide sweep of his muscled arm, "The Hawk and Dove festival is your oyster."

"But, once we leave the talent camp, aren't photographers going to start crawling all over you?" I ask, as Trent strides down the grassy hill.

"Me?" he laughs, "What about you?"

"What about me?" I ask, "My band's just filler. You're heading, for god's sake."

"Don't tell me you're intimidated," he says, swinging his searing gaze my way.

"Of course not," I lie through my teeth, "I'm just saying. We're not exactly on par."

"I wouldn't be so sure," Trent says, digging into his pocket, "Everyone loves and underdog, Ellie. You might be surprised by how much people want to know about you."

He produces a set of huge aviators that match the set perched among his curls. "These are for you," he says, "You'll thank me later, I promise."

"I think you're giving me too much credit," I say, taking the glasses all the same. "I'm telling you, no one's going to recognize me."

"Suit yourself," he shrugs, "But don't say I didn't warn you."

Chapter Six

Ellie

We reach the bottom of the hill side by side and step toward the edge of the teeming crowd. As though they could smell the nearby musicianship, people start looking our way. Unbelievable! I peer at Trent and see that he is in full incognito mode, hiding behind his big old sunglasses and pretending he doesn't notice the stares leveled our way.

Out of nowhere, a petite redhead comes hurtling out of the crowd towards us. She nearly knocks me to the ground with the force of her affectionate embrace. I blink up at Trent, astounded by the display. He merely looks on, amused by my newfound popularity...or rather, by my gob smacked reaction to it.

"Oh my god, oh my god, oh my god," the girl squeals, her face pressed up against me, "I can't believe it's really you! I'm completely obsessed with you."

"Oh. Um. Thanks," I say haltingly, looking to Trent for some help. He just shakes his head happily—I'm all on my own.

"Where's Mitch?" the redheaded fangirl asks, looking around without freeing me from her hug.

"He's, uh, practicing," I say. There are more young women, and a few young men, headed our way. Word of our presence is spreading, it would seem.

"Oh," the redhead pouts, taking a step back. "I wanted to take a picture of you two for my blog!" Her eyes land on Trent, and after a moment, she recognizes him, too. Her mouth falls open into a perfect little circle, and a very high pitched squeal pours forth. "Oh my god!" she screeches, "Trent Parker!"

Now the hordes are upon us. People swarm up out of nowhere, enclosing Trent and I within a pressing circle of humanity. I look to him for some kind of idea as to how one behaves in situations like this, but something's up.

The moment he was recognized, something snapped on in him. There's a showmanship about his motions, his expressions, his very being, that wasn't there a moment before. The transformation is subtle but complete. Even his smile is different—shrewder, more jaded.

He takes a swinging step toward me and rests an arm over my shoulders.

"They'll leave once they've got a few pictures," he mutters in my ear, "Just put on your Famous Musician face. It'll be over in a second."

I smile nervously and lean against him. Even if he's acting like his own evil twin, the warm, casual embrace of his arm is all I can think about. His hand hangs down just inches from my chest. If I just moved a little to the right, those dexterous fingers might brush against my skin, through the soft cotton of my dress. He might close his fingers around my hard nipple, and squeeze just hard enough—

"That's enough for right now," Trent says authoritatively, loosing me from under his arm. "Let's go Ellie."

I scamper after him, away from the crowd of people. This time, I'm sure to bring my sunglasses down firmly over my face. He stalks through the bustling space, and I have to jog to keep up with him. We're moving too quickly for anyone to notice us, now, and thank god—that whole fawning-audience thing is not my cup of tea, I don't think. And even though he's probably used to it, something tells me that it isn't Trent's, either.

When he stops suddenly, I run smack into him, catching his elbow in my stomach. I reel back, coughing, and he finally turns toward me again. I'm relieved to see that his rock star airs have vanished once again. His expression is all concern and affection, just the way I like it.

"Shit, are you OK?" he asks.

"I'm fine," I laugh, looking around. We've stopped on a little rise of earth, beneath a majestic tree. A stage stands before us, rising up out of the ground. Hundreds of people are there waiting for the next act to begin.

Trent leans back against the thick trunk of the tree and takes a deep breath. "This is more like it," he says, "Just you and me, away from the gawking idiots."

"Be nice," I say, standing beside him beneath the swaying leaves, "They're just excited, is all."

"Yeah, well. It gets old pretty quickly," he sighs, "You'll see soon enough."

"You say that like you think I'm actually going to get anywhere in this business," I reply.

His green eyes turn toward me, bright with sincerity and conviction. "I don't think anything of the sort, Ellie. I know it. You're the real thing. Can't you see that?"

"Trent," I say, dropping my gaze to the tall grass, "We don't even know each other. How can you know something like that?"

"I just do," he shrugs, "Maybe I recognize something in you that I've known about myself for a long time."

"What's that?" I ask over the cheering crowd. The band is starting to file onstage, all decked out in their indie folk regalia.

"That you've been searching for something your entire life," Trent goes on, "Somewhere you feel safe, and whole. Somewhere that feels like home. And if you're anything like me, you've only ever found one place that comes close."

"But where?" I ask, "Where do you find that?"

Trent gestures toward the stage as the musicians take up their instruments. "Right there," he says, "Inside of the music. The first time I was up onstage—and mind you, it was really just the back of a shitty bar and grill when I was fourteen—I felt like I was coming home for the first time. I felt like I could take a breath, and settle in to stay for a while. And after that, I knew that no other single place would ever feel like enough. No house, no state, no country would ever feel as right and as safe as a song does."

"But what do you do in the meantime?" I breathe, fighting to swallow the knot in my throat, "When you're not in the music. Can't you ever get back to feeling like you belong somewhere?"

Trent looks at me sadly. "What do you think?" He asks, "If you're asking me, you already know."

"I thought that I was just growing up," I say, blinking back the stinging tears before they can well up in my eyes. "I thought I felt out of place at home because I was growing out of it. But you know, when I'm honest with myself, it's not just home that feels too small for me now. It's everywhere I've ever been. I feel it at school, I even feel it here. And I love it here, I really do...but it's not the same."

"I know it can hurt," Trent says, looking at me intently, "I know there's a sadness that comes with all this. God, do I know it. But Ellie...think about what you get in return. Would you really trade the music for anything else in the world?"

"Never," I laugh. "What could possibly be worth it?"

"Nothing that I've stumbled upon yet," Trent smiles, "All you can do is keep moving through the world, Ellie. No place you go will ever feel quite like home again, but it's not because home doesn't exist. It's because you've already found it somewhere else. You've found it on the stage, in the music. And you know what? That will always be there. That feeling of coming home again doesn't go away."

"Really?" I say.

"Well...At least not yet," Trent grins, "But then again, I'm only twenty five. Ask me when I'm sixty, I guess."

I let out a single laugh, and a rouge tear slides down my cheek. Trent's green eyes blaze with endless understanding. He edges toward me beneath the towering tree and, without a word, takes my hand in his.

Our fingers entwine, his grasp strong and full of compassion. I let my eye flutter closed for a moment, just long enough to memorize this instant in time. I let the warmth of the evening breeze, the solid comfort of Trent's hand around mine, the sad, simple beauty of honest words come together in my mind. I know that it's a memory I'll cherish for the rest of my life.

The band onstage begins its first number, a lyrical ballad that perfectly captures the sweet sorrow that's coursing through me. I love it when the perfect song comes along at just the right moment. I squeeze Trent's hand and sidle in an inch closer to him. He looks over at me and smiles without a hint of expectation.

I can tell that's he's just happy to be in my company. Our backs press up against the rough bark of the tree, and I lean toward him, brushing my side against his. His fingers graze my thigh, and I can't tell if it's intentional or not.

The wailing, soulful sound of music encompasses us in this little world of our own. As I hold Trent's gaze under the swaying, rustling branches, our bodies press against each other tentatively. Our fingers tighten, and I can't help but lift my chin just a hair, offering up my lips should he want to kiss them. I can feel his breath against the skin of my throat as our faces move to meet halfway. I feel like I've just chugged half a bottle of whiskey, my head is spinning so.

The entire world has fallen away from my mind, and it's only me and Trent, suspended here together, on the verge of a kiss.

His lips part, and I can practically see the words building up inside his mouth. He's stopped moving toward me—in fact, I think he's drawing away.

Did I do something wrong?

"I've got to get ready and head over to the main stage," he says, his voice gravelly.

"OK," I mutter, looking away. I don't want him to see the blush in my cheeks.

"Come with me," he suggests, pulling on my hand, "You can watch from backstage. You'll love it, I promise."

"Sounds great," I tell him, swallowing my embarrassment.

I let Trent tow me away from our little place in the world, off toward the center of the festival. My mind is grappling with what the hell just happened between us, but there's no time for overanalyzing. I pick up the pace to keep up with my mysterious guide through this new world of experience. At least he seems to know where he's going—that makes one of us.

Chapter Seven

Trent

"Here you go," I say, gesturing toward a prime patch of backstage real estate. "You can see the whole show from right here. Best spot in the house, I promise you."

Ellie peers past the curtains toward the swelling audience. She's being a very good sport, though I can tell that some part of her wishes she could be out in the crowd, like a normal girl.

It makes me a little sad for her—now that she's a known musician, even a minor one, simple pleasures like watching a concert without being bothered by the paparazzi and crazed fans are a thing of the past.

"This is great, Trent," she smiles. The corners of her mouth are stretched a smidge too widely for her enthusiasm to be completely wholehearted.

I avert my gaze, regret twisting my stomach into knots.

Why did I have to blow her off before? I've never lost my nerve with a girl in my entire life. Well, not since I hit puberty, anyway. We were absolutely on the edge of a moment back under that tree, on that little hill overlooking the festival. I saw what was happening, felt it, and still I ripped us away.

Sure, there was the pressing issue of my concert to consider, but would one kiss have killed me?

I'd wanted to kiss her so badly. Those full, soft lips of Ellie's were inches from mine, and moving closer. In a perfect world, I would have been able to press her back against that tree, pinning her there. I would have been able to kiss her as deeply, and long as I wanted, letting her feel the weight of my body against her own. I would have been able to wrap my arms around her, carry her off to some secluded corner where we could be alone.

But this is hardly a perfect world we're living in. If I had let something happen between us back there, a dozen gawkers would have been along to spoil the moment.

Ellie's name would be splashed across gossip blogs in the same breath as mine, and that would be it. I don't want to put her through the media circus that occurs around every development in my romantic life.

The women I'm seen with are always treated like Groupies of the Week by the music press, and I'm not OK with Ellie being lumped in with the others. She's as far from them as can be. For one, I actually *like* Ellie. And the last thing I want to do is hand over whatever privacy she has left to the tabloids.

If something's going to happen between Ellie and I, it has to be on her terms. I'm not going to pounce on her in the heat of the moment, tempted though I might be. This is quite a departure from my usual "Anything

Goes" philosophy of romance, but it's not like that school of thought was doing me any real favors.

"I have to go get ready," I tell her.

"OK," she smiles gamely.

I can tell she's confused and a little put off by my evasion. I can only hope that this doesn't drive a wedge between us. The last thing I want to do is extinguish whatever's crackling between us. I hope she knows that I'm not trying to avoid her—I'm just trying to avoid making her life more difficult for my sake. No time to worry about it now, though. Hopefully, we'll be able to sort everything out later tonight. If she deigns to wait that long, of course.

"Your stuff gets a little heavy sometimes, right?" she asks.

"Sometimes," I tell her, "I really won't be offended if that's not your thing."

"I like all kinds of things," she says, "I'm not a strictly ukulele-and-harmonica kind of girl."

"I didn't suppose that you were," I smile.

"And besides," she goes on, taking a step towards me, "Even if I may not be well-acquainted with something, it doesn't mean I'm not interested in learning something new."

I swallow hard, and will my body to behave itself. There's a renewed, irresistible determination glinting in Ellie's eyes. I know that look quite well.

But there's something else behind the raw desire, something more private, more secret. She wants me as badly as I want her, that much I'm sure, but it's not just a one night fling that she wants. She's making herself vulnerable to me in a way that women usually don't. Usually, it's a roll in the hay and a peck on the cheek. But with Ellie...

There's something in her that I recognize. Something fragile, and honest, and more than a little lonely. I recognize it because I can feel it too—though I'd be loathe to admit it to anyone in the world.

Being with Ellie would mean stripping away every defensive layer I've managed to build up over the years. But what if we tried it, this whole new kind of honesty, and something went wrong? Can I really risk dismantling these carefully crafted bits of armor without some kind of assurance that things are going to work out?

Or, forget "work out", just not end in a horrible train wreck of heartbreak? How does anyone get to know someone else without that kind of guarantee?

"You'd better get going," she says, taking a quick step forward.

Before I can respond, she gives me a simple kiss on the cheek. Her lips brush against my stubbled skin, sending a scorching bolt of sensation straight through me. I look down at her, more than a bit bemused. This girl has already got quite the hold on me.

"Go on then," she laughs, "Break a leg! Or someone else's. Whatever you rock and roll types are into."

"I'll do my best," I smile, turning reluctantly away from her and tearing through the backstage realm toward the green room. It's time I see to my rock star duties again.

I fumble toward the makeshift tent that's supposed to be serving as our green room. Ducking into the flimsy lean-to, I nearly burst out laughing at the sight of Kelly. She's standing stock still in the middle of the space, surrounded by the rest of my band. Her nose is scrunched up like she's just stepped in a pile of dog shit, and she's practically vibrating with fury. I did warn her this trip was going to be rustic, but I suppose she underestimated the extent to which that would be the case.

"Where the hell have you been?" she screeches at me. I'm glad she seems to be frozen in place—she looks about ready to claw out my eyes.

"Enjoying the festival," I tell her, "Ellie and I caught another one of the act's shows."

"Oh, really?" Kelly hisses, planting her hands on her hips, "You're telling me that instead of preparing for this rather high profile concert, you were off gallivanting with some charity case all afternoon?"

"First of all," I say, feeling heat rising in my face, "Since when have we ever practiced more than the absolute minimum? And more importantly, what the hell do you mean 'charity case'?"

The guys move off to the corners of the tent as Kelly and I square off against each other. They're used to our showdowns by now.

"I mean," Kelly winds up, "That the New Voices contest is a scheme to get more ticket buyers interested in the festival. It's not as though it actually counts for anything. I mean, it would be one thing if your little friend and her playmate were any good, but considering—"

"Ellie is an amazing singer," I interject, "You heard her the other night with your own two years!"

"She's fine, I guess," Kelly drawls. She can tell she's getting to me, and she digs her nails in even deeper. "But as long as she's hanging around with that mopey little string bean she calls a band mate, she doesn't stand a chance in this business. There are plenty of pretty girls in the music scene, Trent. Far prettier than her. You should know, you've screwed most of them by now."

"She's better than that," I shoot back.

"Not with her little boyfriend, she's not. And it doesn't look like they're splitting up anytime soon. At least, that's what the blogs say. And you know their word is law."

"Oh, please," I groan, "That little twerp is just trying to boost his own popularity."

"Manufactured or not," Kelly says, "There's definitely something going on between them. So if you've got any sense in that thick skull of yours, you'll stay far away from her."

"What is this, *West Side Story*?" I laugh incredulously, "You have no authority over who I spend time with, Kelly."

"Maybe not," she says, taking a step toward me, "But as your manager, I have ultimate authority over your music career. Have you forgotten that, Trent?"

"Are you threatening me?" I ask quietly, advancing toward her in turn.

"Of course not," she sniffs, "Just reminding you of the way things stand. I've always been your advisor, Trent. Your trusted advisor, I'd like to imagine. Why you would feel the need to stray away from my guidance is beyond me. Haven't I done a good job for you so far?"

"Sure," I admit, "Sure, I suppose you have."

"Then listen to me now," she says, dropping her voice so that the others can't hear, "That Ellie girl would be terrible for your image. For your entire career."

"Oh, come on," I say, "How the hell do you figure that?"

"Have you seen your fan base, lately?" she asks, cocking an eyebrow, "The people listening to you are hardcore rockers. Your fans are tough, and loyal, and merciless. What the hell do you think would happen if you started carting around some ruffly, girlish nymph, huh? They'd burn your damn records. Write you off as pussy whipped. She's the exact opposite of the kind of woman they want you with, Trent. They hate people like her. You know it's true."

"Well, what about what I want?" I counter.

"You're an entertainer!" Kelly cries, exasperated, "What you want is about as significant as a piss in the Atlantic Ocean!"

"Is that so?" I say, "I don't think I would have signed up for the job if I'd known that going in."

"Don't play the gallant troubadour," she laughs, "You love your fame. You love being fawned over. You love the sex, and the drugs, and the herds of willing, young bodies. Don't you dare try to deny it, either. I've been with you since the beginning, and you've taken to this whole fucked up world like a duck to water. It might seem like fun to try on the noble prince costume for a minute, Trent, but it's unbecoming. It's not worth losing all this just for some indie try-hard."

"She's not like that," I growl, "Even if she was, it wouldn't be any of your goddamn business. You do realize that there's a life outside of the industry, don't you Kelly?"

"No," she snaps, glaring at me, "I don't accept that. This is my life, Trent. You're my life. And you can be sure that I'm not going to let some no-name songstress fuck this up. And you can tell her I said so."

Kelly storms out of the room, pushing Rodney roughly out of the way. The three of them stare at me quizzically, but I'm too livid to bother filling them in.

Instead, I take a long swig out of the nearest bottle and let out a loud shout. The guys rally around me, passing the booze between them. We collapse into our ceremonial huddle, and I focus on their eager, amped up faces.

"OK guys," I say, "Let's get out there and do what we do best!"

They erupt into whoops and cries of boundless enthusiasm, and their bottomless energy starts to get to me, too. I can feel the jolting, unstoppable burst of adrenaline flooding my system, just like it always does before a show. We break free of our huddle and charge out of the holding tent.

Stage hands flock around us as we make our way toward the stage, handing us our instruments. The stresses and conflicts of the real world begin to fall away from me with every step that I take toward the mic stand. Right now, nothing in the world matters but getting on that stage and pouring my heart out through the speakers.

We swing onto the wide, deep platform just as the stage lights blast us with a blinding flash.

Thousands of screaming fans send rapturous shouts up into the dusky sky as we take our places before them. Beyond the audience, the quiet plains stretch on forever, lit up with millions of fireflies. For a second, it's all I can do to stand there and take it all in.

I want to memorize this moment, keep it on my shelf forever, just like I do with every single show. No matter how many of these massive gigs I play, it never gets old.

Out of the corner of my eye, I spot a flash of gold beyond the curtains. I turn and spot Ellie, grinning out at me from backstage. Any trace of doubt or frustration has faded from her features. She's beaming at me, now, her whole body radiating excitement.

I feel a thrill rush from my head to the tips of my fingers—the joy of making her happy, of exciting her, is unlike anything I've ever felt. I take two longs strides and grab the standing mic, dragging it close to my lips.

"To all my hawks, and all my doves," I scream, letting the adoring cries of the crowd wash over me, "Get ready lose your fucking minds!"

They don't need any permission from me. They're already roiling by the time I slam the first chord into the throbbing night air. The guys follow me into our first number, our latest hit single *Eviscerate*. The rhythm of the music overtakes my body, resets the beat of my heart. I'm fully within it, encompassed by the song itself. My entire universe shrinks down to this stage, this wild crowd, the warm night air against my skin...and the beautiful woman standing just beyond the wings.

We pound through verse after chorus after verse, sending the audience into a frenzy. I give myself room to roam around the stage, stalking like a predator about to fell his prey. This primal feeling comes over me every time I begin to sing. It's far more powerful than I am, but I don't mind. I'm enough of a man to accept being overcome every once in a while. Especially when the conqueror is as sweet as this. I let the force of the music sweep me away, transport me to a place where no one can follow.

I turn my back to the audience, letting my eyes sweep across the stage. Rodney, Rodger, and Kenny are out of their minds, pure conduits of the sound. We're all of us alone and as one with the audience right at this moment.

As I pivot back toward the stage, I catch another glimpse of Ellie. I nearly let the microphone tumble from my hands.

She's dancing with abandon, all on her own. Her hips gyrate along with our pummeling tempo, her blonde hair whips all around her upturned face. I've never seen anyone move so freely to my music.

She catches me watching her, and I fear she'll become self conscious and stop her gorgeous, writhing dance. But instead of being drawn out of her state by my attention, she sinks more deeply into it. We draw each other further beyond the realm of the mundane, ever on toward transcendence.

I let an animal wail rip from my throat, and the audience rages at an even greater pitch. I look out over the crowd, surging beneath the clear night sky. These are the moments that I live for. This is everything I've ever wanted. And I realize suddenly that Ellie is becoming a part of that everything.

We soar through the rest of our set, revving the crowd up more and more with each passing number. The audience grows and shifts as the night wears on, and soon it looks like everyone within a five mile radius of the stage has congregated to listen.

There's sweat pouring down my face and neck, soaking my tee shirt. As we transition to another hit, I rip the dripping garment off my back and toss it into the crowd. A little cloud of dust arises as a dozen fans dive for the shirt. I hear a hearty laugh and turn to catch Ellie giggling over the scene my offering has made. I grin back at her and dive into the next number.

I've never felt the presence of another person so clearly during a show. Usually, it's just me—lost inside of the music. But with Ellie, it's like she's traveling with me. I don't need to translate or explain anything to her, she just understands. And if this is what it's like when music is involved...what kind of connection would we have in other, more intimate communications?

I snap my mind back like a dog on a leash. It wouldn't do to start rocking a major hard on in front of a crowd of thousands. I signal for the guys to start our final number. We take a collective breath and throw our entire selves into the show closer.

At this point, it hardly feels like we're even in control of the sound. It just happens. We're just witnesses to what's moving through us. I scream out the final notes and let the adoration of the crowd all but bowl me over. Their attention is intoxicating, but there's another party who I'm far more interested in connecting with.

From the wings, I can feel Ellie's eyes on me, the heat of her gaze. I surface from the depths of the music and make my way to her as the guys file offstage in the other direction.

Without breaking stride, I scoop Ellie up into my arms, picking her up right off the ground. She's laughing with abandon, wrapping her arms around my shoulders. There's nothing jarring about our closeness—no resistance or hesitation. I spin her around in the dark backstage nook, acting for the world like a heartsick Romeo.

"That was...Trent, that was amazing!" she breathes, planting her feet on the floor in front of me. Her dainty hands rest firmly on my shoulders, and her face is turned up toward mine in something that looks an awful lot like rapture.

"Thank you for being here," I tell her, daring to rest my hands on her waist. The curvature of her body feels so good, so comfortable under my fingers. I don't know how much longer I'm going to be able to resist her. She's looking up at me with deliberate intention, and I can read pretty clearly what's running through her mind.

"Thank *you*," she says, taking the smallest of steps forward. "I've never been at a show like this before. It was so *raw*. So intense..." The closeness of her is sending a hot, throbbing need down through my body. If she comes any nearer, she's sure to feel it for herself.

"I liked knowing you were right there," I tell her, letting my hands slip further around her body. "I could feel you, even through all the noise and the chaos."

"I could too," she says softly.

Her teeth close on her plush bottom lip, and I have to swallow down a low groan. I know that we're caught up in the moment, and that this isn't how real life works. But what about my life is anything near real? What's the use in trying to follow rules that simply don't apply?

"Ellie," I say firmly, cupping her chin in my hand, "I need you to kiss me."

"Wh-what?" she stammers, taken aback by my request. I suppose it's a little unconventional to ask for permission at a time like this.

"Kiss me," I tell her, "Please."

The sudden thrill of agency washes over her body, and I see a spark of gleeful authority sizzle in her eyes. She presses her body against mine, gasps as she feels the hard length of me against her. Her arms encircle my neck as she offers up her lips to me. *Close enough*, I think, and bring my mouth firmly down to hers.

Our mouths move together, and I shudder as the taste of Ellie sends shockwaves through my entire system. She opens herself to me, and our tongues tangle and caress as our bodies press closer and closer together. I let my hands wander down to her round, firm ass, grabbing hold with relish. I feel her hands running through my hair, her breasts billowing against my bare chest.

I back her up through a partition of curtains and press her up against the nearest wall. We're cocooned in our own private world, even the middle of this raging festival. Ellie wraps her long, smooth leg around me, and I lean into her embrace.

My stiff member is pressed against her, right where we both want it most. She breaks away from my mouth and starts to kiss my throat, my chest. I let my hands wander all along her body—cupping her breasts through the thin fabric of her dress, letting my thumbs glance over her nipples.

I'm tantalized by the bare stretch of thigh that reveals itself as the hem of her skirt falls back. God I want to fuck her so bad.

I lay my fingers on her tanned, tender skin and close my eyes as she runs her hands down the panes of my chest. Our eyes meet in the darkened space, and I can see she's swept entirely away.

We pause as one, our hands lingering on each other's bare skin. We both know where this is heading, where we want it to head...and we both know that it can't. Not right this second.

I straighten up before her, peering down at her beautiful face in the half light. I'm not going to screw her up against the wall of a concert venue as if she were just another groupie. I've never met someone like Ellie before, and I have no idea how these things are supposed to progress, but I'm pretty sure this isn't the part where we get to have each other, we barely just met.

She lifts her hands off my body and brushes down her skirt.

"Well," she says, "There that is."

"I hope you're not offended," I say, rather self-conscious of the bulge in the front of my jeans.

"Of course not," she says quickly, "This is all just...I'm not used to this."

"Me either," I say.

"Yeah right," she laughs, "You probably get down with women backstage every night."

"I didn't mean that," I tell her, "I meant that I'm not used to actually liking someone enough to save the screwing for somewhere other than on an amp."

That one's stumped her. Her mouth falls open prettily, and I can't help but let out a laugh. God, does this girl do anything that's not hopelessly sexy?

"Oh," she says, "Right. Um...You know, it's not that I'm not attracted to you. Because I am. Obviously. It's just...things feel so unsteady. With all this attention. And Mitch is all—"

"Mitch?" I repeat, caught off guard, "What does Mitch have to do with anything?"

"I mean, there's some unresolved stuff going on—"

"You don't actually have feelings for him, do you?" I ask, Kelly's warnings echoing in my ears.

"Not...No..." Ellie sputters unconvincingly, "But he's important to me as a friend. And as a songwriting partner."

"He seems to think of you as more than that," I mutter.

"Maybe," she admits, "But I can't hold that against him."

"Neither can I," I say, taking in the sight of her. Even flustered, she's still stunning.

It's taking a Herculean effort not to wrap her up in my arms again and carry her back to the tour bus. The surge of desire that overtook me just moments ago does not seem to be quieting. This is going to be a long night of pent-up need, I can tell that much already. Still, it's worth it. I don't want to blow this thing on the first pass.

"Let's get out of here," I suggest, taking Ellie by the hand.

"OK," she says, happy for the subject change. "Where should we go?"

"Anywhere," I say, "The world is our oyster. Or something."

"Let's just see where the night takes us," Ellie suggests.

"Right," I say, leading her through the backstage universe. I savor the feel of her hand in mine as we make our way along. "We've got two great shows to celebrate, eh?"

"I don't think you can put my show on the same level as what you just did," she laughs, "But I'll take it, nonetheless."

"You really need to get better at taking compliments," I tell her, "You're going to be rolling in them soon enough. Did you see that crowd at your show? I think you're about to make it, my dear."

"Is that even a thing, 'Making It'?" she asks, as we approach the back entrance of the space.

"Beats me," I say with a shrug, "Most of the time, it starts to feel just like everyday life. But every once in a while, it can be pretty amazing."

We step out of the backstage tent side-by-side, and are instantly blinded by a searing wall of flashbulbs. I throw up my hand to shield my eyes from the lights, and feel Ellie shrink back against me. There are a dozen photographers gathered around us, snapping shot after shot. Generally, I don't give a damn who gets a picture of me, but I can feel Ellie cowering in shock and embarrassment.

A sudden surge of anger whips through me, and I bowl through the throng of paparazzi, towing Ellie along behind me. Reporters are screaming questions at us as we make our way past, and I answer them all at once with a flip of the ol' bird.

Ellie and I race away from the cloud of eager gossip-mongers and lose ourselves in the crowd. We hurry along, trying to ignore the curious stares as we pass. I slip a pair of sunglasses over my eyes and tell Ellie to do the same. Sure, it's night time—but being the weird guy wearing sunglasses at night is still a lot better than being the clamored-after rock star disrupting everyone's evening. Little by little, people stop noticing us.

I trot up to a nearby food tent and procure us a couple of well-deserved beers. Handing one to Ellie, I can see she's a little overwhelmed. First the kiss, then the photographer ambush—the poor thing's getting completely immersed. I at least got to wade in the shallow end for a while before plunging into the deep.

Ellie's getting no such pass.

"Are you OK?" I ask, taking a wonderfully icy sip of beer.

"What, me?" she says sarcastically, "Oh, yeah. I'm fine. Just trying to figure out how you people do this twenty four seven."

"Don't have much of a choice," I tell her.

"But how do you stand it?" she asks, as we walk toward the outskirts of the crowd, "How can it possibly be worth it to have people hounding you all the time?"

"You already know the answer," I tell her, "Ninety nine percent of being a musician is nonsense, but the one percent that makes it worth it, the music itself, is the only thing worth living for."

"What about a little peace?" she asks wistfully, "Isn't that worth living for, too?"

"That's all up to you," I tell her, "But I'd suggest that you decide soon whether or not you think you can handle all of this."

"It's not a question of whether I can handle it," she says hotly, "I can handle it just fine. I can deal with spats with writing partners, and a chaotic schedule, and not knowing when I'll be able to sleep next, or have my next meal. I can even handle the petty gossip bullshit if I have to. I'm just trying to figure out whether fame is really the end-all be-all that you seem so attached to."

"Hey," I say sternly, "Don't put words in my mouth. I didn't say anything about wanting, let alone needing, to be famous."

"So you don't like it?" she challenges me, "Some part of you doesn't love being famous just as much as you love the music?"

"Don't attack me for being successful just because you're afraid," I tell her.

"I'm not—"

"Sure you are. You'd be an idiot if you weren't, and I certainly know you're not that."

"I just...I don't want to fuck everything up," she says, her anger giving way to upset. "If I put myself in the spotlight, open myself up to the world, nothing's ever going to be the same."

"No," I allow, "But you'll be OK."

"It seems lonely, living the way you do," she says as we walk beyond the crowd, out through the green fields.

"It can be," I tell her, "But once in a while...like right now for instance...it's not so bad."

Out of the corner of my eye, I catch a slight smile cross her lips.

We look back at the bustling festival and linger beyond its reach. There will be plenty of time for complications, and noise, and fervor. But for right now, all I want in the world is to be alone with this person I've managed to find among the masses.

We sip our beers in silence, looking on as the world turns in front of our eyes.

Chapter Eight

Ellie

We spend the night migrating from place to place together, flitting as we please between shows and parties. Roaming around the festival at night, I feel more in my element than I have since Mitch and I rolled up to our campsite in my crappy car.

The throbbing, chaotic energy of this young and vibrant place is something that I can understand. Fame, attention, and celebrity may be far beyond what I'm able to grasp, but this is a world I know how to navigate. In the night, anonymity is ours again. The entire population of the festival gives itself up to the booze-soaked, drug-addled evening and finally leaves us alone for a spell.

I'm not one to let a good party pass me by, and the past few days have certainly warranted a little letting loose on my part.

With Trent in tow, I throw myself into the current of the festivities. Soon, we've stumbled into the fray and procured a couple of drinks, then a couple more. I've made up my mind not to care about propriety tonight.

I've spent my entire time at Hawk and Dove this year worrying about my every move, and what's come of it? I'm fighting with my only band mate, and locked in a frustrated stalemate with the mysterious, irresistible man currently swigging rum by my side.

As the alcohol starts to dull my anxiety, I finally start to forget about the abrupt end that my kiss with Trent came to earlier tonight.

In fact, his entire concert is a pleasant blur in my memory. The show was truly astounding—I never listen to music that intense, and I was blown away by how it got to me. So blown away, in fact, that I all but threw myself at Trent as soon as he came off the stage. It seemed like he wanted me, but I sensed a reluctance in him and backed off.

But I can still feel the pent-up attraction between us growing bigger with every passing moment. What are we supposed to do, if not let ourselves go? What's lingering between us, and obstructing what we both so badly want?

The night rages on, and I match Trent drink for drink. When happy strangers offer us hits off their joints, we accept graciously. I don't usually party this heavily, but all the rules I'm used to organizing my life with seem to be suspended, these days.

As I become more and more intoxicated, my awareness of Trent grows razor sharp. I'm keyed in to his every gesture, his every expression. We move through the festival as a pair, stealing touches and glances, trying to read each other's altered minds.

As my high reaches a fever pitch, a low, throbbing bass line catches my ear. I grab hold of Trent's hand and tow him toward the sound. We race along and surface under a huge tent. A DJ is spinning heavy, pulsing beats, and a crowd of hundreds is gyrating and writhing on the dance floor.

I grin up at Trent in the darkness as wild, flashing lights spin overhead. His face breaks into a wide, wicked smile as I pull him out into the crowd. We weave through couples and groups of dancers, each locked in their own private universes. Even though we're in a sea of people, it still feels more private here than it has since I met Trent just a couple of days ago. It's like we've finally found a place that we can't, and won't, be followed. As long as we keep moving, it's just the two of us alone in the world.

As we reach the center of the bumping, twisting crowd, I spin around to face Trent. His every muscle seems loosened, and even his smile is less controlled. I like this side of him—this unburdened, free-wheeling version.

I take a step toward him, letting my body find its way into the music. He looks down at me intently, eyes locked on the swaying of my hips. I lay my hands on his chest, letting my shoulders dip and sway. My hands have a mind of their own, wander down along the firm muscles of Trent's chest, coming to rest finally on his hips.

"You're quite the dancer," he says over the music. His voice is scraping against the bottom of his register, and the lusty thickness fills me with wanting.

"I know a couple of moves, I guess," I say. Pivoting, I turn my back to him and close the space between our bodies. I let out a low moan as I feel him start to grow hard against me. I felt him before, back behind the curtains at his concert. I could feel then that he wanted me, just like I feel it now.

So what in the world have we been wasting time for?

His hands fall upon my waist once more, caressing the dips of my hourglass figure. I feel his fingers tighten as the bulge in his jeans grows even more firm. He lets his hands wander across my tummy, trailing over the twin peaks of my hips and up, stopping just short of my breasts. I lean back into him, grinding against him with abandon. I love the feel of his hands on me, exploring my body as they please.

Though there are hundreds of people all around us, it feels like we're the only two people on the planet.

I turn back to Trent, looking up into those bright green eyes that never fail to swallow me up. He tugs me against him, wanting me to feel his desire pressed up against me. I bury my fingers in his messy curls, letting my breasts push up between us. There's no mistaking the need in his eyes, and I'm through playing games. I lean in close to his ear and whisper, "If you don't get me out of here, I'll have no choice but to have you right here in front of all these people."

"Well, we can't have that, can we?" he growls, "We entertain these people plenty enough as it is."

He takes hold of my hand and weaves off through the mass of people all around us.

Though simple, the mere touch of his hand sends sparking ripples of desire through me. I'm not usually the one to initiate things like this—to say what I want without fear. But something about Trent gives me courage. Something about how we understand each other makes it easy to speak what my heart, and what my body, wants above all.

We break free of the crowd, stumbling just a little. His strong arms steady me as we route a course back to the campsite. All around us, parties are raging through the night. The sky is still pitch black, with dawn lurking hours away, yet.

We race through the mad, wild world of the festival. All around us, people are shouting and laughing, drinking and smoking, falling on each other as lovers and fighters both. I'd forgotten how intoxicating this place can be, in all senses of the word. But the madness doesn't derail us—if anything it only adds to our fervor.

Clutching onto each other, Trent and I finally find ourselves at the base of the hill on which the talent campsite stands. The incline seems higher than Everest in our current state, but we set to climbing all the same. With every step, I can feel the throbbing need building up in the very core of my body. I know it's been growing there since the moment I laid eyes on Trent in the flesh, despite my attempts to ignore it.

Well, for tonight at least, I'm through trying to turn a blind eye to what I want.

We stagger over the top of the hill, chests heaving. I swear, I could take him right here on this little patch of grass. His arm is hooked protectively around my waist as he leads me forward through the deserted camp. Everyone else is still down among the revelers, it would seem. We have the entire hilltop to ourselves.

We hurry around my own modest little camp, but I see no signs of life. I haven't checked on my band mate since I put him back to bed this morning, but I have no room for Mitch in my thoughts right now. All I can think of is Trent—*all* of Trent.

"My guys won't be back until sunrise," he whispers to me, pulling me onto the tour bus.

"Good," I say, "Because you're going to be occupied for a while."

As the door snaps closed behind us, I throw my arms around Trent's broad shoulders. His hands fall on the swell of my ass, pulling me tightly against him. Our mouths meet in a searching, eager kiss. His strong tongue glides against mine as his fingers dig deeply into my skin.

All the matters in the world at this moment is those hands, that mouth, this amazing person before me.

I let out a gasp as Trent hoists me up into the air as if I were weightless. I throw my legs around his waist, hooking my ankles behind him. He suspends me before him as I kiss him with an urgency I've never known.

I bite his firm bottom lip ever-so-lightly, drawing a rumbling groan from his throat. I can feel him throbbing against me, now. All that separates his thick, pulsing manhood from the aching wetness between my legs is a few layers of cloth and denim.

The friction between us builds to a frenzy, and I tear my mouth from Trent's to cry out, "I can't wait any longer."

That's all he needs to hear. Trent's arms tighten around me, and he carries me swiftly across the cabin of the tour bus. Without breaking stride, he kicks open door after door until we find ourselves in a small, quiet chamber in the back of the huge vehicle. I peer around the space, and a thrill runs through me as I realize that most of it is taken up by an enormous, pristine bed. Well, pristine for now, anyway.

Trent falls to his knees on the sprawling bed, laying me down before him.

He pulls himself on top of me and I eagerly part my legs, wanting to feel that pulsing need against me once more. His lips find the tender skin of my throat, kissing me deeply wherever they land. I let my head fall back against the bed, savoring the feeling of his lips as they brush against me.

He pulls at the loose hem of my top, drawing the garment up over my head and tossing it across the room.

I lay before him in my cotton bra and panties, but he drinks in the sight of me as if I was Venus herself. With a reverence I've never seen from any man, he let lets his hands trail down the length of me, driving me more and more wild with every stroke.

His hands slip around my back, unhooking my bra with one swift, expert motion. My amble breasts spill out, and he eagerly lowers his mouth to my hard, erect nipple. He takes the stiff little peak into his mouth and sucks, hard.

I arch my back, moaning at the sweet sharpness of his kiss.

His hands continue to roam as he lays kiss after kiss upon my breasts. Down across my belly his fingers skirt as I tug at the bottom of his tee shirt. He rips the shirt off his hardened body and presses himself to me.

Our bare torsos come together, and the heat of his skin sends me spiraling into a state of utter need and desperate anticipation. I want there to be no space between us at all. I want to feel all of him, right this instant.

I bring my lips to his, telling him without words what I need so badly.

In a heartbeat, he's tugged his jeans and briefs down his smooth, firm thighs, and I let my hands wander where they will. Trent takes in a sharp breath as my hands close around the hard length between his legs. I can scarcely hold all of him at once.

My hands work up and down his staggeringly long thickness, and I can feel him growing harder by the second. His eyes are closed in utter bliss, and I'm nearly on edge myself, just knowing how good I can make him feel.

His eyes finally focus on mine once more, and he looks down at me in wonder.

I gasp as he pins me back hard against the bed, snatching my hands away and holding them firmly above my head. He looses a hand and wastes no time—I cry out as I feel his fingers glance against the length of my wet slit.

A smile spreads across his face as he traces a slow caress along that eager place between my legs. He's taking his time, letting us both enjoy every minute. I stare up at him, wild-eyed with anticipation, as he slips his fingers between my silky folds. Further inside me his thick fingers dive, flexing against my most intimate flesh. I relish the feeling of him inside of me, but I only want more, I want to take as much as he can give me.

"Oh my god," I moan breathlessly, as he finds the throbbing, tender nub there and begins to rub, hard. He knows exactly what he's doing, exactly how to touch me. He kneads and caresses with expert precision, and my very vision begins to swim. It's all I can do to dig my fingers into the bedding and try to keep from screaming into the night.

He reaches over me to grab a condom off the bedside table, tears the package open and swiftly wraps his member.

I hold my breath, preparing myself for him, as a low, rattling groan rips from my throat as I feel the bulging tip of Trent against me. We lock eyes as he lowers himself to me once more and finally, *finally*, sinks deep inside of me.

Our sharp breaths sound out as one as Trent plunges into my body, parting me as he goes. I pull him in as deeply as I can, marveling at how he fills me so much more than I've ever felt before. We lean into each other with every thrust, transporting each other beyond the tiny room, beyond the festival, to a place that no one can ever travel but the two us of. I buck my hips against his hard, pounding member, barely able to take the length of him, my mouth falling open as I careen toward ecstasy.

"Trent," I breathe, "I'm...I'm gonna..."

His lips part in a wordless howl as we meet each other and crash as one into a state of all-encompassing bliss. Even through the condom, I can feel him emptying himself into me, as waves of dizzying sensation crash over me...leaving me speechless.

We hold each other as the shockwaves of pleasure rush through us, overcoming every other thought. Our limbs entangled, we collapse into each other, curled up on top of the sheets.

Sleep rushes in as soon as the tide of bliss subsides, and we sink into sweet slumber in each other's arms.

Chapter Nine

The sky is still a flinty gray when my eyes crack open.

For half a second, I can't figure out for the life of me where I am. But when I feel Ellie's warm, smooth skin pressed against me, the night comes rushing back into my mind, blowing me away all over again.

In the lightening little cabin, I take in the sight of the beautiful woman resting in the crook of my arm. She's sleeping soundly, her hair splayed out across the white sheets like a halo. I pull her closer against me, relishing in this time that's ours alone.

I gave it my best shot, resisting her. But after that scorching kiss backstage, that intense connection on the dance floor, and a little alcohol inhibition...I didn't stand a chance. Hell, I was a goner from the first time we said three words to each other.

It's hard to believe that only a few days ago, this amazing person was missing from my life. How did I get on, before Ellie wandered into my world? Not very well, all things considered. Not very well at all.

The way she took charge of things last night—that's what had sent me over the edge. She told me exactly what she wanted, in no uncertain terms. There aren't any games with Ellie, no playing hard-to-get, no coyness. She's genuine, and unpretentious, and so utterly real.

I've never been with anyone like this before. And if I didn't know just by being in her company that this was something big, last night certainly proved it. I don't even know how many women I've slept with in my years of being a rock star, but I know that I've never felt before what I did last night.

With the rest of the women I've slept with, sex has always felt like a transaction. Each party gets what they came for and calls it a day. There's never been a connection, or any sense of caring, to any of it.

Not until Ellie, that is. She didn't come to me looking for a good story to tell her friends or bragging rights in the mosh pit. She didn't come to me asking for anything but for me to be there with her, present to what was happening between us.

I feel like a goddamned virgin again with this girl.

Though I have no way of knowing what sex is usually like for her, I'd have a hard time believing that she's been around as much as I have, that's for sure. I just hope that she doesn't wake up kicking herself for diving into bed with me. That would absolutely kill me. But for a few more minutes, or maybe even an hour, I get to hold her like this—with nothing at all between us. I get to hold her here in this little, wonderful world of our own creation.

Just as the room starts to grow bright, almost imperceptibly, Ellie stretches out against me and lets her eyes flutter open. I watch her take in the unfamiliar room, confused for a moment about where she's ended up. But I tighten my arms around her, letting her know I'm here.

Her gaze swings my way, and she almost looks surprised to see me. But her awe soon gives way to contentment, and she snuggles in closer to me. Her simple, spontaneous act of intimacy is more meaningful than it has any right to be.

"Good morning," she murmurs. Her voice is thick with sleep and impossibly sexy.

"Morning, you," I whisper, my lips hovering just beside her ear. "You really don't sleep past five in the morning, do you?"

"And I guess you really don't sleep at all," she laughs softly, turning to face me.

We're lying together on top of the covers, totally bare. I let my eyes travel down the curvy landscape of her body, dipping and bobbing all along the way. Her eyes crinkle with pleasure as she watches me become transfixed by the very sight of her. I can't help it—she's impossible to look away from.

"How do you feel?" she asks, reaching out to lay a hand on my chest.

"Fucking unbelievable," I answer honestly.

She smiles, rolling her eyes. "I was kind of talking about the copious amount of substances we ingested last night. Are you hung over or anything?"

"I don't really get hung over," I tell her, "What about you?"

"I think I'm still all kinds of drunk," she laughs, "I'm a bit of a lightweight myself."

"You could have fooled me," I tease, "It seemed like you were keeping up just fine last night."

"I didn't...I wasn't making an ass of myself, was I?" she asks.

My smile drops a hair. "You...You do remember last night, don't you?"

"What do you mean?" she asks.

"I mean...Everything between us..."

"No..." she says, sounding almost upset, "What happened between us?" She arches her eyebrows and looks genuinely afraid of my answer.

"Oh," I say averting my gaze. Fuck I knew this would happen.

"I'm just kidding you loser!" She says with a hearty laugh. "I'm not the sort of girl who doesn't remember sleeping with someone the next day," she says, "Especially when the evidence is as clear as all this..."

She motions to her naked body, smiling at me with those beautiful lips.

Thank God what a relief.

"I didn't mean to imply—"

"I know," she says quickly, "I just don't want you to think that what happened was an accident. Or a whim. I didn't just decide in the spur of the moment that

I wanted to sleep with you, Trent. I made up my mind about that pretty early on."

"How early on, would you say?" I ask mischievously.

"Since you tried to steal our campsite, I would say," she shoots back, "You dick."

"Guilty as charged," I grin, "And for what it's worth...the feeling is mutual."

"So I gathered," she says, rolling onto her back. I lean toward her, resting my hand on her soft stomach. She arches her back just a little, stretching in a markedly feline sort of way.

I love watching the little movements of her body, the little features that make her unique. I'd never say it out loud for fear of sounding like an asshole, but Ellie is not the sort of woman I'm used to sleeping with. My general type is tall, thin, surgically enhanced, and all but silent. Ellie, on the other hand, is untampered with, soft, and very much the type to speak her mind. I never thought it would be so thrilling to stray away from the mold, but then again I don't think I could ever have imagined someone quite like her.

As if reading my mind, she turns to me and asks, "So, how do these things usually go with you?"

"These things?" I parrot.

"Your conquests," she says, pulling herself up onto an elbow, "I imagine that the rest of the bus is filled with your band mates and whatever young ladies they've carted home themselves. What happens in the morning? Does everyone come together for a pancake breakfast?"

"I hope you don't think this is just a conquest," I say, bristling.

"I just don't want you to feel pressured," she tells me, "I'm not completely naive when it comes to this kind of thing."

"Is that what this feels like to you?" I ask, "Just another 'thing'? Or are you just playing tough for me right now?"

"I don't *play*," Ellie says, sitting up in bed, "And no, honestly, this doesn't feel like anything that's ever happened to me before."

"Me either," I say.

"It's a little...scary," she says hesitantly.

"Are you kidding me?" I say, "It's fucking terrifying."

She stifles a relieved laugh with the palm of her hand. "Well, I'm glad that's out in the open," she says.

"If you think I'm used to actually caring about the people I sleep with, you're sorely mistaken," I say honestly.

"Is that supposed to make me feel better?" she asks.

"I don't know," I say, "Does it?"

"Actually...It does, a little," she admits, "As long as you promise you're not just spinning this shit so that I'll agree to sleep with you again."

"Ellie," I say, taking her hand in mine, "I dare you to look me in the eye and tell me that you didn't feel something...*amazing* between us. Unlike anything else in the world."

She keeps her eyes averted, which is all the answer I need.

"I'm a pretty good actor," I admit, "But even I couldn't fake what was there last night."

"I know," she says, "I hope you know I didn't either."

"So...does that make it any less scary?" I ask.

"Honestly, not really," she laughs, "I don't know if anything could. I just...I don't have any idea what comes next. Usually, it's a goodbye kiss and onto the rest of my life, but...I don't want that with you."

We sit together in silence. I know she's waiting for me to say the same, to assure her that I know how we're supposed to proceed. But I have no idea what comes next, here.

She's a baby, as far as the music scene goes. A college student. With a whole, normal life to lead back home. What am I supposed to do, interrupt all that? Drag her into my crazy, chaotic life? That may be what we both want right now, but what if she eventually grows to resent me for it?

I wouldn't be able to blame her if she did. I wouldn't wish the bullshit of this business on anybody, especially not her.

"Trent?" she says softly, "Tell me what you're thinking."

"I think...we should probably get dressed," I say, "These things are best talked about with clothes on, don't you think?"

A brief, pained expression crosses her face. She thinks I'm going to try and brush off figuring out what's going on between us. And the crappiest part is, she's partially right. The last thing I want to do is decide what happens next. I have absolutely zero experience with relationships that last longer than a week. The fact that I'm even thinking the word relationship is freaking me the hell out.

She unfolds her long legs and hunts down her clothes where they've been scattered about the room. We dress in silence, stealing glances at each other's bodies.

In a moment, it seems like the air has grown thick with unsaid words. Ellie's smile is just a little too tight, a little too forced. What is the matter with me that I can't just speak what's on my mind? I suppose that's a muscle I've never been called to exercise before. I hope she'll understand that I might need to work up to the whole "emotional creature" thing.

Fully dressed, we face off across the tiny room. The mussed up bed sheets attest to the amazing night we shared together. But now, the sky is growing brighter. Through the tiny window, I can see streaks of yellow and pink soaring through the morning as sunrise approaches.

I wish that I could dig my heels into the ground and stop the world from spinning for a while. I don't want this night to be over. I don't want to face the day, deal with the ridiculous politics and pressures of fame. I just want to stay here with Ellie, forever.

But that's not the way it works, is it?

"I guess I should go?" Ellie says quietly, "Before everyone wakes up, you know."

"I guess that would be a good idea," I say, "I don't want you to have to deal with the guys' nonsense in the morning."

"Me either," she smiles, "How are we going to get through the bus?"

"There's a back door," I tell her, taking her hand.

We've only known each other for a little while, but already I'm hooked on the way her fingers feel entwined with mine.

I lead her back through the bus, ducking through the darkness. We come to the door, and I push it open, letting a remarkably cool breeze waft into the bus. We step out onto the dewy grass together, taking in deep breaths of the morning air.

Ellie takes a step away from me, spreads her arms wide, and closes her eyes. She's backlit against the sunrise, her head thrown back. She might be the most beautiful thing I've ever seen, rumpled by sleep and not giving a damn.

I want to ask her to run away with me right then and there, leave behind this ridiculous place and go somewhere where no one knows who we are.

The only problem is, that place doesn't exist. No matter where we might roam, I'd never be anonymous. I'd never be able to start over with her from scratch. But Ellie...she's standing on the precipice of fame. If she wants to, she can turn it all down.

She could drive away from here right now and get to keep the rest of her life to herself. And whatever she ends up choosing in the long run, it has to be her decision, not mine. I'd never force fame on her if she didn't want it.

She looks back over her shoulder and sees my troubled expression.

"Why so serious, dear?" she asks.

"I was just admiring the view," I say, looking at her pointedly.

"Yeah?" she says, doing a little twirl right there on the grass, "You like?"

Fuck yeah, says a little voice in the back of my mind.

And then a sudden revelation knocks the wind right out of me. It hadn't occurred to me, not until this moment, but now that I've thought it, I know that it's the truth. I'm falling, or I've already fallen, for Ellie.

My jaw hangs open dumbly, and Ellie's brow furrows.

"You don't like the hippie look?" she pouts theatrically.

"I...Um...Need some coffee," I say haltingly.

"Good idea," she says.

We set off together across the campsite, toward the smell of brewing coffee. Ellie keeps a healthy three feet of space between us, and I get the feeling that it's more for my sake than for hers.

Does she have any idea just how deep my feelings run for her? Can I even be sure of them, or am I just swept up in the novelty of being with someone so different than me?

But that's the thing, isn't it? We're not so different at all. Maybe we've picked different patches of signifiers for ourselves, but there's something shared between us that's much more important. There's a vital understanding, a shared experience, that I've never had with anyone before. Not with my family, not with my friends, not with my band mates.

I've only known Ellie for a few short days, but she's quickly becoming the most important person in my life.

I shake my head in silent wonder as we collect our coffee. Maybe the world will seem clearer on the other side of a caffeine kick.

Chapter Ten

Ellie

We part ways quietly as the third day of the festival dawns. Off across the open plains, storm clouds are gathering on the horizon. The reds and yellows of the brilliant sunrise start to fade as the rest of the camp rouses itself from sleep.

It's not exactly an auspicious sign to start the day, catching sight of looming thunderheads. I'm determined not to read too much into the weather as an omen of my romantic future, but I've always been a little superstitious. And I'm more than a little overwhelmed by everything that happened last night.

Quick though our courtship of sorts may have been, I have no regrets about sleeping with Trent. My mom used to tell me, when I was a teenager, that there's nothing wrong with sex outside of a relationship, marriage or otherwise.

She said that when you run out of words, when the only expression of how you feel about someone is intimate, then sex can be a beautiful thing. She was right, of course, whether or not I always followed her advice. Between Trent and I, going to bed together was inevitable.

I knew it from the start.

And god, had it been incredible. I've slept with a few men in my life—boys, rather—but I've never felt anything like what passed between Trent and I last night.

I didn't feel like we were going through the motions, or ticking off items on a sexy to do list. We were just...Collaborating. Just as if we were composing a piece of music together, we were contributing to the whole, not trying to get something out of the experience just for the sake of it. We wrote a beautiful, unexpected love song together. It was the most amazing thing I've ever experienced with someone else.

I watch as Trent disappears back into his tour bus to get ready for the day. I linger beside my sedan, cradling my coffee cup in my hands. If what happened last night was so wonderful—and oh, was it wonderful—why do I feel so shook up about it? I wish I knew what I was supposed to do, now. What was expected, or acceptable.

With most guys, the playbook is pretty clear. You sleep with the guy, you decide whether or not you liked it, then you either ignore his advances or agree to go along with the whole dating or booty call thing.

But with Trent, there's no set of rules to follow, no path that's already been blazed a thousand times. Whatever is building up between us is bigger than I could have ever comprehended before. And in its hugeness, it's terrifying. Not to mention, in a few days we'll be parting ways and a million miles away from each other.

Leaning back against the car, looking out over the stormy, sprawling fields. I dare myself to name the thing that's got a hold on me. If I'm honest with myself, I know how I'm coming to feel about Trent.

Honestly...I think that I'm falling for him.

"How the hell did that happen?" I mutter to myself, shaking my head in disbelief. I'm not a girl who falls in love on a whim. So far in my twenty one years on this planet, I don't think I've actually gone and fallen in love with any guy.

I know what it is to love my family, and maybe a close friend or two. I had a hamster once that I loved with all my heart. But loving a man? I have exactly zero knowledge about the matter. Especially when the man happens to be an international rock star. I suppose we have shared a lot together in these past few days, more than most people probably ever share to be honest. There's just something about him, and the timing of all of this coming together at once.

Where can I even go from here? I'm sure the last thing Trent needs is a lovesick songwriter trailing him around the country. The Trent Parker that the world has come to know doesn't do the whole "love" thing. He does the arm candy thing, at least publicly.

What the hell would people think if I suddenly started appearing by his side? They'd probably think I was just trying to steal a little piece of his fame for myself, or that he was trying to draw in a new demographic of listeners by dating some indie chick.

Whatever we did, wherever we went, some swarm of gossip columnists would have an opinion about it.

That's supposing that Trent would want me around at all—or that he could possibly be having the same thoughts that I am. I don't dare hope that some part of Trent is wondering about the depth of his feelings for me.

I doubt that "love" is a word Trent bandies about. He's a rock star, for god's sake. He's practically contractually obligated not to believe in love. He'd probably think I was a lunatic if I ever told him what I was feeling now.

And even if, by some holy miracle of the divine, Trent did have feelings for me that went beyond our one night together, what then? I'm not exactly a free agent in the world. I have a band of my own, fragile though it may be.

I'm still in school—and I have no interest in dropping out to be a rock star's girlfriend, or groupie, or whatever. And what about Mom and Kate? How would they ever understand my wanting to be with someone rich and famous? We grew up with so little, but what little we had was carefully crafted and full of love.

The opulence and excess of rock stardom would probably turn my family's stomachs.

A powerful pang of homesickness wrenches through me as I think about my little home in Barton. I wish I could be back there right now, helping my mom paint the kitchen whatever color she felt like that week. I just want to sit back on my front porch with a notebook and a beer, and forget about fame and fortune forever. But I can't have it both ways. I can't have my peace and quiet and keep my rock star, too.

With a heavy sigh, I peek inside the tent. A wave of guilt catches me off guard as I take in the sight of Mitch, curled up alone on a half-inflated air mattress. I've been a terrible music partner and an even worse friend to him since we got here. He'd been as good a sport as anyone could have asked about this whole thing. Sure, I'd had to drag him kicking and screaming to the festival. And sure, he'd been a huge dick after our first performance. But still, I owe him a little bit of appreciation after all his years of loyalty.

I unzip the tent as quietly as I can and step inside. It's sweltering as ever in here, though the day has hardly even started in earnest.

I cross my legs under my body and sit next to Mitch's sleeping form. His clothes are a mess, and the smell of vodka hangs heavily in the air. I suppose he spent last night getting wasted yet again. I feel like it's all my fault, and I hate that. I never meant to make him this unhappy. I don't have feelings for him, sure, but he deserves better than how I've been treating him.

Gently, I lay a hand on his shoulder. His nose twitches, but his sleep is pretty deep. I give him a little shake, trying to rouse him. Slowly, he begins to notice my insistent presence.

He stretches, groaning pitifully. A night sleeping on the rocky ground will do a number on your back. Finally, his bloodshot eyes crack open and blink up at me. His mouth twists sloppily, and it's pretty clear that he's still a little drunk from his previous evening's escapades.

"Well, look who it is," he mutters.

"Hi Mitch," I say, "How are you feeling?"

"What, me?" he says, rolling onto his back, "I'm just peachy."

"What did you get up to last night?" I ask.

"Not much, not much," he says, staring up into the tent, "I snagged a bottle of vodka from some famous dude's campsite and had myself a little party in here."

"You stayed here?" I ask, spotting the very large and very empty vodka bottle laying beside the air mattress.

"Yup," he says, "It's not like I had anyone to hang out with."

"I'm sorry," I say, "Really, Mitch. I just got caught up."

"With that asshole Trent?" he asks, pained.

"We hung out for a while," I admit, "But really, it was just the whole festival, you know?"

"Uh huh," Mitch says, grabbing for his phone, "That sounds legit."

"Seriously," I insist.

"So, you weren't off sleeping with the enemy while I plastered myself to the wall in here?"

"First of all, Trent is not the enemy."

"Funny that you associated him with the word, though..."

"And second of all, no. I wasn't. But it's good to know that you have such a high opinion of me, Mitch. That means a lot."

I'm lying through my teeth, of course, hoping that Mitch won't notice. I hold my breath as I wait for his response, hoping that this whole thing will blow over like so many storm clouds. He's propped up on an elbow, staring at the screen of his phone. A look of pure fury seizes his every feature. His entire body seems to be trembling with outrage.

Stumbling, he pulls himself to his feet, and I scramble up to the other side of the tent. His eyes are glued to that phone...and I doubt very much if I want to see what it is that's captured his attention so.

"Mitch," I say softly, "Mitch, what's wrong? Did something happen?"

He lifts his eyes to mine, and I feel like the anger there is going to knock me to the ground. Mitch takes a menacing step toward me, thrusting his phone into my face. I look helplessly at the device and feel the bottom of my stomach drop out. There, plastered across the screen, is a perfect close-up photo of Trent and I dancing together. My head is thrown back rapturously, and Trent's hands are all over my writhing body.

I grab the phone from Mitch and scroll through the page. There are dozens upon dozens of images just like it. Pictures of us grinding up on each other among a sea of festival goers, pictures of us emerging from his concert hand-in-hand. There's even a shot of us standing beneath that beautiful tree together, inches away from kissing. Everywhere we went together, there's a trail of pictures to prove it.

I feel nauseated by the thought that someone was lurking beside us all through last night, stealing away our private moments and making them public domain. And this is just one gossip blog. If they have these pictures...

"Oh..." I breathe, as I come to the last photo of the set. It shows Trent and I clamoring up the hill to the talent campsite. Even from a hundred feet away and from behind, you can practically smell the urgency of our flight. There's no ambiguity about what transpired between us last night, as if Mitch had needed photographic proof to know that.

"You want to lie to me again about how you spent last night?" Mitch growls, furious.

"Mitch," I begin, holding the phone away from me as if it was poisonous, "I'm sorry I didn't tell you. I thought you'd be upset..."

"Upset?" he says, with a cruel laugh, "Upset that you abandoned me to spend the night throwing yourself at a cocky asshole? Upset that you had the audacity to lie to me about it? Upset that the girl I've been in love with for years has turned out to be nothing but a fame-hungry, naive bimbo who'll suck anything to get ahead?"

"That's not fair," I say, balling my hands into fists, "Don't you dare accuse me of that. You know that's not me, Mitch. You know full well that—"

"I don't know anything of the sort," he yells, "How could you be interested in that douche bag? You hate the commercial garbage he calls music, you hate the idea of selling out."

"No Mitch, that's you," I say, "And you've never even listened to his music. How in the world can you judge—?"

"Oh, god," Mitch groans, "Can you even hear yourself? Are you so sick with pathetic puppy love that you're actually buying into his whole act? He's a freaking con artist, Ellie. He's nothing but a sham propped up by a record deal and a multi-million dollar marketing campaign. There's nothing pure or true about him."

"And you're some kind of beacon of truth and light?" I shoot back, "Please! You're nothing but a privileged, sniveling child with a batch of first world problems and mommy issues. You spend your entire life trying to knock other people's efforts down so that you'll feel a little better about yourself. You've actually got yourself convinced that you're some arbiter of taste, and all that's good in the world, and it's bullshit. You hate everything, Mitch. There's not one thing in the world that you don't look down on or hold in contempt."

"I didn't hate you," he says, "At least, not until now."

"Don't be so fucking dramatic," I say, "And, here's a little bit of breaking news for you: I'm not a thing for you to love or hate. I'm not an idea, or your white whale, or something you can keep on your shelf to look at when you're feeling blue. You've never thought of me as anything but something that you wanted for yourself. But you know what? You don't get to keep me. I'm taking myself off the market."

"That's fine," he says, his voice soft, "I'm not interested in damaged goods, anyway."

Before I know what I'm doing, I've chucked Mitch's phone across the tent, straight at his sneering, horrible face. The device cracks against his forehead and spins away. He staggers backward, surprise and hurt piling on top of his anger. My chest is heaving with the force of my disgust for him.

"Get out of here," I say, "I never want to see you again."

"You're forgetting, dear," he says with gritted teeth, "That we have a show left to play."

"I don't care," I tell him, "It's not worth it."

"Yeah, right."

"I mean it. This is over. I should have let you go that first night. So, consider this your invitation to stay the fuck out of my life, for good."

He stares at me for a long, brutal moment. Then, without another word, he snatches up his bag and turns away.

Mitch climbs out of the tent and disappears from my view. I know in my gut that this is it, but I can't bring myself to humor him with a goodbye. I stare up into the canopy of the tent and watch as the first fat drops of rain dash themselves against the canvas.

Chapter Eleven

Trent

I make myself comfortable in the main cabin of the bus, sinking into an oversized armchair. The rest of the guys won't be up for hours, and I plan to cherish every minute of this quiet morning.

I have no idea how to go along with this thing with Ellie. If I had any idea in the world what she was thinking, maybe I could at least make an educated guess. I'm not used to not having all the power in a relationship, or at least all the agency. Usually, whatever I say goes.

But not so this time around.

Through the windshield, I can see a massive storm rolling in across the plains. *Perfect*, I think. It's the perfect sort of weather for lovey-dovey brooding. How am I supposed to get back out there and play our next show when, on the inside, I feel like a fourteen-year-old kid again, miffed that he doesn't know whether his crush likes him back?

I need to talk this out with Ellie. This guessing game bullshit isn't going to work. But what am I going to tell her? That I've somehow managed to catch feelings for her in the span of, what, seventy two hours? That's not creepy at all.

Even if I was honest with her about this bizarre feeling, what would happen then? I don't get the feeling that Ellie is the kind of girl who will drop her entire life to follow me around like a puppy. I wouldn't be falling for her if she was. I mean, she's not even out of school yet. She's got her own friends, and family, her own life. I don't want to force my entire world onto her. How the hell would that be fair? She'd be miserable, being with me.

I try to imagine Ellie giving up her own ambitions to tag along and hang out backstage during my shows. The very thought makes my skin crawl. She'd be hounded relentlessly, just like I am. Her face would be splattered across tabloids with horrific rumors printed below. They'd tear apart her look, her personality, her voice, just because they can.

They'd accuse her of being a star-fucker and never let her have a career of her own. And if that became the case...I don't see how she would ever be able to forgive me for it.

There's one thing I know for sure in all of this.

I'm not worth the trouble.

Being with me is not worth Ellie throwing away everything else she's got going on for her. It would be selfish of me to ask her to stay. It would be nothing but pure ego to expect her to want to. But...how am I supposed to let her go, feeling the way I do?

How can I keep her close without destroying everything else about her world? A future between us seems as cloudy as the storm on the horizon, threatening to shatter the sky at any moment.

I hear someone moving around in the back of the bus. Somewhere in the web of rooms and bunks, one of my band mates is rising back from the dead.

Or, so I think at first.

I turn to face the back of the bus and watch as Kelly makes her way slowly into the light of the cabin. She's looking at me with a cold, steely anger that I've seen only a few times since we've known each other. I wonder, wildly, whether she was witness to what transpired in my bedroom only a few hours ago. Dear god, don't let her have been awake for that.

"Good morning," I say hopefully. The last thing I need is a tongue lashing from my testy manager. But the steady, unflinching fury in her eyes doesn't give me much confidence that I'm going to get away from this confrontation unscathed.

She takes a few slow steps toward me, and I see that she's holding her smart phone to her chest. With shaking hands she throws the device sharply into my lap. Confused, I look down at the gadget. It's got some stupid fake news blog pulled up on the screen. I take a closer look and recognize the subjects of the pulpy article.

"Shit," I murmur, as the photos come into focus.

Some asshole photographer must have trailed Ellie and I all night long. Shot after shot cascades down the page, leaving nothing to the imagination. There's us on the dance floor, all but getting it on right in the middle of the crowd. There's us watching that first concert on the tree, almost about to kiss for the first time. Us leaving my concert, and...Oh, god. Us heading back up to the bus at the end of the night.

"This is bad," I say softly.

"Bad?" Kelly repeats, "This is beyond bad, Trent. This is a fucking nightmare."

"Don't get ahead of yourself," I tell her, "I'm sure Ellie will understand. The paparazzi are unstoppable, you know? She'll be OK."

"Why the hell would you imagine that I care what your little girlfriend thinks about this?" Kelly shrieks. "I don't give a rats ass whether her feelings are hurt, Trent. I'm talking about you. You, and your career, and the band's future, and ours!"

"Ours?" I ask, baffled, "What the hell do you mean ours?"

Kelly looks genuinely flustered by her slip of the tongue. "As talent and manager. Obviously."

"Right," I say suspiciously, "Well...Other than this being a pain in the ass, would you like to clue me in on what's so goddamn tragic about a spread of photos in a magazine?"

"Are you kidding me?" she says, looking at me as though I've sprouted two extra heads. "What do you think your fans are going to say when they see you wrapped up in some folk rock pixie's arms on the cover of a tabloid? Do you think that any of them will be able to respect you, if this is the kind of musician you intend to be?

Your fans value sincerity, and a fuck-off attitude, and the fact that you're not a media puppet. That's your entire brand, Trent. That's what the fans pay to see. If you go down this road, you'll be judging reality shows and playing at bar mitzvahs before you can say 'washed up'."

"That's such a load of crap!" I yell, getting to my feet. "Sincerity? Can you even hear yourself spouting off this shit? Nothing about this entire act is real, or honest, or unfiltered. I'm just as commercial as those famous-to-be-famous assholes you seem so keen to knock. I'm just another commodity. That's what you've turned me into.

All these years, you've been trying to convince me that we'd only have to play the game for a little while. That once we made it big, we could play by our own rules. But that was all just a bunch of lies, wasn't it? We're playing by the same rules as everyone else is. We're not doing anything new, or real..."

"And I suppose that little girl is, though?" Kelly demands, her face twisting with contempt.

"Yeah," I say, throwing up my hands, "That *is* right. Ellie is the most genuine musician I've ever met in my life. She's the kind of influence I want in my life."

"She's not genuine," Kelly laughs, "She's just new in town. That fresh scrubbed exterior will be muddied up soon enough. Especially if she keeps hanging out with you."

"Why are you trying to ruin this for me?" I ask, "What do you have to gain from me being miserable and alone?"

"Good music," she spits, "And a flagpole act who's not distracted by cotton candy dreams of happily ever after."

"God...How did you get so cynical?" I ask quietly, shaking my head, "What made you this way, Kelly?"

"I'm sure that hanging around with you all these years hasn't exactly done wonders for my outlook on love," she says. I can hear the hurt tugging on her vocal chords. "If anyone's convinced me that love and affection are fictional, it's you."

"What the hell do I know?" I say, "I'm twenty five years old. I've never met anyone I could care about before Ellie."

"Really?" Kelly says, looking at me hard, "Not anyone?"

Sudden understanding hits me smack between the eyes. I hear, for the first time, what Kelly is trying to tell me through her half-baked accusations.

"Oh..." I breathe, taking in the sight of her. Her model-caliber body is draped in a few thin layers of cotton pajamas, but not much else. I've always recognized the fact that Kelly is a sexy woman, but I've never felt anything for her in the past, she's too aggressive.

How am I supposed to tell her, after all this time, that my indifference to her stands? She's a great manager, but I could never want anything else from her.

Especially not now.

"You really never noticed?" Kelly asks. I'm alarmed by the sultry tone of her voice.

This cannot be happening right now. It just can't be.

"We've always been great friends," I say, trying to lure her away from the subject.

But she's advancing toward me across the cabin, her eyes fixed on mine. I run my fingers through my hair and sit back into the arm chair. How can I get out of this terribly awkward situation without offending her?

"But you can't honestly say that you've never wanted anything more than that. Can you?" she asks, standing before me in her scanty clothing.

"Kelly, stop this," I tell her, crossing my arms in front of my body, "You're making a fool out of yourself."

"I've been doing that for years," she says with a smile.

"Aren't you supposed to be mad at me right now?" I suggest, "I've just tanked my fan approval rating, right? Why don't you go back to berating me about that?"

"How have you never noticed that I want you, Trent?" she asks, stepping in even closer to me. I can see the lust in her eyes beginning to rise.

I need to get out of here. Now.

"Kelly, this is really embarrassing," I say, lurching up from the chair and putting distance between us, "This is not what I want. You're the best manager I ever could have asked for. Can't we just leave it at that?"

"I don't think so," she tells me, "Not anymore. You need to be with someone who understands you. Someone who gets how you think."

"I think so too," I say, thinking of Ellie, "But that person is not you."

"You've just never given me a chance," she whines.

"I don't—Hey!" I say, as she closes the space between us and lays her hands on my chest.

"Forget about the little girl," she croons in my ear, "Think of what an amazing partner I would make. I'd devote every second of my life to you. God knows, I do that already..."

"Why would you want that?" I cry, knocking her hands away.

"Because I'm crazy about you Trent. I always have been."

"This isn't OK. This isn't OK for you to be doing right now."

"Since when do you have qualms about being seduced?" she laughs, "Last time I checked, it was one of your favorite things. Now, come on. I know full well that you want this. Just give into it, Trent. We've waited long enough. This whole stunt with that girl was just you acting out. But I can soothe you. Really I—Trent!"

I shove her roughly away, a surging anger rising inside of me. This is the last thing in the world I need right now. All I want to do is sort things out with Ellie before she gets the wrong idea. How am I supposed to do that while my insane manager is in heat?

A knock on the bus door disrupts our standoff. I turn away from Kelly and march to the door, yanking it open none-too-gently. My mouth falls open as I see Ellie standing there in the threshold, a look of utter bewilderment on her face. The rain that's started to fall across the plains is soaking her through and through. Her blonde hair is plastered across her forehead, and for a moment the downpour obscures her own tears.

"Ellie," I breathe, stepping down to meet her, "What is it?"

"The entire world knows. About us," she says blankly, "It's all over the internet. Pictures...Everyone is going to see."

"I know," I say, pulling her into an embrace, "It's going to pass though. Don't worry about it."

"Mitch is gone," she says into my shoulder, "He just left me here."

"I'm so sorry," I tell her, "That's not...Ellie?" I see her eyes gazing beyond me, into the depths of the bus. With a sickening sense of dread, I follow her line of sight. Kelly has come forward into the little patch of light, her skimpy clothing and tousled hair looking far too sexy for anyone's good.

I turn back to Ellie, panicked. "Come on..." I say, "You don't think that anything—"

"Come back up here, babe," Kelly drawls, "I'm still sleepy."

"Trent..." Ellie says, pulling out of my arms, "What the hell...? How could you...?"

"You know that it's not—Nothing's—Ellie, you know me better than that!"

"I don't know you at all," she says, her chin beginning to quiver. She backs away from me into the rain, looking back and forth between Kelly and me. "I really don't have anyone, do I? Not even you."

"Of course you have me," I insist, "Kelly's just—"

"Kelly's just one woman," Ellie says, "But if it's not her today, it'll be someone else next month, won't it? You could never be content with one person. You're too used to getting exactly what you want."

"What are you saying?" I demand, "That's some other person you're talking about, it's not me."

"I just...I need to go," Ellie says distractedly.

She turns from me and hurries away, but I'm not letting her go so easily. I catch her arms as she tries to move away from the bus, but her rain-soaked skin is slippery. She darts away from me, back toward her meager little camp. But instead of throwing herself back into the tent, she wrenches open the car door and slides inside. My heart twists itself into a knot as the engine roars to life. I spring forward, but the vehicle is already speeding across the uneven land. She takes off like a shot, ripping off through the rain like a loosed bullet.

I stand in the midst of her abandoned camp and watch her taillights disappear into the distance. Soon, every trace of her is obscured by the falling rain. Just as quickly as she fell into my life, she's slipping away from me.

Chapter Twelve

Ellie

I slam down the gas pedal, half expecting my foot to crash through the undercarriage of the car.

The heavy rain splashes against my windshield, outpacing my ancient wipers. I'm hurtling along the muddy road, bumping with every stray rock and grassy patch along the way.

The last thing I'd ever call myself before this week is reckless, but while my head may be begging me to slow down, my body and heart have other ideas. All I know is that right now I need to put as much distance between myself and this festival as possible, as quickly as I can.

I just need to get away.

A thick, irrepressible knot is throbbing in my throat. I can feel the hot tears welling up behind my eyes, threatening to blind me, but I don't have time for them right now.

My thoughts are ricocheting around my skull like fireworks, and the racket they create is just as overwhelming. All I can do is keep my hands on the wheel, force my eyes to stay on the meager sham of a road before me, and keep driving, no matter what.

At this moment, it feels like my life depends on it. *Keep moving*, I coach myself, *keep moving, don't stop*.

The front wheels of my sedan bounce up, dragging me along onto the highway. A long, seemingly endless expanse of asphalt stretches out before me. The road looks like a black river in the rainy gloom, and I intend to ride it as far along as I can. I press my foot down hard and gasp as my car rears forward, behaving more like a bucking bronco than any sophisticated machine.

I take off down the highway, swathes of muted green flying by on either side. Forcing deep breath after deep breath down into my lungs, I do my best to staunch the flood of emotion that needs so badly to be let loose. Between that storm surge and the torrential rain outside, I might just drown if I'm not careful.

Desperate, I fumble through my CD collection for something that will clear my head, and root me back to the ground. I snatch up the first promising disk and slide it into the dusty player, waiting for the sweet release of music to cure what ails me.

The CD whirs to life, and the voice of Joni Mitchell washes through the cockpit of my car. My breath catches in my throat as she glides through the first verse of "River", taking me along with her through this mire of heartache. Silently, the tears begin to slide down my face. I let my favorite songstress carry across the threshold of feeling, guiding me into the depths of my confusion and pain.

I swerve over to the shoulder of the road as a throaty sob rips from my body. The twin headlights of my car illuminate the rushing rain as it pours down against the roof of my beat up ride.

Giving over to the swell within me, I let my forehead rest against the steering wheel, and I weep.

The overwhelming, disorienting events of the past few days play in my memory like a film reel, coursing along with the soundtrack of Joni's music. I feel as though I've lost every point of reference grounding me to real life. It's like I've been washed away into someone's else's story...but all I want is to return to my own.

Gazing out the windshield at the stormy road ahead, I marvel at how my life has been completely rewritten in a matter of days. Before I made this trek to Hawk and Dove, I was just Eleanor Jackson—student, daughter, sister, unknown-musician.

I had a friend and partner in Mitch, a wonderful home to return to, and hopes of sharing my music with the rest of the world. But ever since that first bit of exposure opened me up to the masses, everything's changed.

My relationship with Mitch is destroyed, my private life is a thing of the past, and the staggering presence of Trent Parker has altered my world forever. From this point on, nothing will ever be the way it once was. I don't know how I can possibly learn to be OK with that.

It would be one thing if I were trading in my old life for a brilliant, secure future with this amazing man I've found in Trent. For a moment there, I actually let myself believe that such a seamless transition, and winning bargain, would be possible. Effortless. How naive I was to let myself think, even for a moment, that Trent was mine for the taking.

I let myself forget everything I knew about Trent Parker before the festival began. For years, I'd heard about Trent the rock star—the womanizing, drunk, fuck-the-world musician with a terrible reputation. I'd read the gossip blogs about his uncountable bimbo girlfriends, his bad behavior, his addictions. But the moment I'd met him in the flesh, I let all of those impressions slip away.

I couldn't believe that the media's version of Trent could live in the same person that I'd fallen so hard for. And sure, most of that behavior was an act, but that's not to say that it wasn't also real, wasn't also a part of him.

There's no way that I can have Trent the man without also accepting Trent the rock star. But if there's anything this week has taught me, it's that a career in music comes at a much higher cost than I could have ever imagined.

Do I really want to be a musician *that* badly? How can I know whether Trent is worth the price I'd have to pay to have him? How do I know he's not just going to turn back into the monster the press makes him out to be the moment my back is turned? I don't know if I'll ever be able to trust him around that bitch manager.

My stomach twists in disgust as my last glimpse of Trent comes back into my mind's eye. I see him framed in the doorway of his tour bus, that blonde harpy lingering half-dressed just behind him. I should have known what was going on with her from the start. Why else would she have been so terrible to me this whole time? And even if nothing's really going on between them, the fact that there are women in the world who would throw me off the nearest cliff to get closer to Trent makes my skin crawl. Can I invite that much hatred into my life without it eating me alive?

I see it clearly now. Being with Trent would mean accepting the ire of thousands and thousands of people. Being visible as a musician in my own right would be risky enough, but to enter the media frenzy on Trent's arm would make things exponentially more hazardous. What if the world were to think that I was using him for his fame? What if his fans hated me for making him soft? What if he got sick of me in a week and cast me aside for the gossip vultures to pick clean?

I've seen enough of life to know that happy endings are hard to come by. Do I really think that I'm so special as to deserve one? What makes me think that I can somehow triumph over the pressures of celebrity, sustain a happy relationship with Trent despite all odds? Even just saying it in my head sounds absolutely ridiculous—childishly wrongheaded.

There's no logical reason to think that something between Trent and I would stand even the slightest chance.

But if that's true...then why is it so hard to believe it? Why can't I chase away the hopeful, optimistic longing to be his? I know, rationally, that the best thing for me to do at this moment is turn away from him, and from any career in music altogether. I know that I should just go back to school, find a new path, and let my fifteen minutes of fame run out. I know what I should do...I just have no idea how to convince myself to do it. My heart won't hear of it.

My entire life up until this point has been devoted to creative expression. The one thing in the world that's made me happy has been putting voice to beautiful, sad, universal ideas through song. And the best way I've found to do that is through my music. There's no way I can let this week destroy my relationship to songwriting. The prospect of spending the rest of my life away from music is too depressing to even consider.

No—I'll find a way through this, somehow. I'll deal with the question of whether Trent has any place in this new world later. Right now, I need somewhere to rest my weary head.

Joni's voice trails off, leaving me sniffling but with a clearer mind than when I first took flight. I wipe the tears from my cheeks and straighten up, taking stock of my options.

From where I'm haphazardly parked on the side of the highway, I can go one of two ways—back to the festival, or away from it. I consider turning around, taking back my place at Hawk and Dove...but how can I do that when my band is no more? Mitch has probably hitched a ride out of the state by now. And I can't just go latch onto Trent. Not until I've had some time to think. No...I can't go back there.

Instead, I swing back onto the highway and start to drive. At first, I have no idea where I'm headed. The simple act of motion is enough to soothe my frayed nerves. I let my car glide along the highway, staving off decision-making until the last possible second. I could stay at a motel somewhere...but I don't want to risk being seen by anyone. I just need to be somewhere safe.

Suddenly, I know what my destination has to be. A warm, familiar calm falls upon me like a blanket as I realize that I have to go home. My fingers tighten around the steering wheel, as if this might make the journey go faster.

All I want in the world is to fall into my mom and sister's arms, ask their advice, hear them tell me without a shadow of a doubt that everything is going to be OK. With them in mind, I settle in for the long trip home. It will be worth it once I finally arrive.

Thank god I'm not totally alone for this long, anxious trip. Joni ushers me through the first leg of it, but there are others on hand to carry me through. One by one, I bring them each along with me. Carol King, Carly

Simon, James Taylor, Janis Joplin...their music fills my car and my heart. Each one of them has a piece of advice, a bit of insight I'd do well to remember. With them by my side, the journey doesn't seem so bad. I feel like I can find the strength I need, with these faithful companions to help me.

The hours pass, one by one, as I bear down on Barton once again. I got quite the early start on my travels, and it isn't even dusk by the time I drive across the border, back into my home state. Even after only a few days, the familiar landscape of my hometown seems aged, foreign.

That nostalgia I've come to know is magnified tenfold after the events of this week. Still, I know this is where I need to be right now. I speed along until my mother's home comes, at long last, into view.

Our little Victorian house stands serenely in its place, just where I left it. As I approach, I can feel exhaustion starting to creep through my body. The adrenaline of my flight has carried me this far, but I suddenly feel as though I might collapse into a heap on the porch before I even get inside.

Just knowing that Mom and Kate are close makes me feel safe and sound. I know that they'll be able to help me through this mad time without any agenda. All I need right now is good advice—and this is certainly the right place to get it.

I swing into the driveway of our home, elated to see Kate's car parked on the curb. She must not be working tonight, for once. I wonder whether they've been following all my madness as it's unfolded? I haven't turned my phone on since the first wave of gossip hit, not wanting to deal with anyone's opinions. I couldn't even bring myself to call home before I came back, lest Mom advise me to stay at the festival and wait all the nonsense out. But it doesn't matter. I know that this is one place I'll always be welcome.

Stepping out of my car, I take a deep breath and fill my lungs. The smell and sounds of home soothe me as I make my way to the front door. I cross our crowded, cluttered porch and ease the front door open. It's unlocked, as usual.

"Hello?" I call, stepping inside. I can hear people moving about in the living room, and catch the last snippet of a heated conversation that cuts off the minute I come in. Quick footsteps echo through the front hall, and my mom steps out to meet me.

"Ellie..." she breathes, her face white.

"Mom?" I say, stepping toward her, "What's wrong?"

"What are you doing back?" she demands, "You're supposed to be at the festival."

Her anger cuts me to the quick. I'm so startled by her manner that my words leave me. Here, I was expecting a warm welcome, a loving embrace. But instead, Mom stands before me, quivering with outrage. What the hell is going on?

"Did I...did I do something wrong?" I ask, my voice trembling on the edge of despair.

Mom's eyes widen, and it's like she sees me for the first time right at that moment. Her hand flies to her mouth, and sympathetic tears spring to her eyes.

"Oh, sweetheart," she whispers, pulling me into a tight embrace, "I'm so sorry. With everything that's happening...You must be so overwhelmed. You poor thing..."

I collapse against her, relief and confusion fighting for prominence within me. Nothing about this feels right. "What's going on?" I ask, "Are you mad at me?"

"No, darling," she says, smoothing down my hair, "The world has just gone mad, is all. I wish I knew you were coming. We...We have a situation on our hands, here."

"Is everyone OK?" I ask, "Did something happen to Kate?"

"We're both fine," she says quickly, taking hold of my shoulders, "Everything's going to be OK. It's just...I wish you weren't here for this."

"For what?" I ask, growing annoyed with her vague answers.

"Ellie?" I hear Kate gasp from beyond the foyer. In a heartbeat, I'm wrapped up again in my sister's arms. I can feel her chest heaving with suppressed sobs, even as she holds me.

"Will one of you tell me what the hell is going on?" I ask, looking back and forth between them.

"This isn't fair," Kate mutters, "You shouldn't have to deal with this."

"We didn't even want you to know. It's so..."

"Mom, Kate," I say, "Please. What do you have to tell me?"

In their silence, I look up in surprise as another figure emerges from within our home. I watch as a tall figure makes its way to where we're standing, clustered around the front door. There's been a man here this whole time, listening to our strange and tearful hellos. For a moment, I stare at him dumbly, wondering who it is that has my family in such a state. But as he takes a step into light, an eerie, nauseating sense of familiarity comes over me.

He stands before us with his hands in his front pockets. The clothing on his back is worn—a thin flannel shirt and corduroy slacks that have seen better days. His scuffed-up shoes are planted firmly on the floor, as if he has some divine right to be here among us. The mop of hair on his head is nearly white, though I'd guess it was blonde at some point. A shaggy beard obscures most of his features, save his big, prominent eyes. It's his eyes that finally usher me to a place of understanding.

"Hello, sweetheart," he says to me, opening his arms, "Long time no see."

"What the hell is he doing here?" I ask, my voice just barely above a whisper.

I haven't seen this man in years, hardly once in the latter half of my life. Part of me had hoped to hear one day that he'd died and disappeared without a trace. But apparently, that was just wishful thinking.

"Hey," he says, pouting theatrically, "Is that any way to greet me after such a long time?"

"I think it's pretty appropriate, yeah," I say. I can feel my fingers balling into fists, itching to slam into that miserable, grinning face of his.

"I just wanted to stop by an congratulate you on all your recent success," he says, smiling obliviously. "I never would have thought my little girl would be such a sensation!"

"Let's get one thing perfectly clear," I say, advancing toward him, "I am not now, nor have I ever been, your little girl."

"She's got my stubborn streak," the man says to my mother.

My mouth falls open in wordless anger as my father grins dumbly around the room at the three women he abandoned so long ago. And here, I'd been thinking that things couldn't any worse.

Chapter Thirteen

"What do you mean, you're leaving?" Kelly screeches.

I push past her, my clothes dripping wet. "Did I stutter?" I growl, stomping back to my bedroom, "I'm going after her."

"No you're not," Kelly says, hurrying after me, "You don't even know where's she's gone, Casanova. How the hell are you going to follow her?"

"I'll figure that out along the way," I tell her, slamming the flimsy bedroom door in her face. As fast as I can, I rip the sodden clothes from my body. The storm is well upon us, now, drenching the entire festival. For once, I'm glad to have the rock star treatment. I wouldn't want to be down in a tent during this downpour. The festivities are sure to be put on hold for at least the duration of the storm.

I'll have plenty of time to go and find Ellie, wherever it is she's gone.

"Trent," Kelly says from beyond the door, "Trent, I'm sorry for acting the way I did. I'm under a lot of pressure right now. I'm not sure if you know this, but you're not exactly the easiest person to manage. Keeping everything in line hasn't been easy lately, with your priorities wandering. Why don't you just open the door, and we can talk about all this. I just want things to be OK between us."

"I'm sure you do," I mutter, pulling on a dry pair of jeans.

My every muscle is tensed with pent-up anger. I'm halfway worried that I might throw Kelly bodily from the bus if I spend more than three seconds speaking to her. What she pulled just now was reprehensible, tasteless, and downright mean. She purposefully tried to drive a wedge between Ellie and I, and even worse, she may have succeeded.

If that little stunt proves to have ruined any chance of something between me and Ellie, my turncoat manager is going to have hell to pay.

The look on Ellie's face as she stood outside before me will forever be burned into my memory. The lost, bewildered hurt in her eyes was almost too much for me to bear. And to think that I'm partially responsible for that pain? I won't let it stand. I can't. I have to go find her.

But the trouble is, I have no idea where she's gone. With the head start she has now, she could be well on her way to just about anywhere. Will she camp out in a Holiday Inn somewhere until the media forgets about our little photo spread? Or maybe she's off to find her gloomy music partner, wherever he's run off to?

Neither of those scenarios seems right. If I had to guess, from what I know of Ellie, she'd want to be with people she trusts right now. She'd want to be home. But I have no idea where "home" is, for her.

Still, I have to do something. I can't just stay here and continue along with the festival as if nothing's happened.

I scramble around the room, trying to locate a clean shirt. Frustrated, I rip the covers off the bed, hoping that some stray v neck will be concealed among the sheets. As I toss the linens away, a little dark patch catches my eye.

Looking closer, I realize what it is. A small leather wallet, buried underneath the bedclothes. I grab it up and open it eagerly. A little shout of joy escapes me as I see Ellie's drivers license, with her home address printed right before my eyes. That joy is chased away by the realization that the girl I care about is careening across Kansas without any money or ID.

All the more reason to hurry.

I finally manage to get myself dressed and burst out of the room, nearly bowling Kelly over as I go. She's still chattering at me, but I've long since stopped listening. As I stalk through the main cabin, I hear the grumbling of my half-sleeping band mates. Kelly's racket has finally roused them from their sleep. Rodney, Rodger, and Kenny stumble off their bunks, blinking at us in the dim light.

"What the hell is all this?" Rodger mumbles, rubbing his bloodshot eyes, "Do you guys know what time it is?"

"I thought we had a 'no fighting before noon' rule?" Kenny whines, looking imploringly between Kelly and I as though we're his parents, in the middle of a fight.

"Sorry guys," I say, "I need to take off for a little while, and Kelly's throwing a shit fit about it."

"Take off?" Rodney says, taken aback, "What are you talking about?"

"Something's happened with Ellie. She left—"

"How is that your problem?" Rodger asks.

I look at the guys, at a loss. I wasn't expecting to give them an explanation, although they are entitled to one. Kelly crosses her arms smugly and waits for me to say something.

"I just need to find her," I say finally, "My best guess is that she's gone home, and—"

"Dude. You can't leave," Rodger cuts me off, "Have you forgotten the fact that we have a show to play, here?"

"Not to mention that the only reason we're here in the first place is because you wanted to come," Rodney adds.

"I don't understand," Kenny says, "Are you and that girl, like, a thing now?"

"None of that is important," I say, exasperated, "I'll be back in time for the show. We're closing the festival, I have time."

"And how are you planning to go after her?" Kelly asks sharply.

She's got me there. I can't really go careening through the rain in the tour bus, can I? "I...Um..." I splutter, "I hadn't really gotten to that part of the plan just yet."

"Of course not," Kelly scoffs, "That's because I've been holding your hand through every practical element of your life for years. That goes for all of you. You all need me, especially you, Trent. I try to give you some wiggle room when it comes to bullshit antics, but things have gotten out of control. Look at us! We're camped out here in the mud, while we could be playing shows in New York and Paris, ordering room service and trashing hotel rooms like real rock stars! We've gotten seriously off track, here. I think we've all lost sight of our priorities. What we need to do is finish off this festival, then take a serious look at what we want from this band."

"You keep saying 'we'," I say through gritted teeth, "But I don't think you understand, Kelly. You're not part of any 'we'. And if we're off track as a band, it's because you've been pushing us to sell out from the very beginning. If there's a problem here, I assure you that it's not us. It's all you. You've been manipulating me from the start, and now you've got us all between your teeth!"

"I doubt that the rest of the band feels that way," Kelly huffs, turning toward the guys, "Isn't that right, gentlemen?"

My friends stare at us, slack-jawed. A heavy, awkward silence descends upon the cabin.

For the first time, we can all clearly see exactly how distant we've become from each other. When we started out as a band, the four of us guys were inseparable. Writing music, we were practically of a single mind. Our first album was something that we were proud of, an equal effort between the four of us with no meddling from Kelly.

But now? We've put out three records in three years, and none of them have come close to the raw, unique power of our first. Something has been wrong here for a very long time, and I think I'm starting to realize what it is.

"I know it's rude to speak for the group," I begin, glaring across the space at our manipulative manager, "But I'd like to float a suggestion, here."

"What is it, Trent?" asks Kenny.

"I don't think there's a place for Kelly in the structure of this band anymore," I continue, "And I move that we let her go, effective immediately."

Kelly lets out sharp laugh. "You can't fire me, Trent," she says, "I'm the only reason you have a career in the first place. Let alone the fact that I have a contract, if it wasn't for me, you'd still be tending bar in the valley, playing for tips."

"That may be true," I say, "But I think you've let personal feelings cloud your judgment as a professional. I no longer feel that—HEY!"

I duck as Kelly snatches up a glass bottle and lets it fly at my face. The projectile just misses me and shatters against the wall. She's just about to grab another missile when Kenny gets a hold of her and restrains her with some difficulty.

"Christ!" Rodney yells, "Get it together, people!"

"I second Trent's motion," Rodger puts in, "We need to get her out of here."

"Fine!" Kelly screams, elbowing Kenny in the gut. "I'll go! I'll watch from my cushy apartment while you idiots run this entire business into the ground."

"It's not a business," I snarl, "It's a band. A band that you no longer have a hand in ruining."

"No," Kelly says, "I'm sure you'll be able to do that perfectly well all on your own."

She turns on her heel and stalks off into the back of the bus, hopefully to pack her bags. I look around the cabin at the faces of my three band mates. Everyone is more than a little disoriented.

"So...Now what?" Kenny asks, holding his stomach.

"Now, I need to go," I tell them, "I know it sounds crazy, but I can't let her just disappear. I have to make things right between us."

"But you'll be back for our show, right?" Rodger asks nervously.

"Of course," I tell him, "No matter what, there's no way I'll miss our show."

"Well, let me just put this out there," Rodney says, crossing his arms, "If you're not back in time, I'm walking. Things have been bat shit crazy around here for way too long for me to put up with any more bullshit. We're down a manager, our fans are turning on us, and we're stuck out here on a hill in the middle of a thunderstorm. If you blow us off, that's it."

"I understand," I tell him, "I do. And it's not going to happen. I'll be here for you guys. I just...have to be there for Ellie first."

"But, Trent," Kenny says, "How are you going to go after her?"

"Ah. Right. It keeps coming back to that..." I say.

"We can't take the bus," Rodger says, "It's not fast enough."

"I think you're forgetting something pretty crucial," Rodney says.

"What's that?" I ask.

"Dude," he groans, "You're a rock star. You happen to have about ten drivers and a private jet. You do the math."

I run to Rodney and throw my arms around him, bear hug style. "You're a genius!" I shout.

"Tell me something I don't know," he says, rolling his eyes. "Now get a move on, would you? We'll get Kelly out of here if you hurry up."

I whip out my cell and start making frantic calls to my drivers. I have a good idea of where Ellie's gone off to, and the means to go after her. In the darkness of our predicament, a tiny little light of possibility is flaring. There's the smallest chance that I can make everything right, here. All I have to do is ignore the staggering futility of it all and go full speed ahead.

No matter what the odds happen to be, I have to at least try. I am a rock star, after all.

Destiny is *my* bitch.

Chapter Fourteen

Ellie

"Ellie, why don't you sit down?" my mom suggests, awkwardly patting the couch cushion beside her.

I keep my feet planted firmly on the ground, across the living room from where my parents are seated stiltedly on the sofa, as if it were the most natural thing in the world. Kate has taken to splitting the difference, pacing anxiously across the carpet. My sister is used to being able to control emergency situations as a nurse—it must be killing her to have no way of fixing this particular mess.

"I'm fine where I am," I tell the room, crossing my arms firmly across my chest and keeping my gaze well away from my father.

He's planted himself in our home as if he has every right to be here. The same dopey, oblivious grin has been plastered onto his face since I walked in the door. Mom's ushered us all into the living room for some deranged version of a family meeting, or something. And to think, I came home from Hawk and Dove for the sake of finding a little pocket of sanity waiting for me. Right on the nose, as usual.

"I can't believe how grown up you girls are," Dad spouts cheerfully.

"Go figure. Years pass, children get older," Kate mutters, "Maybe it wouldn't be so surprising if you'd actually been around to watch us grow up."

"That's not entirely fair," he says condescendingly, "I didn't leave you three. Your mother thought it was best to buy a house behind my back and move out on me."

"Gee Dad," I spit, "You think the double life of coke and hookers had anything to do with that?"

"That has been wildly exaggerated," he sniffs, leaning back into the couch.

"I resent that," Mom says quietly.

"Damn right, you do," Kate says.

I watch my mother shift uncomfortably in her seat. Why does she feel squeamish about her role in all this? Getting us away from this man was the best thing she could have possibly done for us. I can barely remember my parents as a married couple, but watching their dynamic now only makes me more furious.

My mother, an empowered and actualized woman, is shrinking away from my dad, as if he still has some kind of control over her. I never realized how entwined they'd actually been, or how hard it must have been for her to pick up and leave him. I feel a new sort of respect for my mom in this moment, and a whole new level of contempt for my father.

"I don't know if anyone's said it yet," I begin, "But I really don't think you should be here, Dad."

"I agree," Kate says, planting her hands on her hips, "Whatever you're looking for from us, I think you're going to be disappointed. There's no place for you in this family."

"That's ridiculous!" Dad laughs, "Of course there's a place for me. I helped make you, didn't I?"

"You provided genetic material," I say, "But you didn't have a hand in raising us, that's for sure. And it's the raising part that counts. You're just a glorified sperm donor."

"Ellie," he frowns, "Don't say such hurtful things! I don't know where you picked up these manners. Maybe from your wild and crazy musician friends?"

"First of all, you don't deserve any cordiality," I tell him, "And what are you talking about, my musician friends?"

"Come on," he says, winking at me, "You've been all over the place the last few days! You've made quite the splash in the music scene, haven't you? I bet it has to do with your name. That was my idea, you know. Naming you after The Beatles' song. Your mom wanted to go with Lucy in the Sky, but I knew better. I knew you'd be a big star someday."

"I'm not a big star," I tell him, growing wary. I knew that this little drop in visit was too well-timed to be coincidental. He's here for one reason, and one reason only—he wants to glom onto whatever beginnings of a career I'm building.

For a fleeting moment before the anger set in, I had almost let myself be excited to see him. As a kid, before I understood the severity of his grievances, I would pray for my family to put itself back together again.

All of my friends growing up came from standard-issue suburban families. Sure, there were some divorced parents, but all the kids still had two parents in their lives—sometimes even three or four if there were step parents involved! Kate and I were always the strange kids with just a mom. And though no one mentioned it as we got older, I still remember being quizzed and teased about my unconventional family when I was younger.

Mom did a good job of keeping her boyfriends away from us, unless they were very serious contenders for her heart. She didn't shy away from dating, of course, but never again did any man permeate our little three-person family once Dad was out of the picture.

We learned to be self-sufficient, without any help. I grew up with the keen knowledge that men were inherently untrustworthy. It was always my understanding that they weren't necessarily bad, as a gender, but that they were so naturally flawed that they simply weren't worth relying on.

I myself have never had a real, loving relationship with a man in my life. The boys I've dated never warranted a real commitment on my part, and I've kept my heart well-guarded.

I feel a hard knot in the pit of my stomach as I realize why my flight from Hawk and Dove felt so desperate. It wasn't as though Trent had really done anything wrong, it was simply the fact that I care enough about him to be hurt by him that drove me away.

If things fall apart with Trent because of my fractured relationship with trust and loyalty, I'll never forgive myself. A new surge of anger ripples through me as I stare down the man sitting beside my mother.

"So, what is it you're looking for?" I all but snarl, "Are you expecting some share of my earnings, or something? Are we finally worth your time and affection now that I might stand to make a little bit of money? Or is it just the vicarious fame you're after?"

"Whoa! Slow down!" he says, holding up his hands, "There's no need to vilify me!"

"You're right," I say, "You do a perfectly good job of it yourself, after all. How dare you come back here just to take advantage of us! You can't just waltz in and pick things up as if you'd never left."

"Why not?" he says, playing dumb, "I've missed out on a lot with you girls, and I take the full blame for that, really I do."

"Well obviously," Kate says.

"I've made a lot of mistakes in my life," Dad goes on. I half expect him to pull out a soapbox for this pathetic little soliloquy. "I never appreciated my family. Your mother and I were very much in love as young people. I can't tell you how wonderful those years were when we had no money. We just enjoyed ourselves with what little we had, without a care in the world. Those were some of the best times of my life.

And then you girls came along, and we really had a little family. I fell in love with you both as soon as you were born. Most of the time, all I wanted to do was stay home and play with you.

But do you know what happened? I started making money, and everything went straight to shit. I was corrupted by the opportunities that money creates. I started wanting more than I needed, more than anyone could ever need. I started being nasty to people, and I grew to be incredibly selfish. I was a man of simple pleasures before I started getting rich, but as soon as I had a little money to throw around, nothing was good enough anymore. I forgot that I already had everything I needed in my family, I lost sight of that, and I started scrambling around for as much as I could get.

After your mother took you girls and left, there was nothing for me. I lived for excess, and ran myself straight into the ground in my pursuit of the next moment of pleasure. I lost my job, all of my money, couldn't even help out with you girls in the end. I was forced to take a good, hard look at my life and discover what was important again. And what I realized was that I didn't need to have the best material things in life.

I got sober, found an honest job in a sporting goods store, and lived as simply as I could. And it's been life-changing, it really has."

"That's a charming story," Mom says, unable to hold her silence any longer, "But you've yet to tell us what, exactly, you're doing here now."

"To be perfectly frank," Dad says, "I did come here because I caught wind of Ellie's success. I haven't done a good job of keeping up with you girls, so at first I didn't even realize that the Ellie all over the Internet was *my* Ellie."

"I'm not *your* Ellie," I mutter.

"But then it clicked," my dad says, ignoring me, "That was my little girl in all the pictures! There was so much chatter to wade through. Gossip about that Mitch fellow, and all that talk about Trent Parker. I have to tell you dear, some of those images were rather difficult to look at."

I blush hotly, remembering the pictures of Trent and I dancing together, racing back up the hill at the end of the night. It already felt like an invasion of my privacy for them to have been printed in the first place, but to know that my dad was looking at them is a whole new level of mortification.

"What's your point?" I ask him hotly.

"My point," he says, "Is that those pictures worried me. You must have more than a little bit of my temperament in you, Eleanor. I never had any interest in booze and parties and drugs before I had a taste. Seeing you out of control like that took me right back to my wild days."

"It's not for you to determine when I'm out of control!" I shout, "For one thing, I'm a grown woman, not answerable to anyone. And, more importantly, don't you dare say that I'm anything like you."

"But you are, dear," he goes on, "As much as it might disappoint you. You're my daughter whether you like it or not. And I'm not jumping to any conclusions—those pictures speak for themselves. You can't let wealth and celebrity spoil you, Ellie. You'll regret it for the rest of your life."

"Thanks for the tip," I say, "But I'm perfectly capable of deciding for myself what happens in my own career."

"Sometimes these things are difficult to control," Dad insists, "They can get out of hand really quickly. By the time you realize that something is off, it might be too late."

"So, what exactly are you suggesting?" I ask, taking a menacing step forward, "That I hang up my songwriting career, go back to school for something practical, and resign myself to being unhappy? Is that your grand idea for my future?"

"Of course not!" my dad says, his eyes wide, "I would never suggest that you back down from your dreams. Your mother was an artist too, remember? I supported her ambitions, and I fully support yours. I just think that you need to be strategic about how you handle your fame."

"Is this coming to a point sometime soon?" My mom asks.

"I really hope so," Kate answers.

"Of course," Dad says, spreading his arms to us all, "I have an idea that will not only bring this family back together, it will also ensure Ellie's good fortune and secure her future."

"Oh, do tell," I say sarcastically.

"I would like to offer my services as your manager and conservator!" he says grandly.

For a moment the room is dead silent. The three of us women stare dumbly at this near-stranger who has barged back into our lives. I think, at first, that I must have heard him incorrectly. He couldn't possibly be so crude, so brazen.

"My...conservator?" I repeat, tasting the sour word on my tongue.

"Yes," Dad says cheerfully, "I have quite the financial mind, you know. I could help you invest and manage your income properly, to make sure that you never go overboard the way I did."

"Let me get this straight," I fume, "You came here, after years of radio silence, to suggest that I put my fledgling career in your hands, because you're the responsible adult in this scenario?"

"More or less," he says.

"You're asking me...for money," I say, my entire body trembling with outrage. "You have the audacity to ask me for anything, after what you've done to us?!"

"Ellie, don't get upset," he says, standing up to approach me. The mere thought of his embrace makes me want to vomit.

"Stay away from me!" I screech, backing up against the wall, "You're unbelievable!"

"It's OK," Kate says, coming toward me, "Ellie, he can't hurt us now."

"I don't care," I scream, beside myself with hurt and anger.

"You must be overtired," Dad says, looking offended by my reaction.

"Fuck you," I spit at him, "You know what? Even after everything you did, I never really hated you. Not once in my entire life...until this moment."

"You don't mean that," he says.

"Oh, but I do," I tell him, "I think that you're a repulsive, presumptuous, pig-headed—"

The chime of the doorbell cuts off my hateful spree. We all look toward the front door, torn from the heated moment at hand. Mom rises from the couch, staggering a bit under the pressure of the situation, and makes her way to the door.

"I suppose...I'll get it," she says, dazed by the bizarre situation that's cropped up in her living room.

Kate puts her arm around my shoulders as we stare down our father across the room, frozen in a tense tableau. His plastered-on smile is beginning to weaken under the force of our distaste. I hear Mom pull open the front door behind us.

A small, strangled sound of shock escapes her, and I tear my eyes away from Dad to see what's wrong. She's standing before the open doorway, her hand raised to her mouth in speechless wonder.

"Mom?" I say, edging toward her, "Mom, who is it?"

Chapter Fifteen

All of a sudden, I feel like a fifteen-year-old boy again.

I shuffle my feet and smile gamely at the woman I have to assume is Ellie's mother. She's staring at me, wide-eyed, and I get the feeling that my presence is not particularly welcome at the moment. I wonder if Ellie's already told her family to turn me away on sight, or if she's so devastated that her mom and sister will never be able to give me a chance.

I knew it was a crazy idea, coming all the way here after Ellie fled the festival, but the sheer madness of my actions is just starting to sink in.

"Mom?" says a voice from within the house. My heart slams hard against my ribs as I realize that it's Ellie speaking.

"Mom, who is it?"

"I...You..." the mother stutters, standing perfectly still in the doorway.

"Hi, Mrs. Jackson," I venture. I very nearly bow, this whole interaction feels so formal. "We haven't met. But I'm—"

"Trent?"

My eyes land on Ellie, peering around her mother's frozen form. She looks absolutely beside herself, and a jolt of guilt sears my every nerve. I'm responsible for upsetting her like this, after all. I hold her gaze, trying to communicate without any words how sorry I am for screwing things up between us.

"Who's out there?" says a deep voice from within.

"Mom, give us a minute," Ellie says, hurrying out onto the porch. Pale and shaken, she closes the door as her mother retreats into the house. She turns to face me, and I can see full well that she's rattled to the core.

"Ellie," I breathe, "What's—"

But the words are knocked out of my mouth as she rushes toward me and throws herself into my arms. I catch her gratefully, wrapping her up in a tight embrace. We stand there together, fervent in our silence, and drink in the comfort of each other's bodies. I never knew before meeting Ellie how much power there could be in a simple embrace. There are lots of things I never knew before meeting her.

She clasps her hands around my neck and looks up at me, blinking back tears. "You're here," she says, a bit bewildered, "How...?"

"I believe this belongs to you," I say, producing her wallet from my back pocket.

"My...I drove all the way here without...? Well. Super," she says, taking the item from me. I can tell that she's completely overwhelmed, beside herself with about a thousand conflicting emotions.

"Ellie, I'm so sorry," I tell her, placing my hands on her hips, "I'm sorry about the pictures, and about Kelly, and about Mitch. I'm sorry that I can't just be good to you without dragging you through the media mud with me. You deserve so much better than that. And what happened between us...if it was too rushed, if you felt pressured, just do me a favor and slug me in the jaw, OK?"

"Trent," she says softly, laying a protective hand on my cheek, "I would never do anything to that jaw of yours. That jaw's a national treasure."

I smile, amazed at her unrelenting sense of humor. "So, you don't hate me?"

"Of course not," she says.

"That's...great. I mean, I had like three more minutes of speech prepared to get you to forgive me, but I—"

"There's nothing to forgive," she says, "I got scared. Everything was happening so fast. With you, with the media, and the fame...I panicked. I know nothing happened with between you and that bitch. I shouldn't have taken that out on you."

"If it makes you feel any better, I think this is uncharted territory for us both," I tell her.

"Oh, good. Something we're both oblivious about, for a change," she laughs weakly. As I watch, her expression becomes strained once more.

"What is it?" I ask, lifting her chin.

"God...I don't even know where to begin," she says, shaking her head.

"Is it something between us?" I ask warily.

"No! Well, not really...It's so messed up, Trent. Everything's just going to hell all at once."

"Did something happen?" I ask insistently.

"It's...my dad," she says finally.

"Your dad..." I say, realizing that I know absolutely nothing about her family. I suppose we didn't quite get to the unveiling of our closeted skeletons back at the festival. "Is he sick?"

"No," she says, "He's...Here."

"He's not...usually?"

"Not since I was a kid," she tells me, "I got back here, and he was waiting for me. Unannounced. After all this time. Apparently, he's been following my escapades from afar, and decided to come get a slice of the action for himself. He's still in there, and I don't know what to do...I don't know how to make him leave."

"He won't leave?" I ask, feeling a deep, protective fury rising within me.

"No," she says, growing angry herself, "He's just parked himself on the couch like he owns the goddamned place. The sight of him is making me sick, I swear to god..."

"I think I can help," I tell her, "I have some experience with dads who would be better off gone."

"Trent, you shouldn't have to get involved with this," she says.

"I don't have to do anything," I tell her, "I want to help, in whatever way I can. Will you let me do that?"

She nods, slowly. I can tell that she's uncomfortable heaping this kind of responsibility on me. If only she knew what lengths I would go to make her life just a little bit better, a little bit easier.

I'm quickly coming to understand that there's just about nothing I wouldn't do for this woman. And while that thought might scare the shit out of me, I intend to rush headfirst into it, rather than risk losing her forever. I square my shoulders as Ellie cracks open the door and leads me into her home.

All that I want to do the moment I cross the threshold is take in the place where Ellie grew up. I want to see every old picture, every scrap of evidence from her childhood. I want to see what her bedroom looks like, what kinds of cereal are stocked in the cupboard— every insignificant little piece of information I can get my hands on.

But there are more pressing things to deal with first. I look into the living room, where a fractured family portrait is waiting.

Ellie's mom is standing in the center of the room, trying to keep the scene from imploding. A young woman in scrubs who must be Ellie's sister is sitting in an old armchair, her face buried in her hands. Ellie lingers in the doorway, looking back at me nervously. And there, reclined on a well-loved sofa, is the man who must be Ellie's father.

His look of unwarranted superiority ignites my already simmering contempt for him. He's just the kind of presumptuous, holier-than-thou, entitled asshole I really can't stand. I can tell, just by the way he holds himself, that he's exactly like my own father—king of the household, supreme arbiter of the family's lives, God in his own right (or at least in his own eyes).

"Well, I'll be damned!" he says, breaking the thick silence, "Trent Parker! This certainly is a treat."

"I wouldn't be so sure about that," I tell him, holding my ground in the doorway.

"I was just telling Ellie that I've been seeing a lot of news about you two lately," he continues, picking himself up off the couch. He extends his hand toward me, and I have a powerful urge to twist it up behind his back and send him flying through the window. But I restrain myself. That's not what Ellie would want.

"Mr. Jackson," I say, as evenly as I can, "Ellie doesn't want you here. She doesn't want you in her life, and I would appreciate it if you'd leave."

"Well," the man says, his hand still suspended in the air, "I don't think that she needs you to fight her battles for her, am I right?"

"I'm not fighting her battle," I tell him, "I'm just the cavalry."

"Trent," he says, crossing the room, "You can't blame a father for wanting to reconnect with the family he was so unfortunately separated from!"

"No," I say, "But I can blame a father for abandoning his children, only to come sniffing around when there's a suddenly a buck to be made. I've been around this particular block myself, Mr. Jackson. And I'm going to tell you the same thing I've told every asshole who's come out of the woodwork looking for a piece of me—you can take your phony affection and shove it so far up your ass that you won't be able to shit it out for a week. Now, why don't you do me a favor and get the hell out of this house?"

"You have no right to talk to me like that," he says, his brow furrowing, "This is not your house to command, young man."

"It's not yours either," Ellie says.

"The hell it isn't!" he shouts back, "Your mother stashed away the money for this place while she was living on my dime! None of you would have anything if it wasn't for me. I brought you girls into this world with a drawer of silver spoons waiting for you. And how did you all repay me? By running off and living like rutting pigs, making a damn fool out of me! You're all a bunch of ungrateful, selfish, mean little bitches. I deserve a cut of whatever this one is pulling in. It's my right as a father. And I'm not leaving here until I've—AHHH!"

I slam the man's shoulders hard into the hardwood floor, pinning him beneath me. He struggles to free himself, but he's no match for me. I cock back my fist, wanting nothing more than to break that stupid face of his in two.

"Apologize!" I shout in his flushed face.

"Trent!" Ellie cries, "Don't hurt him! It's not worth it."

"Go ahead," he sneers up at me, "Hit me! Do some good damage. I'll slap you with the biggest lawsuit you've ever seen."

"You're pathetic," I snarl, "You're a sad, washed-up bully who doesn't deserve your daughter's time of day. I hope you know how outrageously depressing it is to have to humiliate you in front of your family. Former family. Now, I'm going to tell you one more time. Get out of here. Now, before I make that lawsuit worth it."

I push him out from under me with the heel of my foot, and he scrambles up to standing. His face is beet red from the embarrassment and exertion, and he glares around the room at all of us.

"This isn't over," he says, pointing a finger at my chest.

"It had better be," I tell him, "Ellie might not be around to talk sense into me the next time you show up acting like an asshole."

"Stay away from us," Ellie's mother says.

"For good," her sister puts in.

"You blew it a long time ago, Dad," Ellie says, "Don't make it worse for everyone."

He looks around at all of us once more, the full scope of his impotence finally occurring to him.

Without another word, he turns his back and crosses to the door, slamming it hard behind him. The four of us who remain stand still, listening as his footsteps ring out across the porch, down to the driveway. A car engine roars to life, and the sound of pealing tires signals his final departure. For a minute, we're all too stunned to speak.

I look around at the three women, at a loss for words. I haven't done the whole "meet the family" thing in many years, but this hardly seems like the conventional way to go about it.

"So..." Ellie says, "Um...I guess I should introduce you guys?"

"I'm Trent," I say dumbly, "But I guess you know that..."

"I promise that our home isn't always so...dramatic," Ellie's mom says.

"Not unless your students are rehearsing," Ellie replies with a smile.

"I'm Kate," says the young woman in scrubs, "Ellie's sister. This is our mom. Of course. Um...Welcome to our home?"

"It's actually very nice to meet you," I tell them, "Regardless of the terms."

"No need to worry," Ellie's mom says, "We're not really a typical family. No use trying to keep up with normative rituals."

"Right," I say.

"So. What exactly are you doing here, Trent?" Kate asks, cocking an eyebrow. "Barton doesn't really seem like your scene, based on the latest pictorial evidence. I think some of the high school kids may be able to hook you up with some drugs, but other than that—"

"Kate!" Ellie hisses.

"I'm sorry if I've given the impression of being irresponsible. Or disinterested, or...Really any other horrible thing you're probably thinking about me," I say, "I just...I couldn't let Ellie just disappear without trying to make things right. So. I guess. That's what I'm doing here."

"And Ellie," Kate continues, crossing her arms, "Are things right, now?"

"Kate, give it a rest. After Dad's guest appearance—"

"I was just asking," she says.

"I think we could all stand to cool down for a minute," their mother says, "Anyone want a beer? We could order pizza! Trent, do you eat pizza?"

"That's very nice of you," I say, ignoring the absurdity of the suggestion, "But the thing is, I really need to get back to Kansas. I have another show to play at the festival. And so does Ellie, if I'm remembering correctly."

"I don't have an act anymore," Ellie says sadly.

"We can figure that out along the way," I tell her earnestly, "But I've got a cab idling outside, and a jet waiting to take us back."

"A jet? Good grief," Kate snorts.

"Will you come back with me?" I ask Ellie, taking her hands in mine. She looks around at her mom and sister, weighing her options.

"Trent...this whole thing is so huge," she says, "I don't know whether or not I can handle being a famous musician. It's hardly been a week, and people are already trying to tear me down."

"There will always be people trying to tear you down in life," I tell her, "That's the story every time. Whether you're a rock star, or a school teacher, or a college student in Boston, the world will always be pushing you to the edge. But Ellie—you can handle it. You were born for it. You know as well as I do that music is your life, what you have to offer the world. I know you're scared, but it's going to be OK. I'll help you. I promise."

She takes a deep breath and holds it.

My entire body is tensed in anticipation. I've never been more keenly aware of needing someone as much as I need her.

"OK," she says finally, "Let's do this thing."

Chapter Sixteen

Ellie

"I can't believe this is our ride," I breathe, as we make our way toward Trent's private jet.

The plane is waiting for us in the middle of a tiny local airport, looking as out of place as my rock star escort in my little hometown.

Seeing Trent here in Barton is as surreal as anything that's happened to me in the past week. Watching this incredibly famous person stride through the front door of my childhood home and meet my family finally forced me to accept that whatever crazy ride I'm on right now is real and true. As insane as this all is, I'd do well to sit back and enjoy it.

Trent offers his hand to me and helps me up the stairs into the plane. "What, are you telling me you've never flown in a private jet before?" He says with a grin, "Gee, how the other half lives..."

"Well, maybe in a couple of years, when I'm the most famous leftover half of a folk duo America has ever seen, I'll be able to get myself one of these puppies," I say, stepping into the jet.

"Dream big, babe," Trent replies as the door closes behind us, "Dream big."

I look around the inside of the plane, shaking my head in wonder. I've been so continually floored by every extravagant detail of Trent's life that I'm out of words for my amazement. The jet is even fancier than the tour bus, with deep, cushy seats lining the windows, a big screen TV, a built-in bar, and door leading back to more private rooms.

"I'm assuming that the Jacuzzi is back there?" I say, gesturing toward the rear of the plane.

"Ah," Trent says, "We had to remove the Jacuzzi when we put in the laser tag arena. My apologies."

"I suppose this will have to do then," I sigh dramatically.

"You're too kind," Trent says, taking my hand in his. A crackle of excitement skirts up my arm, even at this slight touch. It's like my body is hardwired to respond to Trent's every move.

So much happened so quickly after we spent that night together that my body's had no time to come down from the high of sleeping with Trent. I feel like I've been suspended in this state of hyper-awareness and sensitivity, just waiting until we could be together again.

I thought that giving myself up to my desire would sate my need for a while, but if anything it's only gotten more intense, now that I know what it's like to be with Trent that way.

I grasp his fingers just a little tighter, wondering if he's feeling the same way. If his flying after me despite my behavior is any indication, we might just be on the same page.

"Come on," he says, pulling on my hand, "You've got to sit down for takeoff."

I allow myself to be towed over into an enormous plushy chair. Trent is kind enough to give me the window seat, since this whole thing is still novel for me. I can't help but be as excited as a little kid as the plane roars to life. I haven't been on a plane for years—not since our trip to the Grand Canyon when I was fifteen. I can't imagine a life where flying across the country wouldn't be thrilling, but that's Trent's day to day.

"How quickly do you get used to all of this?" I ask, as the jet rolls around toward the runway.

"Honestly?" he says, "Far too quickly."

We pick up speed, and I grab onto Trent's arm as the jet lifts off. My hometown falls away beneath us, shrinking down to the size of a kid's block city in no time at all. The place looks so insignificant from up here—just another woodsy corner of the country with nothing spectacular about it. But maybe being a little unremarkable isn't such a bad thing.

My nose is practically pressed up against the window as we sail through the dusky sky. My race home took up most of the day, so we'll be enjoying the view of the darkened world as we fly back to the festival. Bright lights dot the landscape below us, clustering around town centers and bigger cities than mine. Soon, they'll give way to huge swathes of black as we fly over the plains and mountains.

"Night flights are the best," Trent tells me, peering around me through the window. "You really feel like you're in a world apart."

"You must always feel that way," I say, turning to face him.

"True," he says, standing up from his seat, "But when you think about it, doesn't everyone?"

"What do you mean?" I ask.

"Well, everyone's reality is a bit unique," he says, crossing to the bar and taking two glasses down from the rack, "Mine just happens to be unique in a terribly specific way."

"That's one way of spinning it," I say, going to join him.

"It makes me feel less lonely, to think of it that way," he tells me, "Let me have my coping mechanisms, would you?"

"They're all yours," I smile.

"Thank you," he says, "Now, for the much more important question...Would you like whiskey or vodka, and how much?"

"Whiskey," I answer, "And I'll let you decide how much."

"Very well," he says, pouring two generous splashes of booze into our waiting glasses. He hands me my drink—the smoky scent of the fine booze is a welcome relief after the day I've had. I raise my glass to him, trying to formulate a toast to encompass everything I'm feeling.

"...To you," I say finally. It's the only thing there is to say. "Thank you, Trent."

"For what?" he asks, clinking his glass against mine and taking a sip.

"For...everything," I say simply, "Everything that's happened. Everything that might happen."

"I'll gladly drink to that," he says with a smile.

We raise our glasses to our lips, eyeing each other across the bar. Those green eyes of Trent's bore right through me, rendering every defense useless. There's no hiding anything from him, that much I know for a fact.

There's something shared between us that can't be ignored or set aside. It's a level of understanding that I've never felt with anyone else. I don't need to put words to it—it's far more intuitive than that. Even though our lives have been completely different, it's as though we're occupying the same little sliver of reality. I don't understand it, but I feel it wholly.

"I'm so sorry you had to see that little family drama," I tell him, perching myself on a bar stool, "That's really not how we are, usually."

"There's nothing to apologize for," he says, leaning into the bar. The muscles in his arms glide and ripple beautifully as he rests his weight on them, and I'm so distracted by them that I almost don't hear what he's telling me. "If it makes you feel any better, I don't exactly have a stellar relationship with my father, either."

"Really?" I ask. I know so little about Trent's life before stardom that I'm instantly intrigued.

"Really," he says, "I mean...it's nothing scandalous. I don't want you to think I'm belittling what you and your family have gone through. I don't have any cause to complain about my own family. We were pretty functional, overall."

"But...?" I prompt.

"But...You know. My parents and brothers aren't exactly artistically-minded. They've always been perfectly content to lead average, run-of-the-mill lives. My parents have been in the same tiny house for decades, my brothers all went out an found honest nine-to-five jobs. I'm the only one who really strayed from that path."

"Well, they must be impressed by everything you've done," I say, "I mean, you're one of the best rock musicians in the world. They have to appreciate that kind of excellence, right?"

"You'd think that," he says, taking another sip of whiskey, "But I'm afraid that's not really the case."

"Well, the money must help a little, right?" I say, trying to lighten things up.

A pained expression crosses Trent's face. "No. No, my family's never accepted a dime from me. They don't really think of it as honest money, to tell you the truth. I suppose they're glad that I've done well for myself, but they don't respect my success. They don't understand the drive to create, and to share what you've made with the rest of the world. They've never understood that part of me because they can't comprehend it. It's not something I can make them experience with me."

"That must be so hard," I say.

"It's gotten easier," he tells me, glancing out the window at the nearly black sky, "When I first started playing music, I thought it would be something that my family could appreciate. I think if it had stayed a hobby, something I did after work and on the weekends, they would have been a lot more receptive. But once I started centering my life around playing my guitar, they started to disapprove.

They didn't think it was responsible, or fair. My brothers were all off working crappy, thankless jobs while I moved out to California to be a musician. Even once I started getting noticed, they thought it was a fluke. As though I hadn't earned it. Regardless of the fact that I've been working for this for over a decade.

It's pretty shitty to know that there is absolutely nothing I can do to impress them, or make them respect my work. And my dad's the worst of all..."

He looks up at me, catching himself mid-rant. His features rearrange themselves, and the anger subsides just a bit. "I'm sorry," he says, "I don't mean to go off on you. I guess I've never said any of this out loud before..."

I reach for him, laying my hand on his forearm. "It's OK," I tell him, "Thank you for talking to me about it. I was starting to feel like I was the only one with a less than perfect home life."

"That's the thing though," he says, frowning, "There's nothing about my family that's messed up, necessarily. I was loved as a kid, and fed, and cared for...So why isn't it enough? Why do I also have to feel validated by them?"

"I don't know why, Trent," I tell him, "But I can tell you, from personal experience, that the feeling isn't imaginary. I know what it's like to feel like there's nothing you can do to make yourself feel at home, and wanted, and loved as yourself. The only time I've ever felt understood and accepted for who I am was...is...Well, to be perfectly honest, it's when I'm talking to you."

He lifts his brilliant green eyes to mine, and a new shade shines through—it looks to me like hope. Trent reaches across the bar and tucks a loose lock of blonde hair behind my ear, letting his fingers brush against the skin of my cheek.

All of a sudden, he actually looks his age. Looking at me, Trent's world-weary rock star mask falls away. He's all youthful hope, and earnestness, and intent concentration. But there's something else in his gaze too...something that sets my knees to trembling. I can see that he's been waiting, too—brought to life by being with me and waiting to feel that connection once again.

"I have no idea how this happened," he laughs, leaning toward me, "I know we just met...But it doesn't feel that way, does it?"

"No," I say, running my hand down his muscular forearm, "To tell you the truth, I've lost track. So much has happened, so much has changed. The only thing to do is let it happen, I suppose."

"That sounds like a solid plan to me," he says, smiling wickedly.

I can't help myself any longer. With a rush of unstoppable need, I bring my lips eagerly to Trent's, leaning across the bar toward him. His firm mouth meets mine, moving with a desire paralleled only by my own.

He takes my face in his hands, and I open myself to him. A shudder of illicit delight runs through me as his tongue glides against mine. There's no hint of strategy or technique about his kiss—he's simply listening to my body, responding to what I want and need. Who knew that the act of listening could be so sexy.

Charged by the power of his kiss, I lift myself off the stool and swing my legs over the side of the bar. Trent's eyes flutter open, gleaming excitedly. I close the space between us, sliding my legs around his tapered waist. I'm balanced on the edge of the bar, straddling Trent as he slides his arms around the small of my back. I let my fingers trail through his messy curls, down against the stubble on his fine jaw. My lips find his once more, and our mouths move against each other insatiably.

Trent pulls me tightly against him, and I groan as I feel the hard length of him press up against the throbbing, wet place between my legs. I throw my arms excitedly around his shoulders, grinding against him. He presses against me, letting me feel how stiff he's grown for me. I bring my lips to his neck, flicking my tongue against his skin as I let my hands wander down to the front of his jeans.

His eyes close rapturously as I stroke him through the thick fabric. I need both hands to tend to him properly, and I sigh in anticipation, remembering how good it felt to pull him in, deep inside of me. My hands move quickly, running along the full length of him as I kiss him hungrily. I can feel his quickening breath hot against my skin. I love knowing that I can do this to him.

I gasp as Trent's hands work their way up the front of the oversized sweater I threw on during my getaway. He lifts the thick garment up over my head as tosses it away, bringing his hands eagerly to my breasts. My head falls back as he kneads them tenderly. I reach around and unhook my bra, tugging it away from my body.

I don't want anything between us.

Trent pulls the straps of my tiny tank top down over my shoulders and tugs down my top.

His eyes drink in the sight of me, straddling him topless. I let out a little cry as he scoops me up into his arms, hoisting me up off the bar. I wrap my legs tighter around his body, kissing every part of his face I can reach.

He carries me across the jet, shouldering his way through the back doors. They slam shut behind us, and I see that we've tucked ourselves away into a surprisingly spacious bedroom.

I lower myself onto the soft carpet and lean against the wall, pulling Trent hard against me. He leans into my body, his manhood throbbing against me. We kiss earnestly, feverishly, even. I lift the hem of his tee shirt, peeling it off his firm upper body. My skin meets his, as I tug him closer, my breasts pressing firmly against his chest. I let my lips wander down to the flat panes of his pecs, counting off each defined ab as I make my way further and further...

A low moan escapes Trent's throat as I back him up toward the huge bed behind us. I guide him across the space, push him down onto the mattress so that he's sitting before me, his eyes blazing with reverent wanting.

Meeting his gaze as steadily as I can, I whip open his belt buckle and tug his jeans down away from his body, taking his briefs along as well. His stiff, pulsating member springs from its linen sheath, and I don't even get his jeans fully off his legs before I wrap my hands around it. I can't help it, I need to feel him.

I work my hands up and down the length of him, as slow as I can stand to. Trent arches his back, and I can feel him growing even harder at my touch. Keeping my hands firmly wrapped around him, I wet my lips and lower my mouth to the tip of his member. Ever so lightly, I kiss the bulging head of his manhood, relishing the sharp intake of breath that escapes from his throat. There's no way I'll be able to fit all of him in my mouth, but dammit if I'm not going to try anyway.

Running my hands along his stiff shaft, I wrap my lips all around the tip of him. He groans deliciously as I let my tongue glance against the tender underside of him. Tracing long, luscious circles around his head, I work my way down, pulling more and more of him deeper into my throat.

Trent buries his fingers in my hair as I lick and suck along the length of him. I need both hands and my mouth to take all of him, and I do—working every inch of his pulsing manhood. I lose myself in the taste of him, the amazing sensation of feeling him in my hands, against my tongue, between my lips.

"Ellie..." Trent rasps, "You've got me so close."

That's exactly what I wanted to hear. I lift my lips from around him, letting my hands travel up and away from his stiff member. As much as I want to keep sucking until he comes for me, filling up my mouth with all I can swallow, I want to feel him inside me even more.

I push his shoulders down onto the mattress, straddling him once more. He pops open the button of my jean shorts and slides them down over my ass and legs. I hook my fingers into my panties and tug them off as well. Looking intently into my eyes, Trent lowers his hand to my slick slit. A low, rumbling moan rattles within him as he feels how wet he's made me already.

I rest my hands against his firm chest as he runs his fingers along the length of me. Trent looses two fingers and slides them slowly up inside of me, pressing against the tender flesh between my legs. I close my eyes, pressing down against his masterful hands.

I let out a cry of delight as he presses his thumb against the throbbing, swollen need between my legs, rubbing me in just the right way. I rock myself against his touch as he sends me hurtling toward bliss. I hold out, savoring the build of my own ecstasy until I'm on the edge.

As I reach the apex of my impending pleasure, I knock Trent's hands away. He takes my cue and grabs for a condom. He tears the package and slides the rubber onto his rock hard manhood. I push his shoulders back onto the mattress again, straddle his hips, and slowly lower myself onto his throbbing member.

We cry out together as I slide down onto him. His thick stiffness parts the silky flesh inside of me, plunging deep into my body.

I look down at him in wonder as he presses ever further, opening places I never knew existed. The feel of him inside me is dizzying, and I need more. As much as I can get. I rock against him as he meets me thrust for thrust. Leaning over his pounding hips, my breasts bouncing, I bring him closer, and closer.

My mouth opens in a long, throaty moan as his thrusting body presses up against that hard, throbbing nub—the very center of my pleasure. Suddenly I'm back at the edge, poised on the brink of bliss.

"I'm gonna...I'm—" I whisper breathlessly. But Trent doesn't need any prompting. He lifts me ever-so-slightly away before pulling me down hard onto his deepest, most forceful thrust yet.

Our faces screw up into silent howls of overwhelming pleasure as we come together, crashing through wave after wave of utter bliss. I let my head fall back as I bounce ecstatically on his final emphatic thrusts. The rippling shockwaves of pleasure travel through me, searing along every cell and nerve as I settle into the warm wave of orgasmic bliss.

I fall heavily against Trent's chest, rising and falling with his every heaving breath. We lay together, still connected in the most intimate way, as our breathing becomes as one. Words don't exist to describe what happens when we meet like this. I never knew that the kind of desire existed that only intensifies even as it's sated. I don't think I'll ever be able to get enough of Trent like this, though I'm certainly going to keep trying.

The exhaustion of my wild flight from the festival begins to overwhelm me. The long, emotionally-wrought drive, the confrontation of my deadbeat father, Trent's miraculous appearance, and now this, all slam into me at once. Sleep descends, whisking me away to the dream world...

Chapter Seventeen

I listen to Ellie's breathing as it slows, feeling her body relax on top of my own. As gently as I can, I lower her onto the bed, slipping free from our intimate point of connection.

I pull her against my chest, spooning her as she falls more soundly asleep. Though I close my eyes as well, I know that sleep is still far off. I never doze for more than a couple of hours at a time, after all.

Truth be told, I'm perfectly content to stay here with Ellie, holding her as she claims some well-deserved hours of shuteye. It's been a longer day for her than I'm sure she's used to. I tug her a little closer, grateful that her long, desperate drive didn't end in disaster.

Even more grateful still that she accepted me once I arrived to ask her back. I honestly couldn't have said when I started out whether she was going to come away with me or not. Of course, now that I do have her here with me, the next step in our journey is a total mystery to me. Once we get back to the festival, what happens then?

I've just fired the one and only manager my band has ever had, and we're playing a huge show in less than twenty four hours. On top of that, Ellie's got a show to play right before ours, and she happens to be down one half of her band. I doubt that Mitch is going to be waiting in Kansas for her with a box of chocolates and an apology. Taking responsibility for his own actions doesn't seem to be his style.

I can't help but feel responsible for breaking up Ellie's duo. Sure, they would have gone their separate ways eventually, but they probably would've gone a little longer without falling apart if I hadn't come into the picture. My presence forced Mitch's jealousy to the surface, leaving Ellie no choice but to reject him. I know she doesn't blame me, but I still feel like I need to find a way to make it up to her.

Then there's the question of my own band. We had an excellent show the other night, and the guys have been really patient with me throughout the festival, but I don't know how much more they're going to tolerate. They've already threatened to jump ship, and I know full well that they weren't messing around. That's not their style.

I haven't been a good band mate since I met Ellie. But that's not her fault, and it's not because what we're doing is wrong—it's all on me. I've got to make all of this right.

Part of me wishes that I could stretch this short flight on into an eternity. Just stay here, curled up with Ellie, and never have to think about the rest of the world again. I let my imagination supply a picture of us, tucked away somewhere together.

For some reason, I picture a little house on a lake, with a long dock running out into the water. I see us, lounging in beat up beach chairs, nursing a couple of cool beers, our toes dangling down into the water...if only things could ever be that simple.

Even if I really did want to leave my music career behind, which I have to admit I emphatically don't, it's not like I could ask Ellie to drop everything and run away with me. Her career is just beginning and who knows how successful she's going to become in her own right.

With a voice like hers, and the way she has with words, she stands a good shot at becoming huge. I wonder if she even realizes how good she is? Or whether she knows that she never needed Mitch in the first place?

I can't even let her know how badly I wish we could just exempt ourselves from all the music industry bullshit and do what we love to do without all the extra drama.

As the sky regains its charcoal gray, pre-dawn color, an idea occurs to me. There's a way I can help Ellie without forcing her out of the game before it's even begun. It's incredibly risky, and it may very well blow up in my face...but it might work. I rest my arm against Ellie's and give her a little nudge, trying to draw her back out of sleep. She snuggles in closer to my body, unwilling to be roused.

"Ellie," I whisper, kissing her lightly on the cheek, "Ellie, we're almost there."

"OK," she mumbles. She has no intention of waking up just yet.

"I have an idea," I tell her, "For your show."

"I don't have a show anymore," she sighs, still mostly asleep, "Mitch left."

"I know," I tell her, "That's the thing. I think I know someone who can replace him."

"Who?"

"Me," I tell her, "I could play for you instead."

A moment passes as her slumbering mind finally shakes out of its stupor. She cranes her neck, looking intently into my eyes to see if I'm serious. But there's no ambiguity in my intentions. I'm one hundred percent serious about this.

"Trent," she says, turning to face me, "My music is completely different than yours. And there's not enough time to learn it, anyway."

"I know how to play things other than hard rock," I tell her, "And I don't think that Mitch's instrumentation was quite as complicated as he led you to believe. I can pick it up, easy."

"But what about...you know. Your image, or whatever?" she says uneasily, "I feel like you're going to get enough shit from your fans now that we've been seen together. But if I turn you into my backup guitar? There'll be a riot."

"I'm not worried," I say.

"I am," she replies, "You're not the one they're going to hate for it."

"Who is 'they'?" I ask.

"Everybody," she says anxiously, "Everybody in the world is going to think I'm just a fame-hungry hanger-on, using you for your success."

"Is that what you're doing?" I ask.

"Of course not," she says.

"Then why does it matter?"

"Because I'm not used to this," she says, "I'm not used to being the target of people's interest and ire. I need to be taking baby steps here, not running full speed ahead into public disapproval."

"Ellie," I say, "You're forgetting one very important thing in this equation."

"What's that?" she asks.

"The fact that you're one of the most lovable people most of the world will have ever laid eyes on," I say.

"You...think I've lovable?" she asks slowly. My heart starts to beat faster in my chest. I hadn't meant to bring the "L" word into all of this, but now that it's hanging in the air between us, I can't very well back down either. I take a deep breath and meet her rapt gaze.

"I think you're incredibly lovable," I tell her, "Which is why, I suppose...that I'm falling in love with you."

Not exactly the most graceful speech of my life, but I don't have time to dwell on it. Her mouth hangs up just the tiniest bit, and for a second I worry that she's going to tell me to shove it. But then her lips pull up into a contented bow, a smile of pure delight.

"I suppose it turns out that I'm falling in love with you too," she says with a smile.

A big, dumb grin spreads across my face, and I hug her tightly against me. For a decade, I've been cultivating my tough, crude, unsentimental image for the rest of the world. Who would have thought that one small town girl could have cracked that rocky exterior right open?

Somehow, she's managed to see straight through the layers of false bullshit, straight to who I am really am. And even knowing that, she still cares about me.

"I think we should do it," she says.

"Do...what?" I ask, perplexed.

"Play together," she says resolutely. "I think it's a great idea."

"That's more like it," I say, "It's going to be amazing, you'll see. It's going to be great."

Chapter Eighteen

Ellie

The festival finally comes into view across the plains just as the sun is beginning to peek over the horizon. I gaze out the window, fighting to keep my breathing steady.

I've been swallowing down as much high-octane emotion as possible, but I don't know how much longer I'm going to be able to go without a good cry. Between Mitch's abandonment, my dad's sudden appearance, and the overwhelming feelings I have for Trent, I'm firing on all emotional cylinders.

Watching the festival loom up before us is adding a whole new feeling to my already jam-packed heart: apprehension.

I trust Trent's judgment, and I'm sure that he only has both our best interests at heart, but I can't help but be terrified about this idea of his. We already brought a storm of attention and disdain down on our heads when we went gallivanting about together after his first concert at the festival. I know that this little stunt of ours is going to set off a media firestorm. The gossip blogs will be raging about our collaboration, and everyone will have an opinion about it. But I know that I need to come to terms with all that sooner or later.

I just have to keep reminding myself that however the media chooses to represent me, it doesn't change who I really am. The people who know me the best won't be swayed by some music blogger's opinion. My mom and sister will still think the world of me. And even though I've only known Trent for a little while, I feel as though he knows me better than anyone.

His esteem of me won't be altered by some fluff piece on a second-rate gossip website. With practice, I'll be able to ignore all the critics, just like he does. I'm glad to have him as a guide through this crazy industry.

The rainstorm yesterday flushed all the haze and humidity out of the air, and the sky lightens into a clear, crisp canopy over the festival. Even with the ugly things that have happened at Hawk and Dove this year—with Mitch, and that skank Kelly—this place is still one of my most favorite spots on earth. There's something wonderfully equalizing about pitching a tent beneath a canopy of stars with thousands of people you've never met.

I hope that Hawk and Dove never loses that charm, however successful I might become. Though of course, that success still has yet to be determined.

"Bright and early," Trent says, taking my hand in his, "We've got all day to prepare."

"Yep," I say, smiling a little too widely to be convincing.

My nerves are getting the better of me.

"I know it's scary," Trent says, turning to me in the backseat of the car. I can't believe I've been hitching rides with Mr. Private-Jet-Personal-Driver for the last few hours. His entire lifestyle still seems so surreal to me.

"It is scary," I say, "But I believe you if you really think this is a good idea."

Trent squeezes my hand in response as our car turns off onto the dirt road leading to the talent campsite. It feels strange to return again, after my dramatic exit.

Part of me worries that Mitch will be waiting for me inside our rinky-dink little tent, waiting to tell me off again. But probably that's just me being paranoid. I'm sure the last thing Mitch wants right now is to see me. I wonder, with a cloying sense of guilt, when we will see each other again? Or if we ever will?

I feel as though I've seen his true colors over the course of this trip, and they're far from beautiful.

I don't know whether I feel more betrayed or disappointed that Mitch was only interested in my friendship as a stepping stone to a sexual relationship. The fact that being friends alone wasn't enough for him would, in another time, have meddled with my self esteem.

But I have a lot more going for me these days than I did when Mitch and I first started playing together. I have a greater sense of myself as an artist, a vision for what my music should be, and a new partner who understands my every thought. Everything's going to be just fine, I hope.

The private car swings around and stops in front of Trent's tour bus. I crack open the door and step out onto the springy grass. The air is filled with the smell of rain, and the ground is muddy beneath my feet. I don't envy all those poor souls who had to camp out during the storm, though roughing it through the festival was always a source of great satisfaction for Kate and I.

The campsite is just coming back to life after another night of wild partying, it would seem. I gaze longingly at the craft services tent—I'd forgotten all about that whole eating thing during that mad dash across the country and back again.

Before Trent can reach the bus, the door swings open before us. A large, burly projectile comes barreling out the door, slamming into Trent at full speed. The human-shaped missile happens to be Rodney, and he's soon followed by Kenny and Rodger bounding after him. The three band mates swarm around Trent excitedly, leaping all around like jack russell puppies.

I glance warily at the door, waiting for Kelly to step out and ruin the party, but no one else materializes in the doorway.

"You're back!" Kenny cries, hopping up and down.

"Of course I am," Trent says, punching the younger guy playfully on the arm, "I said I would be, didn't I?"

"Sure, but we didn't...you know," says Rodney.

"My word is always good," Trent says, "You know that, guys."

"We sure do," Rodger says, "And check it out! We don't even play until tonight. You got back with time to spare!"

"And some recovered cargo!" Rodney says, finally noticing me standing there a few paces away.

"I'd prefer not to be referred to as cargo," I say smiling, "But, hello to you, too."

"Sorry," Rodney says, his smile dimming.

"He doesn't know how to talk to women. Other than groupies, that is," Kenny says.

"Hell, he doesn't even know how to do that," Rodger laughs, "Most of the groupies aren't very talkative."

"Why don't you all shut up?" Rodney says defensively. "The only woman we've been hanging out with consistently for the last few years is Kelly. Forgive me if my idea of women has been skewed."

"Well, no need to worry anymore," Rodger laughs, "Now you can start your rehabilitation!"

"Why?" I ask, "What happened?"

"Didn't Trent tell you?" Kenny says, eyes wide.

"Tell me what?" I press.

"I...Uh...Had to let Kelly go," Trent says finally.

"You...fired her?" I ask, my heart skipping a beat.

"I did. Yeah," Trent says, trying not to grin at my shock.

"Can you...Could I borrow Trent for a second?" I say to the guys, beckoning my rock star to follow me around the other side of the tour bus. We make our way around the massive vehicle and come across the sad remains of my own little tent.

The storm all but destroyed that testament to my brief run as Mitch's musical partner. It looks like unnecessary hangers-on are being cast off all over the place.

"I hope you didn't fire her just for my sake," I say to Trent, "I admit, I was upset finding her coming on to you, but I can handle it. I trust you enough, Trent, and it won't be the last time I witness a girl throw herself at you."

"I know," he says, "Believe me, what she tried to pull on you was just the final straw. She's been running this band straight into a bleak, commercial wasteland. We need a change of direction, and we need it badly."

"Are you sure?" I say, taking his hands in mine, "Doesn't a band sort of need a manager?"

"A band needs a manager that has its best interests at heart," he tells me, "That's not what we had in Kelly. She was more interested in making enough money to buy herself a private spa in Malibu than preserving our artistic integrity."

"To be fair," I say, "A private spa would be amazing..."

"Don't you start," he says, pulling me against him. He tilts my chin up and kisses me firmly. His touch reassures me, puts me at ease. But we can't get carried away right this moment. We have work to do, after all.

"Come on," I say, planting my hands on his firm chest, "We've got a lot to practice before tonight."

I march Trent back around and into the bus where the guys are lounging in various states of excited contentment. Trent grabs the nearest acoustic guitar and leads me back to the little bedroom that I've already become intimately acquainted with. Closed off from the rest of the band, Trent and I settle down onto the still-rumpled bed and work out a game plan.

"How will you know what to play?" I ask, as Trent expertly retunes his guitar by ear.

"Easy," he says, "Just sing through your songs for me, and I'll be able to figure out the chords."

"We've got, like, twelve hours," I say, amazed by his confidence.

"I don't know if you've been told," Trent says with a grin, "But I'm something of an excellent musician. We'll be fine."

"But—"

"Just start singing," he insists, cradling the acoustic against his chest, "I'll follow along."

I set aside my reservations and decide to go with the flow. Taking a deep breath, I begin to sing:

And if I might,
I think I'll just sleep
In your green shirt tonight.

And spend the night
Dreaming of a porch swing
Rocking in the twilight.
So baby, sleep tight.
And rest easy knowing
That I'm doing alright...

As my simple words float out into the air, Trent begins to pluck at the strings of his guitar. I nearly forget the words to my own song as I watch his hands dance along the instrument. I've only ever seen or heard him play hard, slamming rock music. But there's a delicacy to this instrumentation that takes me completely off guard.

He catches me staring at him and smiles. "You thought I only knew power chords, huh?" he teases, executing an amazingly complicated plucking pattern before my eyes. "Just keep singing, would you? I'm just starting to get the feel of the song."

I soar into the next verse, weaving through the world of the song. Trent follows wherever I go, listening and responding to my voice as if it were his own. And as I round back into the chorus, he comes along. His voice harmonizes perfectly with mine, balancing and filling out my sound. The addition of Trent's voice and music completely changes my song—for the better.

"That was..." I breathe, as we rest between songs.

"Amazing? Incredible? Genius?" Trent suggests.

"All of the above," I tell him, "I had no idea you were a real—" I catch myself, literally biting my tongue before I can finish the thought. The shadow of a scowl crosses Trent's face.

"A real what?" he asks, coolly. "A real musician?"

"I'm sorry," I tell him, "That came out so wrong. This is just so different from anything I've heard from you before. I didn't mean—"

"It's OK," he says, cooling off before he explodes, "I'm just a little touchy about that. No one considers rock musicians to be artists anymore, you know? I mean, people worshipped Jim Morrison and Mick Jagger as musical geniuses, but these days...I just wish I could be recognized for being a good musician, rather than a bad boy with a penchant for trashing hotel rooms and selling albums."

"Well, maybe this will give you that chance?" I suggest.

"Maybe," he says, "That's what I'm hoping for, anyway."

"Hell, we could just break off together and start a whole new group," I laugh.

"That's an idea..." he says, looking thoughtful.

"Oh no," I say quickly, "I was just kidding. There's no way in hell I'm going to be the Yoko Ono in this little scenario."

"Don't worry," he laughs, "I'm sure we can work it out. Later. Right now, we'd better focus on getting your songs down pat. The world will be watching, babe."

"You really think so?" I ask.

"I really do," Trent says, "Do you feel ready for that?"

"Does anyone ever?" I laugh.

"Maybe not," Trent admits.

"What was it like for you?" I ask, "When you first started getting popular."

"It's hard to say," he starts, "I wasn't in the best place back then. I was drinking a lot, doing more than my fair share of drugs. Things were pretty out of hand when Kelly snatched me up in the first place."

"I didn't realize..." I say, "Sorry to bring it up."

"Don't worry about it," Trent says, "That's a part of my past, no getting around it. But I'm better, now. Or at least I like to think so. I don't feel like I need any of that to get through the day, anymore. Especially not lately..."

"Shucks," I say, batting my eyelashes, "You mean I'm a good influence?"

"You're a nut, is what you are," Trent grins, "But a very talented, very grounded, very beautiful nut who does terrible things to me every time you come into my sights."

"Oh?" I say, edging a little closer to him on the bed, "Every time, huh?"

"You stay back!" he says, "I can't be held accountable for what happens when you make those sexy eyes at me."

"I don't make sexy eyes," I protest.

"Sure you do!" he cries, "You're doing it right now!"

"That's just how my eyes are, asshole!"

"Well...Fine. Sexy-by-default eyes. But all the same, we need to keep working. There will be plenty of time for...other sorts of collaboration later. Come on, lead me into your next song."

Reluctantly, we get back to rehearsing. But every moment I spend close to Trent is another leaves me more and more desirous of him. I've never felt so insatiably crazy for someone in my entire life. If this is what falling in love is always like, no wonder people rave about it so much in all those songs! If things keep going the way they have been, I'll have a few sappy love songs of my own to write soon enough.

We spend hours in that room together, flowing from song to song in an ever-deepening state of unity. We've never played together like this before, and working with Trent this way is almost as thrilling as it was to sleep with him for the first time.

There are more than a few similarities between music and sex, of course—both require a keen ability to listen and respond, both can change the way you think about the world, and both are much better when you have a fantastic partner.

Chapter Nineteen

Ellie

The little patch of sky outside the bedroom window lightens to a vibrant blue as the hours wear on, but we keep practicing straight through the gorgeous afternoon.

Playing with Trent doesn't feel like work, the way playing with Mitch sometimes did. This expression feels like such a natural extension of our dynamic that moving from song to speech is seamless. I feel completely in synch with Trent, as though we're of one mind. I've never felt this kind of easy engagement with anyone, and I'm eager to keep exploring it.

A knock on the door interrupts our marathon jam session, and Kenny pokes his head into the room.

"What is it, Kenny?" Trent asks, a bit irritated by the interruption.

"Sorry to intrude," Kenny says, "But you guys do know that it's, like, five o' clock?"

"What?!" I screech, "How is it five o' clock already?"

"I dunno," Kenny shrugs, "Just is."

"Trent, we've got to get down to the stage!" I breathe, springing to my feet.

"Don't worry," he tells me, slinging the guitar over his back, "Everything's under control."

"But—"

"It's all cool," he insists, leading me out of the room, "Just trust me."

I nod, fighting to keep my chin from quivering. This is it, the moment of truth. Time to see whether the world can stomach us. Time to see if anyone will give a damn about what we have to share. But whatever the reaction, at least I know I've found something beautiful in this surprising collaboration.

Trent leads the way through the tour bus, and the three guys fall in step behind us as we make our way out into the early evening.

"Are you guys...coming?" he asks.

"Of course we are!" Rodger says, "You think we'd miss it?"

"No, I just...Thank you," Trent says, "That's pretty cool of you."

Rodney hands Trent a flask, and my partner takes a hearty slug. He holds it out for me, and I raise it to the group before taking a swallow of smooth vodka for myself. A little liquid courage will go a long way, right about now.

The five of us turn and head down the hill together. I have to admit, it's nice having a little posse to be a part of. Especially one that knows the ropes of this whole "fame" thing.

As we approach the bottom of the hill, a crowd begins to form. People peer up at us as we come ever closer, and I can feel my chest growing tighter with each step. The guys spread out around me, forming a protective little "V" to keep me from getting overwhelmed by the crowd.

Beside me, Trent walks with long, authoritative strides, challenging anyone to be disparaging about our joint appearance. As we make our way to the stage, he throws his arm around my shoulders and pulls me tightly against him. I wrap my arm around his waist, grateful beyond measure for his infectious courage.

People are clamoring at us left and right, but we keep on trucking until we close in on the stage where Mitch and I were set to perform. We duck backstage, finally leaving the throng behind.

From among the intricate system of curtains and audio equipment, Pearl the stage manager comes bustling toward us. She's even more excited than when we first met—which is not something I'd thought possible.

She's beaming from ear to ear as she comes up and wraps me in a hug.

"You sure have had a busy festival!" she laughs, eyeing Trent.

"You could say that, yeah," I tell her.

"We're just about ready for you out there," she says, looking around the backstage world, "But where's your partner?"

"Right here," Trent says, stepping forward.

"No, no," Pearl giggles, "I meant your songwriting partner. Where's Mitch?"

"Trent is my new songwriting partner," I tell the stage manager, "Mitch and I had a bit of misunderstanding."

Pearl's eye widen. "Oh...Oh, dear. This is rather unexpected. We don't really have anything set up for the whole band..."

"It's just me," Trent says, "We're doing the acoustic duo thing, don't worry. As long as a couple of mics are set up, we'll be fine."

"But...The crowd is expecting to see Ellie & Mitch," Pearl says anxiously.

"They're getting something better," I tell her, "They're going to see the first ever performance of a whole new group...Jackson & Parker."

"Nice one," Trent says.

"I don't know how this is going to go over with these fans," Pearl says, biting her lip.

"Well, we don't know either. So why don't we find out, huh?" I say.

"OK," says the stage manager, backing away, "I'll just...get out there and introduce you, then."

She hurries away as the rest of the band wishes us all the broken limbs in the world.

It's just Trent and I, standing alone backstage. I can hear the rumble of a huge crowd beyond the curtain—I'm sure there are far more people out there than last time. A stampede of butterflies breaks loose in my stomach, and it's a struggle to set aside my doubts.

What if they really do hate us as a duo? I know that I shouldn't care, but my skin isn't that thick yet. There's always going to be a part of me that just wants to be liked, to be the best.

"Trent, this is crazy," I hiss, squeezing his hand.

"That's true," he smiles, brushing my hair out of my face, "But it's exciting too, isn't it?"

"What if they just despise us?" I ask nervously, "What if they see you, me, and a guitar, and call bullshit on the whole thing?"

"Then they must not be listening," he says, "Your music is great, and we're wonderful together. Just have faith in us, Ellie. I know I do."

"I do too," I tell him, "This is all just a little bit much."

A cheer goes up from the audience as Pearl's voice crackles through the speakers. "Welcome to tonight's first performance!" she says, reluctantly enthusiastic, "I know that you all came to see Ellie & Mitch, but unfortunately there's been a slight change in program."

"Unfortunately?" Trent snorts. But I can hear a groan of disappointment coming from the crowd. I don't know whether to feel flattered that they were excited to see my act or terrified that they're going to hate what they get instead.

"Instead, I'm proud to introduce a brand new act, featuring some musicians that you already know and love. Please welcome to the stage, Jackson & Parker!"

Trent grabs onto my hand and walks me out onto the stage. As soon as the audience catches sight of us together, they lose their collective mind all at once. A wave of sounds breaks over us as we make our way center stage.

At first, it's impossible to tell what the tone of that noise is. But once the shock of its intensity has subsided, I can tell that it's not ire or disappointment these people are showering us with—it's excitement and delight. They're happy to see us, after all!

I'm smiling ear to ear as Trent and I take our places before the standing mics. Our setup is simple, our stage unadorned, but the crowd is still going nuts for us. I look out over the audience—it must be three times the size of our first crowd at Hawk and Dove.

I feel the love pouring in from all of them, and have to swallow down happy tears before I grab the mic and say, "Hi everyone." Another roar of applause forces me to wait a moment before I continue, "Thank you all for coming out to see us tonight. Even if you were expecting a different us. Trent and I just met here at Hawk and Dove and, well...we've really hit it off. We've been working on some music that we really think you're going to enjoy."

A ripple of whispers spreads through the audience. I look over at Trent and he smiles at me, with him at my side, I feel more than brave enough to break into song.

I count Trent off and let out a low, melancholy wail to begin our first number. The crowd is screaming and reaching out for us as we swing our way through the first song, an ode to foiled expectations and the pain of realizing that no one has all the answers.

We fall right back into our place of wonderful dual-solitude, even though there are hundreds of people watching us. It might as well just be the two of us alone in our little rehearsal room, I still feel that close and connected to him.

His fingers draw the most beautiful patterns up out of his instrument, complimenting my songs in a way I never knew was possible. And when he adds his voice to mine in breathtaking harmony, it's like my words are actually coming to life—taking form in the air that hangs between us and the audience.

I've never been a part of anything so beautiful before in my life. Together, we transport the entire crowd beyond this field in Kansas, straight into the world we're creating with each passing note and word. It's a true and beautiful collaboration of the purest sort.

As we wrap up the first half of our set, the audience is practically pulsing with ecstatic delight. They can sense that they're witnessing something more than just the creation of music—they're watching two people falling in love right before their very eyes. And the fact that one of those people happens to be Trent Parker doesn't hurt things one bit.

I hold the microphone away from my mouth and lean toward him.

"I think they like us," I say with a smile.

"They love us," he replies, wrapping his arm around my waist. He brings his mouth down to mine in one sure, sweet motion. I press my lips firmly against his, throwing my arm up over his shoulder. I can hear the crowd going wild, but I don't even care. All I care about is the feel of Trent's lips on mine, the sweet coolness of the breeze off the rain washed grass, the deep pink color of the darkening sunset. I don't know how this moment could be any more perfect.

Trent takes a step back and slings the guitar off of his body.

I blink at him, not comprehending at first.

"What are you doing?" I ask, "We still have half a set to play."

"I know," he says, "I think you should play your song first."

"What?" I breathe, staring at him.

"Play the song you were telling me about earlier. The one you were working on before you hit the road to come here."

"You want me to play the guitar?" I hiss, "In front of all these people?"

"Why, yes," he laughs, "I do. Come on—you're a real musician now. Time to start taking some risks."

I wrap my trembling hand around the neck of the guitar and take it from Trent. "This is either the best or worst idea in the history of the world," I tell him.

"Don't be such a goofball," he says, rolling his eyes, "Just play your song. I'm right here, Ellie. There's no reason to be afraid."

I glance out across the hundreds of upturned faces. "Oh yeah. No need to be afraid at all..."

Approaching the standing mic, I sling the guitar around my neck. The audience is buzzing with curious chatter as I lean into the mic and say, "I've been working on an original bit, lately. I'm not much of guitarist, so you'll have to bear with me, but I wanted to share this with you anyway."

And as I say it, I realize that it's true. I do want to share my song with the rest of the world—that's why I'm here in the first place. Just last week, before I left for the festival, I was practicing this little ditty in my childhood bedroom. Now, it's about to belong to everyone standing before me. And it's all thanks to Trent, in the end.

I steal a sidelong glance at him and draw courage from his assured, comfortable gaze.

I draw in a deep breath, arrange my fingers on the guitar, and begin to sing:

Remember me just like this,
Picking feathers and burrs
Off the hem of my summer dress.
Remember how I was that day,
Laying down my bread crumbs,
Lest I go astray,

All for the sake of a man
I don't even know by name...

A hush falls over the audience as I delve deeper into my song. The chords that I strum out are simple, drawing even more focus to the words themselves. The story I weave is impressionistic, even surreal at times, but the audience stays right there with me through the whole thing.

As I sail into the chorus, I hear Trent's voice joining mine, adding a gorgeous richness to my melody. He stays with me through the rest of the song, and the audience's response is deafening. Their adoration carries us all the way through the rest of the set, straight into the encore. We practically float offstage together, hovering on the overwhelming power of their praise.

"That was amazing!" I exclaim, throwing my arms around Trent.

"You were amazing," he tells me, "Truly."

"We make a good team, huh?" I laugh.

"The best," he says, cupping my cheek in his hand, "But we'd better not linger here too long."

"Why not?" I ask.

"Well, there's this little matter of a rock concert I need to play in about an hour..."

"Oh!" I cry, "We should go..."

"Do you want to come?" he asks.

"Of course I do, are you crazy?" I say, "I'll watch from the wings like last time."

"Maybe," he says, "But I think I have a better idea. Follow me..."

We race off together, plunging into and through the sea of photographers that follows us everywhere. But this time, they don't scare me. With Trent's hand in mine and a guitar hanging across my shoulders, I feel truly invincible.

Chapter Twenty

We scramble into the green room of the Hawk and Dove main stage.

Ellie's cheeks are beautifully flushed after our mad dash across the festival grounds. I can't help but mirror her wide, beaming smile. I knew that we'd sound great together, and that the audience would love us, but even I didn't expect our surprise collaboration to go over *that* well.

And here I was, worried that playing together might complicate whatever relationship is springing up between us. Turns out, music is just another expression of the fact that we're a perfect fit.

Ellie throws her arms around my shoulder and brings her lips to mine. I happily accept her kiss, grabbing her by the hips and drawing her tightly against me. We're the only ones in the little green room tent, and I intend to take advantage of our momentary solitude.

I let a hand wander down Ellie's round, sumptuous ass, grazing along the back of her shapely leg...she doesn't stop me. Her teeth close lightly on my bottom lip, and I have to fight to keep myself from laying her out in the grass right then and there. Every time I touch this girl, the need to be close to her only intensifies.

There's no extinguishing my desire for Ellie, but luckily enough, the feeling seems to be mutual.

"Trent," she says, her breath warm against my neck, "I've never felt like this after a show."

"I should think not," I grin, wrapping my arms around her waist.

"How did you learn how to improv like that?" she asks, peering up at me with bright eyes. "I felt like we were sharing one mind the whole time we were playing. I mean, I know you're more experienced with the whole band thing..."

"Honestly Ellie," I tell her, "That's the first time I've ever felt that on stage, too. That communication, I mean. It's never been like that with any band I've played with—not even with the guys I play with now. I don't know what to say..."

"Does that make me your first?" she smiles wickedly.

I let out a laugh. "I suppose it does," I say, kissing down her throat.

She lets out a little moan and presses herself harder up against me. What I wouldn't give to blow off my concert and whisk her off somewhere a little more private. I imagine us hopping back into that jet and taking off for the Virgin Islands, or Tahiti...or Siberia, for all I care, as long as we can be alone together.

"They really loved us, didn't they?" Ellie sighs happily.

"The audience? You bet your sweet ass they did," I say.

"I really felt like they understood me," she says, "I've never experienced that before. Usually, it feels like only snippets of what I mean are actually getting through to the audience. Like, they're too distracted by the costumes or the duo gimmick to get anything from my songs. But this time...it's like they were really with us every step of the way. No distractions or anything."

"Damn," I say, "Could it be that there were no red suspenders or stupid facial hair onstage to draw focus away from what was actually important?"

She gives me a little punch on the arm, just to keep me in line. "Be nice," she says, "Mitch will find his way."

"As long as he doesn't expect that way to be at your side, it's fine by me," I say, "Because the thing is, sweetheart, I'm calling dibs on every single side you've got."

"You're a creep," she laughs.

"Tell me about it," I say, sliding my hands down the curvature of those coveted sides of hers. "Do you have any idea how much of a turn-on making music with you is?"

"Oh, I think I have an idea," she says, leaning into me. I'm sure she can feel me growing hard against her. "But darlin'...I think you're forgetting something at the moment."

"What's that?" I all but growl.

"You have another show to play. Like...right now," she reminds me.

"Ah, shit," I sigh, putting a couple of healthy inches between my stiffening groin and Ellie's gorgeous body, "You're right about that. It's completely unfair that I have to be somewhere other than on top of you right now, though."

"Be that as it may," she says, taking a step back, "You do have other people who are counting on you. They may not also double as excellent bedmates, but your band mates still depend on you. Think you're ready to get out and play another set?"

"Are you going to be back in the wings?" I ask.

"Of course," she says, "I wouldn't miss it."

"In that case," I say, "I'm going to be just fine. Maybe you could even come out and do a little surprise appearance?"

"Yeah, OK," she laughs.

"I'm serious!" I tell her, "I'll call you out for one of the songs."

"You think your band would be OK with that?"

"You're forgetting something rather crucial," I say, "Our act is just Trent Parker, not Trent Parker and Friends. At the end of the day, I'm still the one calling the shots."

"How the hell do you manage to make arrogance so goddamn sexy?" she asks, shaking her head in wonder.

"A lot of practice," I tell her, "I've been looking out for myself for most of my life. This whole 'partner' thing is kind of new."

"For both of us," she says.

I start to bring my lips to hers, but a raucous cheer distracts us both. Kenny, Rodger, and Rodney come barreling into the tent, whooping and hollering as they always do before a show. Ellie grins at them, and the hint of shyness creeping through her smile makes my heart ache with affection for her. This girl's going to turn me into a huge softy if I'm not careful—but it's OK. That's what take-no-prisoners stage personas are for.

"Trent! Since when do you play *music* music?" Kenny bellows, slapping me on the back.

"You guys sounded awesome"! Rodger says, "I couldn't believe that was you up there, Trent."

"After all these years of hard core screaming, who thought you'd still be able to carry a tune?" Rodney puts in, "You were like...Like fuckin' Frank Sinatra or something up there!"

"You're just saying that because he's the only singer you can name," I reply.

"Maybe," Rodney says, "But you get the point, right?"

Kenny turns reverently to Ellie, full of admiration. "And you're like...scary good."

"Why thank you," she laughs.

"I mean...I don't even know how you could possibly sing that well," Kenny goes on, "And those words, too? They're like...poetic and shit."

"How eloquent," I say, rolling my eyes.

"Look," Rodney says, squeezing Kenny's cheek, "You've made a fangirl out of Kenny!"

"Hey c'mon," Kenny grumbles, pulling away from Rodney, "I was just being honest."

"You guys think the fans will forgive Trent for playing with me?" Ellie asks. She's struggling to keep her tone light, but I know that she has reservations she's trying to mask.

"Oh, whatever," Rodger says, "Screw anyone who's got a problem with it. People got down on Joni Mitchell when she went all jazzy, but that didn't change the fact that she's a musical genius."

"You like Joni Mitchell?" Ellie asks excitedly.

"Who doesn't like Joni Mitchell?" Rodger replies.

"Straight men, generally," Rodney guffaws.

Rodger draws himself up to his full height. "I happen to be confident enough in my masculinity to admit that Joni Mitchell makes me all gooey inside. So suck my balls, asshole."

Rodney tackles Rodger to the grass, and Kenny falls into the playful wrestling match as well. I shrug my shoulders at Ellie, but she doesn't seem the least perturbed.

As rambunctious and destructive as my band mates are, she's having no trouble at all fitting in. I imagine what it would be like to bring Ellie along for a tour. The five of us, cruising around the country in the jet, partying together—she and I sneaking off whenever we please. It's a damn appealing picture, I must say. But she's still in school, with a plan of her own. Who knows whether she'd even want to schlep around with us assholes?

"OK, OK, break it up," I grumble, nudging the guys with my foot, "You may have forgotten, but we have a show to go play."

"Oh, right," Kenny says, pulling himself up off the grass, "Ready when you are, chief!"

"We've got the set list down," Rodney says, sitting on the grass like an oversized toddler.

"Let's do this," Rodger says.

"Wait a minute, guys," I say, "I've got an idea for something we can try tonight."

"Ohhhhboy," Rodger mumbles.

"In case you've forgotten, we've got the rare opportunity here to play a show without having to answer to a manager afterwards," I say, "We can do whatever we want, play whatever we want, without any fear of having to deal with some bullshit afterwards."

"You're right," Kenny says, "It's like Christmas morning!"

"So, what should we do?" Rodney asks.

"I think we should forget all the garbage we've been writing to sell records," I say, "We should get back to basics. Play the stuff that earned us a fan base in the first place. I'm talking way back to our first album—when we actually meant it."

"Yeah!" Kenny cries, all but leaping in the air, "We can play the hard stuff again. Really get people going."

"That's what I had in mind," I say, "Let's toss out the rule book and start playing the kind of music we want to make, not the kind that's engineered to get us to the Top 40."

"Hey, if they don't like it, you're the big name," Rodney says, "It's no skin off my ass."

"Nose," Rodger says.

"Whatever," Rodney mumbles.

"So, anything goes," I say, drawing them all in for a pre-show huddle. Ellie tries to give us some space, but I pull her in anyway. She belongs here as much as anyone. With Ellie here, I feel a whole new source of energy opening up to me. It's a raw, unstoppable power that only comes from knowing you have the support of the people who mean the most to you in the world. I feel like I can do anything, just knowing that she's here with me.

"Let's make this one hell of a show!" I roar.

The guys answer with cheers and shouts of their own, and we break to get to our places. I take Ellie's hand and lead her back through a maze of curtains and equipment. We come to the edge of the stage, and I take her up in my arms. She kisses me deeply, letting her tongue glide against mine. The surging sound of the crowd blocks out my low groan, but the vibration of it moves through each of us. I pull away and see Ellie's wide eyes shining in the low light.

"Go get 'em," she grins, giving me a firm slap on the ass.

"You're going to pay for that later," I tell her.

"Is that a promise?" she asks.

"You bet is it," I say, and turn toward the stage.

The lights blaze to life as I stride to center. The rush of taking the stage never fades, no matter how many concerts I play. Every time, that terrified little fourteen year old experiences a moment of ice cold panic, followed by a rush of intense, indescribable power. I raise my arms up to the crowd and let their applause and cheering rush over me like a crashing wave. I'm the conduit for their energy, the source and the beacon of everything they're feeling. For this fraction of time, I feel like more than a man.

I grab a standing mic and drag it across the stage, screaming as I go, "Hawk and Dove! Are you ready for one last show?" A roar of sound erupts through the air in response. "We're holding nothing back tonight. No half measures, no way. We're going back to the very beginning, back to the music that made you lose your minds for us in the first place. How about that?"

A massive swell of noise bursts, and a wild grin spreads across my face.

My band mates are waiting, poised at their instruments. Every cell of every body onstage is pumping with energy begging to be expressed in song. I look back at Ellie and catch her staring at me with a rapturous glint in her eyes. Her excitement puts me right over the edge.

I lean back and bringing the mic to my mouth, letting loose with a wild, throaty, animal yell. The pent up aggression and pain and joy that have been muddled for so long by catchy refrains and ticket sales rip through me now, filling the entire sky with blazing, unmitigated fury.

I stalk across the stage, right up to the very edge. A sea of people roils before me, moved by our every note, my every primal grunt and cry. I reach out to the up-stretched hands, drawing more and more energy from the desperate, exuberant excitement of my fans.

In the center of the crowd, I watch as an enormous gap opens up. Bodies fly into the abyss, arms swinging, legs kicking. The mosh pit grows and surges, people throw themselves into the dangerous fray left and right. I'm suddenly tempted to join them down there, among the thrashing limbs and furious movement. It's been so long since I've felt like this at a show, like anything in the world could happen.

We tear through our first number, a song we wrote years ago at the very beginning. It feels so good to be back here, retracing our way to a place of truth and meaning after all these years of commercial nonsense. And I never would have had the courage to do this if it hadn't been for Ellie falling into my life.

Suddenly, the need to have her there beside me takes over. I stride back to where she's standing, just beyond the curtain. There's so much happening onstage and off that the crowd hardly even notices that I'm missing.

I rush up to Ellie and take hold of her hands. She looks at me like I've lost my God damned mind.

"Come on," I scream over the music, "Come out here with me!"

"What are you talking about?" she shouts back.

"I want you with me," I tell her, "I want you with me wherever I go, and I want to go with you too."

"That's all well and good," she says, "But I don't think I belong onstage at a rock concert."

"I don't think I belong in an indie folk duo," I shoot back, "But that didn't stop me. Come on! You know that part of you wants to see what it's like."

"What if they hate that I'm there?" she asks, her nerves getting the better of her.

"Who cares?" I say, "It doesn't matter what anyone else thinks."

"But—"

"No more but's," I say, "You're coming with me!"

And with that, I scoop her legs out from under her and cradle her against my chest. She kicks out, laughing like wild.

That laugh of hers was one of the first things that drew me to her. In no time at all, she's won me over like no one ever has before.

"Either you're walking yourself, or I'll carry you!" I yell.

"Fine, fine!" she says, thrashing in my arms, "I'll go willingly, you lunatic!"

"That's what I like to hear," I tell her.

She grabs onto my hand and squeezes tightly. "Start a song I might know, would you?"

"You don't even listen to my music," I remind her.

"Shit," she says, "You're right...Well, whatever. I'll just make it up."

Hands clasped, we make our way back onto the stage. Little by little, as we make our way to the center, the audience starts to notice the change. The air alters as they realize that I have company, and I grab onto the microphone as we reach center.

"We have a special treat for you tonight," I tell the humming crowd. "This is Eleanor Jackson. You might not have know who she was before, but you sure as hell will now. And not because she's here with me tonight, but because she's an amazing, brilliant musician.

Ellie's mouth falls open as the audience's reaction rises to a boil. My band mates and cheering like crazy as the crowd rages before us. I pull Ellie to me and kiss her hard on the mouth, unable to restrain myself. She throws her arms around my neck and kisses me back for the whole wide world to see.

"This is some first date," she says into my ear as we pull away from each other.

"A little unconventional," I agree, "But no time to worry about it now."

Behind us, the band powers into the next song, and we're swept up into the sound. I start to sing, letting the words burst out of me on their own volition.

Ellie is there beside me, feeling the shape of the song, letting it move through her body. I don't think I've ever seen anything sexier than her writhing body, lit up against those stage lights. We cross each other and move around the stage, always finding our back. She's singing now too, and I bring her near me so that our songs can tangle and soar, amplified against the starry sky.

We're here together, harmonizing and balancing, giving and taking. It's a conversation, a collaboration, a string of compromises that cost nothing. It's beyond exhilarating—it's orgasmic.

We make our way to the edge of the stage once more, reaching down into the crowd. Hands grab out, trying to latch onto ours for just the briefest of moments. Usually, this kind of intense affection just makes me feel lonely. All those people out there, in love with the image that I offer up as sacrifice to the masses. But with Ellie here, I feel rooted to who I really am. I don't feel lost or alone anymore. I know who I am, and what I want, and who I love for the first time in my life.

Ellie and I lock eyes as dozens of hands stretch up toward us. Her eyes are on fire.

She jerks her head toward the crowd, and I can tell what she has in mind. This girl never ceases to amaze me. I nod, grinning like an idiot, and take a few steps away from the surging crowd. Together, we take off at a run and leap into the sea of clamoring hands. We're carried over the waves of humanity by the adoring hands of my—our—fans. I feel my fingers tightly clasped around Ellie's not wanting to lose her as we let the audience bear us along.

I look straight up into the clear night sky, the warmth of Ellie's hand in mine burning like a signal fire among all this noise and chaos. I always feel alive during concerts, always feel like I'm living at full throttle—but this is the first time that I've ever actually felt *happy* during one. I've always felt like I needed to share my music, but tonight I give it gladly, joyously.

Laying back in the arms of our fans, Ellie and I let the current take us wherever it will, trusting that we'll be safe and sound as long as we're crossing the expanse together.

Chapter Twenty One

Ellie

The band and I take our third, fourth, and fifth bows, trying to satiate the audience. They just can't seem to get enough of us.

I can't stop laughing as I look out over the massive group of people. I keep expecting to wake up from this crazy dream any second, but it just keeps stretching on. There's Trent Parker beside me, the festival main stage beneath my feet, an enormous cheering crowd stretching out as far as the eye can see. It's *real*.

We finally start to make our way offstage, the roar of the audience throbbing and pulsing like a living creature. Trent and I hurry off into the wings as the guys clear offstage, and I all but collapse into his arms. I'm so overjoyed, not to mention overwhelmed, that for a moment all I can do is let him hold me.

It's a pretty intense high, being out there in front of an audience like that. And something about Trent's music just transcends anything I've ever felt playing my own stuff. He channels something in the music he creates that I've never felt before—something sad, and true, and timeless.

"Holy crap," I whisper, resting my cheek against Trent's firm chest, "Is that what's it's like to be you?"

"I suppose so," he says, holding me tightly against him, "You were amazing, Ellie."

"I was terrified," I admit.

"Still," he says.

I look up at him in the half-light, listening as the audience slowly begins to migrate away from the stage. "I guess they didn't hate us together too much, huh?"

"How could anyone hate us together?" he asks, "When something makes this much sense, feels so right...people can see that."

"I guess so," I smile, my knees starting to tremble. It's been one hell of an evening. "Let's get out of here," I suggest.

"Yeah," he agrees, "Though it looks like I might have to carry you after all."

"Maybe a little," I laugh, swinging my leg over his back, "Do you object to piggy back?"

"It's not my favorite position," he jokes, lifting me up onto his back, "But I'm willing to compromise."

"Save the banter for later," I tease, wrapping my arms around his shoulders, "Take me away, my steed!"

"Stud? I'll take it," he says.

I don't bother correcting him as he carries me out from the backstage world, weaving through fans and photographers and reporters as we head back toward the hill. I rest my head against his shoulder, exhaustion finally settling into my bones.

It's the final night of the festival, a night I've always spent partying with the whole congregation of

Hawk and Dove. But tonight, I just want to be alone with Trent.

As we start to climb the hill, it occurs to me that we've never spoken a word about what's going to happen tomorrow. My original plan was to drive back to Barton with Mitch and commence with summer vacation. And surely, Trent has some other concert or recording session to run off to as soon as the festival wraps.

For all our proclamations and admissions, we've never once touched on the practicalities. I suppose that's what being a rock star is—leaving the practical worries to the little people. But I, for one, still feel very much like one of the little people, and I'm more than a bit anxious about this completely uncertain future we're staring down at the moment.

Has Trent even paused to consider it?

We reach the top of the hill and trudge over to the tour bus. The rest of the band hasn't returned, probably choosing instead to revel with the fans and groupies down at the after party. I slide down off Trent's back and lean, exhaustedly, against the tour bus.

"Wait here," he tells me, "I have an idea."

He skirts around the bus and rushes inside to fetch something. When he returns, he's got the makings of a tent and a bottle of whiskey in his arms.

"What is this?" I ask.

"Well, I had been planning on camping out during this whole fest," he tells me, dumping all the tent parts on the floor, "But some little indie folk asshole told me I wasn't allowed."

"To be fair," I say, "You were in our space."

"Well," he says, "Do I have your permission to resurrect my tent?"

"By all means," I tell him, forcing the doubts from my mind. Better to just enjoy his company tonight than worry too much about what happens in the morning, right?

I settle down onto the grass as Trent takes a big swig of whiskey.

He sets to putting the tent up, and I can't help but shake my head in wonder at this strange, amazing, beautiful person who's crash landed into my life.

A week ago, I would have told you that Trent Parker was just some rich asshole churning out pseudo-hard rock dance tunes for the masses. I would have assumed that he was just another womanizing, vain, soulless creation of the pop music marketing machine, devoid of any real feeling or intelligence. I would have thought all these terrible things, and I would have been dead wrong.

It makes me wonder how often I completely misjudge the people around me, by virtue of not taking the time to know them as people, rather than personas. I'm glad that, at least this once, I was able to see beyond someone's mask. Thank god we were open to seeing each other for who we really are. What a tragedy it would have been not to have met this man.

"You're good at this," I tell him, as he finishes setting up the tent.

"I grew up with a bunch of brothers," he tells me, "Camping skills were just another way to be better than everyone else."

"Well, at least your competitive streak comes in handy sometimes!" I say.

"That is does," he says, securing the tent down into the soft ground, "Your suite awaits you, my dear."

I climb into the tent, marveling at the absurdity of the situation.

"I'm going camping with the most famous rock star in American," I mutter, "Just another weekend away from home, right?"

"I'm about to be the second most famous rock star in America," he says, climbing in after me, "You made quite the impression this evening."

"With your help," I remind him.

"You would have anyway," he says, zipping up the tent behind us and handing me the whiskey. I take a slug, trying to wash away the sourness of our impending departure. I'm not sure how much longer I can put it out of my mind. We just got so caught up in everything that's happened this week that the rest of our lives managed to slip our minds somehow.

"Trent," I say, as he unrolls a big, comfy sleeping bag for us, "Is this how you envisioned spending the last night of Hawk and Dove?"

"Not at all," he laughs, "How could I have imagined this?"

"Yeah," I allow, "I know what you mean."

"It seems appropriate though, doesn't it?" he says, opening his arms to me, "To have spent the festival with a dove, I mean."

"Or a hawk," I say, curling up on his lap, "This has been amazing, Trent."

"You don't have to tell me," he laughs, "I've been here too, you know."

"I just mean...I won't ever forget all of this. Whatever happens next..."

I hold my breath as the question falls between us. Someone had to bring it up eventually. I guess it might as well be me. Trent looks down at me, his eyebrow cocked.

"Whatever happens next?" he says, "That sounds a little ominous..."

"It's not supposed to," I say, "I just...We've never really talked about what the hell we're going to do tomorrow."

"About what?" he asks.

"About...Everything, Trent!" I exclaim, "You are aware of the fact that we live completely separate, disparate lives, right?"

"Well sure," he frowns, "But why are you so upset about it?"

I can't help but feel hurt that he's not worried about our future. Maybe he just took it as a given that we'd go our own way tomorrow? That can't be how he truly feels.

"What are we supposed to do?" I ask quietly.

"Exactly what we're doing right now," he says, pulling me to him.

"You want to be with me?" I ask as bravely as I can.

"Of course I do," he answers, "You didn't doubt that, did you?"

"Well..." I say, "No. Well, maybe. A little."

His face grows stormy at the suggestion. "What, did you think I was going to leave you behind in the dust like some groupie?"

"No!"

"I wouldn't do that to you, Ellie. You should know better than that."

"Then what do you intend to do, Trent?"

"I hadn't...thought about it," he says, turning away from me.

"Well, think about it now," I tell him, "Morning isn't that far off."

"What do you want to do, Ellie?" he asks.

I let out a defeated little laugh. "I have no idea. Part of me wants to run back to Barton, get a job at an ice cream shop, and pretend like none of this ever happened. Everything's already changed so much just this past week...I'm scared to think of what else might change. What else I might lose if I keep on this path..."

"Yeah," Trent sighs.

"This is the part where you're supposed to tell me how wonderful it is to be a musician, and how I shouldn't worry about what I might lose because there's so much to gain?"

"Is that what I'm supposed to say?" Trent asks, "Because that isn't the truth, Ellie. You're smart enough to know that without me telling you. It's true—if you see this whole thing through, every single thing about your life is going to be completely different. Even if you try and maintain some level of normalcy—go back to school, live modestly—nothing will truly stay the same. If you turn around now and walk away from all of this, from your career, your fame, you have a shot at regaining the life you had before. But if you stick it out, then yes. There's a lot to lose."

"Right," I say, sitting down on the soft earth, "I suppose I knew that."

"So what you have to ask yourself," Trent says, sitting before me, "Is whether or not what you have now is worth never knowing what might have been."

"How can I possibly know that?" I ask, "How can I predict whether or not this will all be worth it?"

"You can't," he says, taking my hands, "That's the bitch of it. You just have to think long and hard about whether or not you'll regret not taking that leap. This is a once in a lifetime moment, Ellie. You don't get a second shot at your big break. So, if you think you can live without everything that comes along with a life in music...maybe going home is the right call."

I look up at him, wishing like hell that he would just tell me to stay. If he said those words right this second, if he told me not to leave because he couldn't possibly bear the thought of a life without me, I'd make up my mind in a heartbeat.

I know, now more than ever, that I want to be with Trent. But I also know too well what can happen when you give up the life you've always known for a man. My dad proved pretty well that men can't be counted on to stay. Mom gave up the life she'd built to follow him. If I went along with this famous musician charade, would I be doing the same thing?

"We couldn't be together if I turned my back on this, could we?" I ask.

"No," he answers simply, a pained expression taking hold of his features, "If we tried to stay together, you'd get sucked in no matter what. There's nothing I can do about that."

"You could walk away too," I say, "We could both just turn away and never look back. Go find a cabin in the woods somewhere and write music together in peace and quiet."

Trent smiles sadly. "That's a nice daydream," he says, "But we both know full well that it could never happen. We have to share our music with the world. That's why we're here in the first place."

"But what if—" I start. There's no graceful way to say this. "If I throw myself into this crazy world, and you decide later on that you're not...you don't..."

"What?" Trent asks.

"Want me," I say.

He looks at me long and hard, a dozen emotions flitting across his face. There's anger there, and sadness, and hurt.

"Let me make this perfectly clear," he says, "The only thing I want is for you to be happy, Ellie. Do I hope that means being with me? Of course I do. But if you decide that all you really want is a quiet life away from the spotlight, I'll respect that too. I'll miss you for the rest of my life, but I'm leaving the decision up to you. You have to want this for more than just being with me in the moment. And, if I can be honest, I think you do. When you're onstage, I can see it—you're home. I can see how much you love being up there, bringing people together. I know that you want this, and I know that you're scared as hell."

"Maybe I am," I say, "Can you blame me?"

"Not at all," he says, "You'd be crazy if you weren't. But don't let that fear control you, Ellie. What's the point of going after your dreams if you're just going to politely pass on seizing them? I know it's terrifying, but I know that, for me at least, it's been worth it every step of the way. Especially now..." His strong hand runs up my arm. "I think about what it would be like to share all of this with you...This life is amazing, you know. It's insane, and scary, and infuriating, and strange, but it's absolutely incredible. And to watch you discover all of that, to be there with you through it, would be an honor. Truly."

"You make it sound so easy," I whisper, my body responding to his gentlest touch, "Making that leap, I mean. Jumping without knowing where you're going to land."

"It's not easy," he says, his voice husky, "But eventually you just realize there was never a question. You know what you need, and you just go for it. You take what you want."

I rest my hands on the hard panes of his chest, leaning into him. Warmth spreads through me as he slides his hands around my waist, pulling me closer.

We're kneeling together in his little tent, like two kids off at sleep away camp who don't want to go back their real lives at home.

Suddenly, I don't want or need to worry about what's going to happen tomorrow. What's important is being here with him right now, on this amazing night. All I need is to be right here in the moment with him, soaking up every single breath before the night is through.

I press my body against his, bringing my hands to the small of his back. He brings his lips to my neck, kissing me hungrily, firmly. I let my head roll back, accepting his every fervent kiss. My hands bury themselves in his back pockets, memorizing the feel of his firm ass.

His arms close around my waist, and the nearness of him is making me wetter by the second. I rub against him, thrilling at the feel of his hard, bulging member swelling against my body. We hold each other as tight as we can, our bodies knowing exactly what they need.

His lips brush against the tender skin of my throat as they find their way back up to my own. Our mouths meet, closing the space between us. His stubble has grown in even thicker—I can feel it against my palms as I rest my hands on his sharp jaw. Trent's mouth forces mine open, his tongue gliding against my own, filling me with the taste of him. I can feel him against me, growing stiffer with each moment that passes.

We kiss as if it's the last time we'll ever get the chance.

Trent's hands glide down over my shoulders, skirt down my stomach, and seize the hem of my shirt. He rips the garment up over my head and lowers his lips to the tops of my breasts.

I offer myself up to him, closing my eyes with joy as he deftly unclasps my bra, letting it fall away from my body. I hold onto his shoulders as he takes my hard nipple into his mouth. A gasp escapes my throat as he sucks just hard enough for a little ripple of pain to be sent dancing through me.

I feel the ground fall away as he lifts me up and sprawls me out across the mattress. Rolling onto my back, I let my knees fall open, beckoning him to me.

His eyes shining, he lowers himself back onto me, the hard length of him pressed up against the wetness blooming between my legs. I reach down and yank the tee shirt off his body. His fine, muscled torso is almost too perfect, too defined and unbelievable to look at as he lays on top of me.

The feeling of our hot, bare skin pressed against one another will never, ever leave me.

Trent's lips stray down my neck once more, glancing over my collarbones and down my ribs. In a heartbeat, he's popped open the button of my shorts. He slides the denim down my thighs, tossing the garment over his shoulder. He kisses my belly, the little peaks of my hip bones.

Then his fingers grasp onto my panties, and I understand. I look down at him, slowly rolling the thin cotton bottoms off my body. My heart begins to hammer against my chest, and a sudden wave of shyness hits me.

"What are you..." I breathe, as he pulls my panties down off my feet.

"I just want to make you feel good," he tells me.

I'm utterly naked before him, sitting up on my elbows and my chest heaves with excitement. I've slept with men before, but no one has ever done anything like this to me.

Trent can see that we've reached the edge of my experience, and I don't know whether to be embarrassed or relieved. A look of pure reverence is glowing in his eyes as they wander down the full length of my body. I can't help but let my legs part just a little more. I open myself to him, spreading myself wide. He groans at the sight of me, surrendering to whatever he has in mind.

Trent brings his hands to my tender inner thighs, and I lay back on the mattress with a low moan of anticipation.

I feel his lips brush against my stomach, lingering there as his hands work further and further up my legs. I dig my fingers into my hair, bracing myself. Trent pushes my legs apart, opening me up completely.

Holding me there, he moves down along my body, positioning himself between my legs.

He kisses the little indent between my hip and my thigh, dwelling there, his warm breath against my skin causes me to writhe in anticipation.

I can feel myself growing even wetter for him as he lays kiss after sweet kiss against these most private inches of my body. Closer and closer his lips travel, his hands firm against my skin. I can feel his tongue tracing a long, slow line just beyond where I want to feel him most.

But then, he's there. I breathe in sharply as he licks along the full, wet length of my slit. The feel of his tongue against me there is pure bliss, unlike anything I could have ever imagined. It feels so illicit, and so undeniably right at the same time.

Trent's tongue roves everywhere, exploring my every dip and fold. With each pass, I can feel him a little deeper, a little firmer. I cry out as the tip of his tongue brushes against that throbbing nub.

He closes his lips around it, rolling it with his firm, dexterous tongue. I dig my fingers into his curls as he flicks and kneads me relentlessly. I try to speak, to tell him how wonderful it feels, but words fail me. I'm beyond language and beyond thought.

I can feel that hot pressure growing up inside of me, begging to be let loose. Trent can feel it in me, too. As he traces little circles around my swollen flesh, I feel two strong fingers slip up into my body. All at once, he's everywhere.

As he strokes the silky flesh within me, running his strong tongue against me, I know that I'm done for. My legs begin to tremble, my fingers tighten in his hair, and my mouth falls open in a wordless, blissful cry.

I come for him, my body quivering with the rush of sensation. For that moment, the only thing in the world is Trent's beautiful body, his insatiable mouth. It's just the two of us alone in the universe—and what a universe we make.

I don't want this feeling to end. I want to stay here with him for as long as I can. Blinded by the intensity of my own pleasure, I fumble for Trent, grabbing at the waist of his jeans.

Drawing himself up towards me, he tears free of his clothing at last. I press myself against him, feel the hardness of him pulsating against my thigh. He brings his lips to mine, and I shiver with delight as I taste myself on him. I've never experienced anything so intimate, so boundlessly sexy.

There's nothing in the world that I don't want to experience with him—and I want him to know it. Breaking away from his kiss, I roll onto my stomach, planting my knees firmly into the mattress. His eyes widen as they meet mine and he catches my meaning.

Slowly, reverently, he swings himself around and comes to rest behind me. His hands fall on my hips as I push myself up onto my hands and knees. Looking back over my shoulder, I grin at Trent in the darkness of our little tent. He smiles back, a look of blissful wonder spreading across his face.

He grabs a Trojan out of his pants and expertly applies the condom over his throbbing member.

I feel the bulging tip of him against my slit. With a deep breath, I lean into him as he glides inside of me. A low, raspy moan flies from my mouth as he opens me up, deeper than he ever has before.

I fall down onto my forearms as he draws back and thrusts again. The little space seems to spin around us as we buck against each other, working ourselves into a shared frenzy. I can already feel myself once again teetering on the edge of bliss as he comes barreling to meet me.

With each stroke, I can feel him getting bigger, harder, until finally he reaches his peak. His fingers dig into my hips as he pulses and comes inside of me, sending a deep shudder of sensation racing through me.

Spent, we topple forward together, collapsing into a heaving, tangled pile of limbs.

I stare up into the canopy of the tent, burrowing into his strong arms. We lay in perfect silence, the quiet interrupted only by our slowing breath. I listen as his breathing becomes slower and slower, dropping off finally into sleep. I'm almost sad to feel him slumbering against me—the last thing I want is for this night to end. But morning will come, as it always does, and we'll face it then.

I close my eyes, resting my head against Trent's chest. On his heels, I drop off into a deep, well-earned sleep. My dreams that night are full of him, and the amazing life we can have together if I prove brave enough to risk it all.

Chapter Twenty Two

Trent

The hard, baking sun turns our tent into an oven by daybreak. I can feel the heat descending on Ellie and I, driving us out of our deep, spent slumber.

Today's the final day of the festival, the last day of this crazy, improbable fairy tale that Ellie and I have fallen into. The likelihood of us finding each other like this was as slim as a whisper—nothing short of a miracle. But now, the wild, unlikely dream that has encompassed the last week is drawing to a close. It's time to rub the sand out of our eyes and see what reality has in store for us.

I can feel Ellie begin to stir against me, and I know that waking can't be put off any longer. What I wouldn't give to stretch this moment into an eternity in and of itself. Right now, it feels like we're standing right at the edge of a cliff, with our entire lives leading up to the next move. Will we jump together, or lose our nerve? Will we be able to throw caution to the wind and be together, or is that just the stuff of dreams?

It's time to find out.

"Trent?" Ellie mumbles sleepily, rolling over.

"Good morning, sunshine," I say, smiling sadly.

She curls her body tightly against mine, as if trying to hide from the impending day. I tug her tightly against me, despite the rising heat of the tent. We wrap our arms around each other, collecting every last touch and sensation to sustain us. I wish I could come right out and ask Ellie what's on her mind, but I refuse to pressure her like that. Whatever she chooses to do next has to be on her own terms. That's the only way.

"It's a freakin' sauna in here," she says finally.

"It is," I agree, "Should we...?"

"Yeah," she says, pulling away from me.

Feeling her move away twists my heart like a wrung towel. I don't know what the hell I'm going to do if she decides to end it today. I'll force myself to respect her decision if she wants to steer clear of all this rock star business, but I'll feel in my heart that she's made a mistake.

There's a lot to lose, being a musician; but nothing ventured, nothing gained. And the gains always outweigh the losses, in the end.

Ellie straightens up, not a stitch of clothing on her body. I stare up at her, memorizing every inch. I want to remember the way her hips sway as she walks, the round, full swells of her ass and breasts, her soft and womanly belly. I want to learn every single thing about her by heart—the way she tucks her short blonde hair behind her ears again and again whenever she's anxious, the way she wrinkles her nose when she's concentrating. I want all the time in the world to know these little things, but time is something we no longer have much of.

I follow her lead, poking around the tent for my jeans and tee shirt. We dress ourselves in silence, though I can feel her eyes lingering heavily on my body, too. There are so many unspoken words hanging in the air between us, it's a miracle we don't choke on them. I buckle my belt and turn to face her, offering up my best attempt at a smile. Ellie mirrors my half-assed cheer and slowly unzips the tent flap. Hand in hand, we step out into the brightening day.

All around us, the festival is collapsing in on itself. Down the hill, tents large and small are being stripped and taken down, stalls and booths are torn down and hauled away. People are trekking away from the center of the festivities in droves—the entire population of the weeklong community is evacuating. Even up in the talent campsite, tour busses are pulling away, fancy amenities are disappearing and the craft service tent is serving up its last batch of rations. We stand still in a world of rapid motion, and I know that there's only so long we can linger here together.

"There you are!" says a voice behind us. I turn to see Rodney climbing out of the tour bus. "We're just about packed up in there. The driver's all set to go. You just about ready to ship off?"

"Oh. Yeah," I say, "I've just got to break down the tent first."

"You and your freakin' tent..." Rodney scoffs, crossing his arms. "You guys just didn't want to have a slumber party with us, huh?"

"Sorry Rod," Ellie says, "We just felt like roughing it for the night."

"So that's what the kids are calling it these days," Rodney says, a wicked glint in his eye. I punch him on the shoulder, just a bit harder than may be necessary. I can't help it—my nerves are coiled up like springs.

"Just give us a second with this," I grumble.

"Whatever, man," Rodney says, rubbing his arm and retreating to the bus.

I move past Ellie and start to disassemble our tent. Out of the corner of my eye, I watch her sink down onto the grass, absentmindedly pulling blades up out of the ground. I work as slowly as I can, stretching out these final moments. As I let the air out of the mattress, I hear her speak up.

"You know, Trent...I'm going to need a ride out of here."

My heart thunders in my chest as I turn toward her. "Oh, right...I guess you left your car back in Barton, huh?"

"That's right," she says, "We took your fancy pants jet back here."

She doesn't need to remind me of that. I'll remember hoisting her up onto the bar in that jet for the rest of my life. I have to fight to keep from getting rock hard at the mere thought of it.

It's no easy feat.

"Well...I could call you a car if you want," I offer, "We've got a freakin' fleet on call for the band. I'm sure I could get someone here to take you...wherever you want to go."

Her features fall, and it's abundantly clear that I've said the wrong thing. I have no idea how to navigate this. How am I supposed to be impartial when what I want is so sharply defined in my mind? I want her to come with me, to stay with me. That's all I know for sure.

"I guess that would be OK," she says softly, her eyes imploring.

"Is that what you want?" I ask, my fingers clenched.

"It's what I know I should want..." she says, blinking away tears, "I should just go home, and forget all about this, and live my life like a normal person, and find some peace."

"If that's really what you want..." I say, the words like sand in my mouth.

"It's what I should want," she insists, "An average, comfortable, safe life. A life that anyone would be happy with."

"This isn't about anyone but you," I tell her, dropping to my knees before her in the grass, "This isn't about 'should'. This about your life. Your happiness. Please, Ellie...Tell me what you want. Tell me what will make you happy, and I'll make it happen, I swear. Just tell me the truth, because I'm about ready to burst at the seams, here."

"Trent..."

"Tell me what you want," I press.

Her gaze swings up to mine, and I know for certain that I've never seen anything as beautiful as her eyes welling up hopeful, terrified, utterly trusting tears.

"I want you, Trent," she whispers, laying her hands on my chest, "I want all of this. I've never wanted anything more in my entire life. Let me come with you, whatever that leads to. Just don't let this be goodbye. Please—"

But her words are silenced as I pull her to me and lay my ecstatic lips on hers. She throws her arms around my neck, kissing me deeply and earnestly. I feel her hot tears against my own scruffy skin, falling between us like warm rain. Her entire body is trembling, and I hold her flush against me, willing every ounce of comfort and strength I can muster to rush into her and allay her fears.

"Thank god," I whisper, as she lays her head on my shoulder, "Ellie...I love you."

"I love you too," she says, sniffling, "But I'm scared shitless, you know."

"I know," I tell her, stroking her ash blonde hair, "It's a scary thing, following your dreams. But you know what? I'll be right here with you every step of the way. It's hard as hell, starting an entirely new life, but you're one of the toughest, brightest, bravest people I've ever met. You're going to be just fine. And when it feels like too much, when you need help, I'll be right next to you to carry the load."

"Do you promise?" she asks, looking up into my eyes.

"I promise that there's nothing in the world that will keep me away from you," I tell her, holding her perfect face in my hands. "I promise that I'll do everything in my power to make sure that you're happy, and cared for, and loved. I promise to love you, Ellie, with all my heart. I can't promise that you won't get hurt, or feel betrayed or lost. This life is full of heartache. But you can be damn sure that I won't ever the one to hurt you."

"I know," she says, smiling through her tears, "I don't know how, and I know that it's probably insane to hope for some kind of happy ending, but I trust you. I believe in you."

"Don't worry about happy endings just yet," I tell her, brushing away her tears with my thumbs, "We're still in the beginning!"

"I guess you're right," she says, laughing. The world seems to grow brighter every time this girl laughs. Her happiness is the light of my world, now. And I'll do everything I can to keep it burning.

"Look," I say, resting my hands on her waist, "We're heading out of here and getting right back on the road for our summer concert series. I don't want to force anything on you, but you're more than welcome to come along. In fact...it would be amazing if you would come. I'd understand if you wanted to take it slow—"

"No," she says, "I want to come. I want to see the country with you. I've never even seen the Pacific Ocean in my life! I can't go back to Barton, as easy as it would be. There's nothing for me there except diner food and lonely nights. It would be comfortable, sure, but I don't want comfort. I want to see how long this ride can last. I'll regret it for the rest of my life if I don't."

"As long as you're sure," I say, my heart swelling.

"I'm sure," she tells me adamantly, "I have no idea what I'm doing, or how I'm supposed to go about all of this...but maybe you could teach me?"

"Teach you how to be a rock star?" I laugh.

"Exactly," she says, kissing me happily on the cheek. "What do you say?"

"I say...welcome to lesson 101," I smile, pulling her to her feet.

"What's lesson 101?" she asks excitedly.

"Getting on the tour bus before it accidentally leaves you behind," I tell her.

We gather up all our camping supplies, giggling like the smitten young lovers we are. If only my fans could see me now, swooning over my dream girl like a goddamn Backstreet Boy. But you know what? I couldn't care less.

The world will have to come to terms with the fact that Trent Parker has fallen head over heels for the most amazing woman on the planet. Once they get to know Ellie, I'm sure no one will have any trouble understanding how she's managed to lock my heart up with about fifteen deadbolts.

She's not the only one leaping into a whole new way of life—I've never had one woman stick around for longer than one tabloid news cycle. This is quite a departure for both of us, but it's better that way. We'll learn from each other, teach each other, as we go along. It seems like a pretty good way to do things.

The tour bus starts up just as we leap inside. Ellie and I stumble into the main cabin where the guys are lounging in various states of disarray. They look up, happily surprised by our new traveling companion.

"You're coming with us?" Kenny asks excitedly.

"That I am," Ellie replies, dumping her half of the tent onto the floor, "Wherever it is we're going. Where are we going?"

"We've got about a day's worth of down time before we head to New York to kick off the summer tour," Rodney says, "I actually have no idea where we're going...Now that we're down a manager, we're sort of free agents."

"Yeah," Rodger says, "Where exactly are we staying tonight, Trent?"

"Beats me," I say, "Does anyone have any ideas?"

A moment of silence passes in the cabin as the bus wheels itself around to the dirt road. Finally, I hear Ellie clear her throat beside me.

"Well...Actually, I do have an idea. It's a little nutty, but I think it would be fun."

"By all means," I tell her, "Why don't you go give our driver a destination?"

She spins around and speaks in hushed tones with the bus driver. I can't help but grin like an idiot at the sight of her on the road with us. Whatever unfolds in the coming months, no matter how bat shit crazy things get, I know it will be the best time of my life. Ellie comes back toward us, looping her arm around my waist.

"So?" I ask, "Where are we headed, Miss Jackson?"

"You'll see," she says impishly, "But I promise, you'll be happy once we get there."

"Whatever you say," I tell her, throwing my arm over her shoulders, "I trust you."

"You'd better," she grins.

Beyond the windshield, the fields of green begin to blur into a long, rippling ribbon. The festival grounds shrink in our rearview mirror, and just like that, Hawk and Dove has drawn to a close. But my arm is still wrapped firmly around Ellie's shoulders.

It's hard to imagine that I didn't dream her up—but here she is, from now on. Wherever this next leg of the journey takes us, we'll be there together.

Chapter Twenty Three

Ellie

"Are we there yet?" Kenny whines, sprawled out across a cushy armchair.

I roll my eyes from the front of the bus. Who knew that rock musicians could be such babies?

"We're getting there Kenny. Keep on being a brave little soldier," I tease, earning a chuckle from Trent and the rest of the guys.

We've been on the road for the better part of the day by this point, killing time before heading up the East Coast to New York City. The full reality of my decision to come along for this summer-long joyride has yet to kick in. Right now, I'm riding a tidal wave of adrenaline and possibility. For the first time in my life, I feel like I'm charging full speed ahead toward my wildest dreams.

It's a feeling I could definitely get used to.

"Take the next exit," I instruct the bus driver, a middle aged man named Chuck with deep, rutted wrinkles and a big, goofy smile. We've bonded quite a bit today, he and I, as I've been in charge of navigation. For lack of a better idea, the guys turned the day over to me. And I have some pretty great accommodations in mind for us this evening.

"You got it, sweetheart," says Chuck, flipping on his turn signal.

Thick trees swallow up the bus on either side as we make our way further off the beaten path. I have a feeling that this is not exactly the established way to spend the eve of one's first national tour, but I can't think of a better way to bookmark this crazy week and get ready to spring off into a whole new chapter of my life. And the novelty will be good for the guys, too. They could use a little humbling once in a while.

"Are you getting to tell us what you've got up your sleeve, Jackson?" Trent asks, wrapping his arms around my waist from behind.

"This should all look pretty familiar to you," I say, twisting around to face him.

Trent peers through the windshield at the thickening foliage, the small town landmarks coming into view as we make our way along. Comprehension finally begins to dawn on that ruggedly handsome face of his.

"Well shit," he says, "I must have been pretty distracted the last time. I didn't even recognize the route!"

"*You* know where the hell we're going?" Rodney asks.

"Sure," Trent says, "Welcome to Barton, gentleman. The little town that raised our very own Eleanor."

"Barton?" Rodger says, chewing on the name of my hometown, "Never heard of the place."

"No one has," I tell them, "But I figured we could swing by my house, crash for the night, be normal people for a minute before setting off on our whirlwind adventure. You guys need a minute to catch your breath too—now that you're free agents, you'll need clear heads to put your band back on the right track. So, what do you say? A night of R&R sound good to you?"

"Do you think that there's a home cooked meal in our future?" asks Kenny excitedly.

"I think we can probably count on it," I smile, "Though don't be surprised if it's plant-based and comprised of super foods, knowing my mom."

"Plant-based? Super foods?" Rodney says quizzically, "Are you speaking English?"

"Don't worry," I tell him with a laugh, "I promise it'll be great."

"Hell, I'd be down for something low key after this week," Rodger says, "We're all of us small town boys ourselves, you know. Different small towns, of course, but all the same. It'll be like home for us, too."

"Super," I say, turning back to the road.

"You've got quite the imagination, don't you?" Trent says, laying a hand on the small of my back. I wink at him mischievously, letting him know without words that he hasn't seen anything yet. I have a feeling that my presence on the tour might turn a few conventions on their heads, but it'll be good for the guys to have a little feminine energy around. At least, that's what I keep telling myself. So far, it doesn't seem like anyone's annoyed by my presence, anyway.

Especially since they're used to dealing with Kelly.

The tour bus chugs along through the winding roads that lead home. As we start to pull onto familiar streets, I start to feel giddy. Passersby stop and stare at the enormous vehicle making its way through our sleepy town. I'm sure nothing like this has ever quite been seen in Barton before.

I wonder, with a little flip of my stomach, whether the people I've known all my life have been following my rock star escapades from afar? To everyone here, I'm still half of Ellie & Mitch, after all.

Mitch was never a favorite in Barton, but I hope that my coming here with the guys doesn't hurt his feelings any, as if he'd even find out about it.

I haven't heard a word from Mitch since he left the festival. I've just assumed that he headed back up to Boston again, to wait for another school year to start. He never felt at home in Barton the way I used to as a kid.

A sudden stab of sympathy for my estranged friend hits me in the gut. He acted atrociously at Hawk and Dove, but I can't help but feel a little responsible for his behavior. I knew that he had feelings for me, and I certainly didn't let him down easy.

Maybe there's a reconciliation somewhere in our future, but I'd call that a long shot. I think that Mitch was always destined to go his own way—open some tiny music venue in a small city and spend his life perfecting his technique on the dulcimer, or something. I do hope that he can find some kind of happiness without me, though.

As ugly as things turned between us, Mitch was one of the first people who really thought I was any good at writing songs. I owe him a lot for that scrap of recognition.

"There it is," I say proudly, all thoughts of Mitch fleeing my mind as my home comes into view.

"Cute," Kenny says.

"Cute?!" Rodney scoffs.

"Pull over here, Chuck," I tell the driver. He promptly swings the massive tour bus over to the side of the road, just in front of my drive way.

"Why do I get the feeling we look a tad out of place here?" Trent says.

"Let me go in first," I say, "This might be a bit of a shock for good old mom."

"I'd say," Rodger laughs.

The bus doors swing open, and I leap out, all but running to my front door. The sight of our shabby old Victorian nearly brings a tear to my eye. Hopefully, the place will be rid of unwanted pests this time around.

I have a feeling that my dad's money grubbing ass won't be coming around here any time soon after Trent's smack down. The further out of my life that man stays, the better off we'll all be. I got over the daydream of us ever coming together as a family again many years ago.

As far as I'm concerned, Kate and Mom round out my perfect family.

We're all each other needs.

I take the front porch steps two at a time and swing open the front door. Immediately, the smell of ginger tea with honey, mixing with a hint of pine wood, washes over me. It's the unmatchable scent of home, and it warms me through and through.

"Mom!" I cry, hurrying into the kitchen.

"Ellie?" I hear her say in astonishment. I round the corner and see her perched at the kitchen island with a big steaming mug in her hands.

I run to her, throwing my arms around her neck. "I didn't know when we'd see you again after...Ellie, I'm so sorry. I should have kicked him out the minute he got here. I didn't know that you'd be coming back, or I never—"

"It's OK Mom," I say, mumbling into her long white blonde hair, "It's over. I think we're rid of him."

"After all these years," she sighs, "I just can't say no to that man. I know you must think I'm weak for not throwing him to the curb—"

"Weak is the last thing I'd ever call you," I say adamantly, "You didn't do anything wrong. He's a rat, is all."

"I'm afraid that's right," she says, laying her hand on my cheek. "But Ellie...what are you doing here? I'm happy to see you, but...Good god, my dear, what is going on in that whirlwind life of yours?"

"You haven't been following the tabloids?" I laugh.

"I thought I'd wait and get the real story from you," she says.

"Is Kate here?" I ask.

"She is," I hear my sister's sleepy voice from behind me. I whirl around and see her enter the kitchen, rubbing sleep out of her eyes. I fly at her, wrapping her up in a bear hug. She squeezes me back, strong as ever.

"You're back," she says, "I'm so glad you're back. We were so worried."

"I'm sorry I didn't keep you guys in the loop," I tell them, "As soon as we got to the festival, everything started happening so fast."

"It's OK," Mom says, easing me down into a seat at the kitchen table. "It's impossible to live your life and be worried about reporting back."

"But for the love of god," Kate says, as she and Mom sit down at the table with me, "What the hell has been going on with you?"

"You want the cliff notes?" I ask.

"Go for it," Mom urges.

"OK," I begin, "This is all going to sound insane, just so you know."

"I delivered twins over a toilet last night," Kate drawls, "I'm OK with insane."

"Well," I say, "When Mitch and I got down to Hawk and Dove, we found out that we had a space reserved for us in the talent campsite. Only, as we went to set up our stuff, we found Trent Parker trying to pitch a tent right in our spot."

"Mitch must have thrown quite the little temper tantrum," Mom says.

"You've got that right," I laugh, "But I ran into Trent one on one the next morning, and he was perfectly...wonderful. Not anything like the character he puts on for the fans. Mitch and I had our first show, and Trent came out and everything...but it turned out that the gossip blogs had taken some of my words out of context and assumed that Mitch and I were an item. He got all excited and tried to act on his little crush, then got all upset when I rebuked him. We had a pretty nasty fight. Trent was there to step in, but...It got ugly.

"How ugly?" Kate asks,

"Ugly enough," I say, remembering the look in Mitch's eyes when he raised his hand to me. "But after that, Trent and I started getting close. And closer..."

"You don't need to go into the details on that one," my mom winks.

"Thanks," I blush, "But it eventually got out to all the media, and that got under Mitch's skin enough that he up and left. I was devastated, obviously, and then there was this horrible manager of Trent's that kept trying to shake me off...Everything came to a head, and that's when I came back here."

"You poor thing," Kate says, taking my hand, "The last thing you probably needed was to see Dad."

"Yeah," I say, "But thank god Trent came and brought me back. He was...amazing. The last night of the festival, he stepped in and played a set with me, and even brought me on stage with his band. It was incredible."

"How did you guys leave it?" Mom asks, "I mean, you're back here now..."

"I got scared," I admit, "About diving into this rock star world he's living in. But he asked me to come on tour with his band this summer and, well...I couldn't refuse. I know it's risky, and might be a huge mistake, but I had to take the risk. I have to see where this leads."

"You're a brave girl," Mom says, smiling, "But...shouldn't you be off with them right now, then?"

"Well, that's the thing," I say, "The tour kicks off in New York in a day or so...And the band needs somewhere to hang out in the meantime..."

"What are you suggesting?" Kate asks.

"Why don't you guys take a took out the front windows," I tell them.

Mom and Kate spring up from the table and rush to the front of the house. I hear their twin gasps as they see the tour bus idling on the curb.

"Here?!" My mom cries excitedly.

"We're going to have a rock star sleepover?!" Kate exclaims.

"Is that OK?" I ask, "I realize it's a bit late to be seeking permission..."

"Are you kidding?" Mom says, "This will be like living in New York all over again! I used to hang out with musicians all the time, before I got all domesticated."

"Wait until I tell the girls at work about this," Kate breathes, "They're going to turn bright green!"

"And here I thought I'd have to convince you," I laugh, meeting them at the front door.

"We're no squares, Missy," my mom says, brushing her hair out of her face, "Bring them in! I should make...something. What do rock stars eat?"

"Whiskey and the adoration of fans?" I suggest.

"I'll figure something out," Mom says, rushing back into the kitchen.

Who would have thought, when we first moved into this place, that we'd one day be running a B&B for rowdy rock star types? I guess you never can tell what's going to happen in this crazy thing we call life.

"I need to change..." Kate says, rushing up to her room, "Would fishnets be trying too hard?"

"Yes," I chuckle, "Trust me, they're much more approachable than you'd think."

"Easy for you to say!" she cries, "You're one of them!"

"I guess you're right..." I say, as my mom and sister disappear inside the house.

I step back out onto the porch and wave toward the tour bus, signaling Chuck to pull into the driveway. The enormous vehicle moans up the incline and grumbles to a stop. The bus is practically as big as our house. I head over just as Trent and the guys are stepping down out of the hotel on wheels.

They look around our quiet little street, a little confused by the lack of bright lights and loud noises. I wonder when the last time was that they had a little small town hospitality.

"Come on," I say, taking Trent's hand, "Welcome to Chateau Jackson, gentlemen. I'm sure you'll find everything is to your liking."

We trudge on up the front walk, me and my escort of rock royalty. I'm glad we live in a relatively secluded part of town—no prying eyes have popped up to spy on us yet. I wonder how long it takes the paparazzi to catch up with Trent's comings and goings?

Hopefully, I can spare my mom and Kate that much, at least. I lace my fingers through Trent's as we climb the steps of my front porch. If I only could have known leaving this house for the festival what kind of amazing souvenirs I'd be bringing home with me.

The door swings open, and my mom and Kate appear in the threshold. I have to bite back my own laughter as I see the excited looks on their faces. They look for the world like two kids on Christmas morning. Kate's slipped on a very becoming little sundress, and even Mom is trying to affect her hard-won Lower East Side cool for the benefit of our musical guests.

"Everyone," I say, addressing the band, "This is my sister Kate, and this is my mom."

"You can call be Abby," my mom says quickly, offering a wide smile to the attractive young men on her doorstep. "Why don't you all come inside?"

"You really don't mind us staying here?" Kenny asks.

"Not at all," Kate says, "This will be a story for the grandkids, for sure."

"Not my grandkids," Mom says quickly, "I'm not a grandmother, or anything."

"Smooth, Mom," I mumble, grinning at her.

"I just want that point to be clear," she sniffs, opening the door for us.

The band mates follow me into the house while Chuck hangs out in the bus. I watch as the guys take in the homey details of our little abode. We really do have the kind of house that could only possibly have been lived in by three women. Every tiny detail has been attended to over the years, and even I have to admit that our home is one of the coziest there is.

It's incredibly strange to see four hard, rough and tumble bad boys making their way through our foyer. They look about as out of place as can be, though I guess that's probably what they thought about me too, the first time I came around.

"This is it!" I tell them gesturing to the kitchen and living room, "Plenty of couches to crash on, all the organic goodness you could eat, the works."

"It's really nice of you to have us, Ms. Jackson," Rodney says.

"Abby," Mom corrects him, "And it's no trouble. I don't have class all summer, so it's nice to have a little company around here."

"Do you guys want to see the back yard?" Kate offers, "We've got a nice little fire pit and everything."

"Cool," Rodger says, giving Kate a not-too-subtle once over. My sister leads the guys out the back door, but my mom steps forward and places a hand on Trent's arm holding him in place.

"I wanted to have a word with you, away from the others," she tells him.

For a moment, I'm afraid she's going to dive into a "what are your intentions" sort of speech, like she used to with the boys I dated in high school.

"Is everything OK, mom?" I ask.

"Oh, of course," she says, leading Trent and I into the living room. It's hard to believe that just a couple of days ago my father was here, perched hideously on our couch as though he ruled the household.

The very memory makes me grind my teeth in anger.

"What is it, Mom?" I ask.

"Actually Ellie," she says, "I was hoping to talk to Trent for a moment on his own, if you don't mind."

I look back and forth between my mother and the man that I've fallen so swiftly in love with. I'm a little surprised—I don't want Trent to feel cornered. But he just smiles kindly.

"It's cool," he says, "We'll meet you out back."

I leave the room, wondering at the absurdity of the situation. But if I stop and marvel at every outlandish thing that happens to me from now on, I'll never have a moment of peace.

I head out to the backyard, leaving my mom and Trent to have their little heart to heart.

Chapter Twenty Four

Ellie's mother looks after her retreating daughter, waiting to hear the swing of the back door as it settles back into its frame.

Her eyes swing toward me, and I notice once again that they're practically identical to Ellie's. Only, there's a wisdom and a certain resigned toughness to Abby's eyes that has yet to settle in Ellie's. Hopefully, it will never have to.

"I'm glad you're here Trent," Abby says, gesturing for me to take a seat, "It's nice to see you again under less...awkward circumstances."

"I hope that I didn't step out of line the other day," I tell her, "Really, I only came to make sure that Ellie was OK, and to try and convince her to see the festival through. I never meant to stick myself in the middle of any...family stuff."

"I'm not upset with you," she assures me, "Although you do have rather outrageous timing. That's the first time the girls' father has been here in about a decade."

"It must have been rough, seeing him again," I say.

"It was," she replies, "I'd like to think that the whole issue of our divorce is resolved, but those things never quite stop hurting. I like to be strong for my girls, and I'm afraid that they saw a rather vulnerable side of me that day."

"There's nothing wrong with being vulnerable," I say.

"According to the above-it-all rock star?" she laughs.

"You've got me there," I smile. "But honestly, I thought you handled yourself very well. Given the situation, and all."

"Thank you Trent," she says, "But I didn't keep you here to tell me how wonderful I am as a mother. I just need to make a few things perfectly clear."

"By all means," I say.

"This family has been through a lot," she begins, "From before the girls were born, things have not been...ideal. There's been a lot of heartbreak in Ellie's life."

"You can hear it in her music," I say.

"It's true," her mom replies, "I'm not suggesting that she's some kind of wilting flower that needs to be handled delicately. She's a scrappy little thing, always has been. There's nothing she can't do when she puts her mind to it."

"I don't doubt that at all," I say.

"She gets what she wants," Abby continues, "And it doesn't take a genius to see that what she wants right now is to be with you."

"I hope you're right," I say honestly.

"Is that what you want as well, Trent?" she asks, "Do you want to be with Ellie as much as she wants the same? I need you to be honest with me."

It's a frank line of questioning, but I step up to the plate anyway. "If anything, Abby, I want it more than she does."

She scans my face for any trace of bullshit, and I can practically feel the heat of her gaze as it sweeps over me. But she can't find any hint of a lie there, because I'm telling her the truth. There's nothing I want more than to have Ellie at my side.

"All that I ask then," Abby says softly, "Is that you keep her best interests at heart, always."

"Of course," I say.

"Even if that means one day letting her go," she finishes.

That one's tougher to swallow.

"I thought you wanted her to have what she wants?" I reply.

"I want her to be safe, and healthy, and happy," Abby says, "But that doesn't always go hand in hand with getting what she wants. I need you to be accountable for this, because once she's got her mind set on something, there's nothing that will shake her loose. I need you to promise that you'll let her go, if being with you becomes too...much."

"Too much?" I ask.

"Too dangerous," she says, "Too traumatic, or risky."

"That's no small thing you're asking," I tell her.

"I know," she says, "But I need you to promise all the same. If you think she'll be better off without you, you have to do the right thing. You have to let her go."

I stare at Abby, the weathered, proud matriarch. As much as I'm loathe to think of life without Ellie, I have to admit that she's right. If I thought that being with me was doing harm to the woman I love, I'd have no choice but to end it.

"I promise, Abby," I say quietly, "If I think she's better off without me...I'll do what I have to do."

"Thank you, Trent," she says, resting her hand on mine.

"You don't think it will come to that, do you?" I ask, feeling like a teenager again.

"What do I know?" she says, laughing off the gravity of the situation, "I'm just an old lady, now. I don't know anything about the lives you crazy kids lead."

I smile at her, happy for the break in heavy conversation. "And you promise you're not mad that I threatened to beat up your ex?"

"Oh please," she says, waving my comment away, "If I had a nickel for every time someone wanted to punch that man in the face, my mortgage would be paid off and then some."

"You don't think he's dangerous, do you?" I ask her.

"Ellie's Dad?" she says, "What makes you think that?"

"I don't mean, like, stalker dangerous," I say quickly, "I just...I didn't have the best relationship with my dad growing up, and it's never really...gone away. The harm he did. I guess I'm just asking whether you think seeing him again is going to, you know..."

"Set Ellie off?" she says, "Don't worry about that. He can't hurt us anymore, or you, for that matter. He'll disappear back into the woodwork and mind his business now, I'm sure."

I nod, but I'm far from convinced. There was a relentless, selfish need in that man that I don't think is going to be extinguished so easily. If he shows up again, and hurts Ellie in my presence one more time, I don't know what I'm going to do.

I picture myself taking a swing at him, really kicking the shit out of his sorry ass...but as I try and picture him in my mind's eye, his face keeps becoming my own father's. I know that some of my outrageous ire toward Ellie's dad has everything to do with my own unresolved issues.

Unlike her father, my own has been completely disinterested in my career so far. I've never gotten an ounce of respect from that man, and I know that no amount of success will ever change that.

But now, with Ellie in my life, I feel like there's something about me that he'd actually be proud of. My family would love Ellie—everyone does. Will there come a point when bringing them a wonderful girl as a peace offering will stitch up our family? Somehow, I doubt I could stomach such a thing.

Abby rises and leads me toward the backyard. I can't help but run through the growing list of people who have been cast off this past week. Ellie's dad, that Mitch kid, and of course Kelly, are all far too close to us for comfort. Kelly especially could try and do some real damage to our band if she puts her mind to it.

I spurned her pretty dramatically—I wouldn't put it past her to try something crazy. The schemes she could be cooking up right now hang heavily over my head.

As I follow Ellie's mom out into the backyard, I'm all but forced to let go of doomsday scenarios.

Their yard is like a fairy world in miniature. String lights hang over the wide patch of green grass, illuminating the scene below. A charming picnic table stands at the center of the space, all set out with glassware and oilcloth. Tall pine trees form a protective ring around the yard, secluding us from the rest of the world. Fireflies flit and fly all over, blinking in and out as I look on.

I laugh as I catch sight of my band mates. Kate has put them to work already. They sit at the picnic table with a dozen ears of corn between them, shucking of the husks. They look like three overgrown boys, helping Mommy prepare for dinner. It's too much for me to handle.

Ellie has a gigantic pitcher of iced tea balanced on her hip, and Kate is tending to the fire pit. This has got to be the most unlikely assortment of people ever to collaborate on a backyard feast. I've seen a lot of crazy things as a rock star, but this scene is right up there among the greatest hits.

"You OK?" Ellie asks softly, hurrying over to me.

"Sure," I say, "She just wanted to get to know me a little."

"That's all?" Ellie asks pointedly.

"That's all," I say, bending the truth like a goddamn pretzel. "What's going on out here?"

"Oh! We're going to have a cookout," Ellie smiles.

"Do you want one ear or two?" Kenny calls out to me, his pant legs rolled up like he's goddamn Tom Sawyer or something.

"Two for me," I tell him, "And keep them coming. Can I do anything to help?"

"Actually," Ellie says, setting down her pitcher, "I was wondering if you'd come on a little errand with me?"

"Sure," I say, "Where to?"

"You'll see," she says, "I just want to set the record straight about a couple of things. I'll explain everything on the way. I'm sure we'll be back in time for dinner."

"Whatever you want," I say, wincing unnoticeably as Abby's warning comes back into my mind.

"Be back in a bit!" Ellie calls to the group, taking me by the hand. She leads me back through the house and over to her little banged-up sedan.

As we settle in, I lean over the cockpit and lay my lips firmly on hers. She kisses me back, a little surprised by my force but as game as ever.

"What was that for?" she asks, starting the car.

"Nothing," I say, "I'm just really glad to be here."

"Me too," she smiles.

I keep my mouth shut tight as we skirt around the tour bus and out into the little town. I'll probably never have to act on the deal I made with her mother, after all. Why bother bringing it up at all? This moment is too nice to spoil with "what if's", anyway.

Chapter Twenty Five

Ellie

"I thought we were having dinner at your place?" Trent says.

I smile, turning into the parking lot of Vera's diner. "We are," I tell him, "This is just something of a business meeting."

"Whatever you say," Trent sighs. He's not the only one who's bound to initiate flights of fancy in this relationship.

We step out of the car and make our way into the restaurant. A string of bells rings our welcome as I push open the door and step into the familiar, homey space. Everything's exactly the same as it ever was in my favorite haunt, except for one feature.

"I'll be damned..." I breathe, taking a gander at the gigantic picture of me that's tacked up in the restaurant's front lobby. "Vera wasn't kidding."

Trent smiles at the picture, and image of me from my first concert at Hawk and Dove. No doubt Vera had one of her young employees print it off some gossip website or another.

"You're a hometown hero," Trent teases, wiggling his eyebrows, "You should be proud."

"Or something," I say.

"Well, look who it is!" I hear a familiar voice crow. In a heartbeat, a pair of meaty arms have me all wrapped up in a hug—my face pressed uncomfortably close to some very familiar cleavage. Vera holds me like I'm a long lost daughter, returned from the war. She's nothing if not hopelessly dramatic whenever she gets the chance.

"What did you think, I could stay away from your home fries forever?" I laugh, straightening up in her crushing embrace.

"So it's just the cooking you're back for?" she sniffs, "I thought you'd want to come grace me with all your tales of celebrity."

"I don't have all that many yet," I remind her, "But I promise not to leave you out of the loop."

"You're damned right," she says, "I'm singlehandedly responsible for feeding you and that Mitch character all through high school. The least you could..." but she trails off, catching herself having mentioned Mitch.

"It's OK Vera," I tell her, "It's not like we were star crossed lovers or anything."

"Tell that to him," she says, "You know that boy was crazy about you. In fact, it seems like you're collecting smitten musicians left and right these days..." I follow her gaze to Trent, who's been standing at the door, waiting for a break in her bumbling affections.

"Hello," he says smoothly, sidling up next to me, "I'm Trent Parker."

"I know who you are," Vera says, eyeing him up and down. "You're the fancy pants rock star who's stolen our Ellie's heart away."

"Vera!" I exclaim.

"I just call them like I see them," she says, raising her hands in the air.

"That you do," I say, tugging on Trent's arm. "Come on, we've got someone else to meet."

I tow my rock star away from Vera, over to my favorite booth in the place. As we approach the table, I see a familiar face waiting for us. Just like I planned.

"Hello Teddy," I say, drawing up to the booth.

The young man looks up, doing a bad job of masking his nerves. "H-hi Ellie," he smiles, "It's good to see you again."

"I'm sure it is," I say coolly, "This is Trent Parker, as I'm sure you know."

"Of course," Teddy says, "It's an honor to meet you, Mr. Parker."

"It's Trent," he says, looking confused. "Ellie, who's this?"

"This," I say, sliding into the booth, "Is the little man who's responsible for my first landslide media coverage. You know—the one I got trapped under just as I was arriving at Hawk and Dove."

"You didn't like the story I wrote?" Teddy asks, as Trent sits down beside me.

"I didn't like that you lied about where your story was going to be printed," I tell him archly. "I thought we agreed that our interview was going to go in the Barton Bugle?"

"We never...*actually* specified," Teddy says, his voice rising a note with every word.

"You're going to make a great journalist," I tell him, "You're already weaseling through loopholes like a pro."

"You have to admit," he says, leaning onto the table, "That article did cause a pretty big spike in your popularity."

"It also caused a huge falling out between Mitch and I," I tell him, crossing my arms, "A falling out that wouldn't have happened if you'd quoted me correctly."

"I'm...I'm sorry if you were hurt," Teddy says quietly, eyes darting nervously toward Trent, "That wasn't my intention at all. I just knew how talented you were, and figured that I could earn myself a reputation in the music journalism world with an exclusive story about you."

"It was a shitty thing to do," I tell him.

"I know," he sighs.

"But," I go on, "The fact of the matter is that breaking off my partnership with Mitch was for the best."

"Oh?" Teddy says, his ears all but perking up, "You don't say?"

"I do say," I tell him, "In a weird, roundabout way, you're sort of responsible for the start of a much more...exciting collaboration."

Teddy's eyes grow wide, skirting between me and Trent. "You mean...you two?" he says breathlessly, "I did that?!"

"I wouldn't go that far," Trent says under his breath.

"Your article created the circumstances that let Trent and I...get to know each other," I tell Teddy, "So, I can't be that angry with you. In fact, I wanted to offer you another exclusive, if you're interested."

"Of course I'm interested!" Teddy squeals, "An interview? With both of you?"

"Is that OK, Trent?" I ask, "Since we're here."

"Oh...Why not," Trent says, "You're the mastermind, here."

"Lovely," I say, "Here's the thing, Teddy. There have been a lot of rumors going around about me and Trent, and I want the record set straight. I'm offering you the chance to be the person who does that straightening. There are a couple of conditions, though. For one thing, you have to actually report what we say accurately. Trust me, you won't need to take quotes out of context to make our story more interesting. Also, you need to publish the story in the Bugle first. It'll get picked up by every single music magazine and blog out there, but I want to give back to the place that taught me how to write in the first place, you understand?"

"Absolutely," Teddy says, "Can we do this right now?"

"I don't see why not," I say.

Teddy plunges his hand into his pocket and digs out a tape recorder. Trent raises his eyebrow at the device.

"How did you know to bring that?" he asks suspiciously.

"A reporter always comes prepared," Teddy says, self importance oozing from every pore.

"Right," I say, "Why don't we get started?"

"Just one minute," Vera says, bustling up to us with three mugs and a pot of coffee, "No good conversation ever happened without a cup of Joe to keep it going."

I think of my and Trent's early mornings at Hawk and Dove, sipping on coffee together as the world dawned over the festival. "You may be right," I allow.

Satisfied, Vera pushes a mug of coffee toward each of us and hurries away. I take a sip, stealing a glance at Trent. He looks benignly mystified, happy enough to go along with my master plan. I like that in a man.

Teddy fumbles with the settings on his tape recorder and finally sets the thing down on the table, just like he did not too long ago, back before any of the Hawk and Dove madness ensued. He looks up at us, eyes big and hopeful.

"So," Teddy begins, "You two are back from the Hawk and Dove festival with some exciting news for the rest of the world..."

"That's right," I tell him, "During our time in Kansas, Trent and I struck up a new musical partnership that we plan on exploring from here on out."

"We're both very excited to see where it takes us," Trent puts in.

I have a feeling that's he's not just talking about the music, now.

"Do you have any big plans for your collaboration?" Teddy asks eagerly.

"We do," I say, "This summer, I'll be touring with Trent and his band as they make their way around the country."

"In what capacity?" Teddy asks.

"Oh...You know," Trent smiles, "Muse, and such."

"Trent and I might play some new stuff we've been working on," I suggest, "Or maybe I'll open for the guys a couple of times. We haven't worked out the specifics. But we were so excited to find so much musical common ground that we want to keep up our partnership."

"Trent," Teddy says, "Don't you think that fans who've grown used to your harder, tougher image might take issue with Ellie's presence during this tour?"

"Anyone who thinks that way just doesn't have any idea how tough Ellie really is," Trent says, throwing me a smile.

"Let me rephrase," Teddy says, "Your styles of music are so different. Trent, you play hardcore rock, and Ellie, your songs are far more folksy and lyrical. How do you expect resolve that disparity?"

"Just because we're different, doesn't mean we don't complement each other," Trent jumps in, "A little variety makes for an exciting partnership. Ellie and I seem very different at first glance, but there's a lot that we see eye to eye on. Our differences only strengthen our resolve about the things that are really important."

"That's very insightful," Teddy says.

"You sound surprised," Trent sneers.

"No! It's just...Your tone during interviews is usually not so..."

"Intelligent," Trent says. "I know that. My fans should brace themselves from here on out for a different shade of Trent Parker than they're used to. I've been doing some spring cleaning, in terms of my personal brand, my approach to music and my public persona. I've let myself become pretty predictable these past couple of years, and I admit that I've sold out some.

This tour will be a great opportunity to take back my autonomy as an artist. I'm done putting on airs for people, or pretending to be something that I'm not. I plan to make a full return to authenticity this summer, and that might piss some people off. But you know what? I'm sick of trying to live my life for the sake of record sales.

The true fans will stay loyal, no matter what. And those who don't like the new direction I'm taking can go find some other Top 40 machine to worship."

"Strong words," Teddy says excitedly, "Ellie, do you see yourself as part of this transformation in Trent? Do you feel like you're the catalyst for this change?"

"I don't think it's a transformation as much as a revelation," I say carefully, "I feel very honored to have Trent trust me the way he does. We're very open with each other."

"Pardon me for saying so," Teddy starts, "But this sounds like more than a strictly musical partnership to me..."

I look over at Trent, hesitating. Is this it? Do we come clean to the public, our fans, as a couple? We've never even really discussed any titles or labels where our relationship is concerned. I'd feel rather strange calling Trent Parker my "boyfriend".

He's much more to me than that, after all.

Trent takes my hand under the table and smiles cavalierly at Teddy. "We're partners in many senses of the word," he says. "Maybe even every sense."

"Meaning...?" Teddy leads.

"Did I stutter?" Trent barks, "I just fed you your headline. Take it or leave it, twerp."

Teddy turns eighteen shades of red, and I have a feeling that I'm blushing just as deeply. Just like that, we've declared ourselves a pair to the rest of the world. There's no turning back now.

"Good luck with your story," I tell Teddy, standing up from the table, "And remember, no fudging the quotes."

"You got it," he says softly, as Trent and I begin to walk away. Vera waves at us as we make our way back to the car, and I'm pretty sure I see her tacking up a second picture onto my wall of fame—one that includes Mr. Trent Parker.

"You're pretty good at this media thing, Jackson," Trent tells me, as we slip back into the car, "Maybe you'll be our new manager?"

"Please," I scoff, "I've got my own brand to deal with, thank you very much."

"Well...Maybe you could stick around in a more permanent capacity anyway," Trent says, "Like...as an actual band member?"

I let my keys fall away from the ignition. "What?" I say dumbly.

"You should be a part of the band," he repeats, "You're already coming on tour with us. And now that we're between managers, we can make any drastic changes that we want."

"I've only played with you guys once," I exclaim, "You haven't even talked it over with the others."

"They love you," he insists, waving away my protests, "And besides, I'm the front man. I call the shots."

"Why do I feel like they would take issue with that?" I laugh.

"Hypothetically, then," he says, laying a hand on my knee. His smallest touch still sends chills straight through me, "Is that something you might possibly be interested in, in the future?"

"God Trent, I don't know," I tell him, my breath coming hard and fast, "Why don't you let me get through this tour, and then we can talk?"

"Why wait until the end of the tour?" he persists, "If you decided now, we could make our debut right away!"

"Why are you pushing this?" I ask, a little alarmed by his attitude.

"I...I'm sorry," he says, "You're right. I'm getting ahead of myself...I guess I just want you to feel safe with us. Like you're not going to get hurt, or anything."

"I don't think that," I tell him, a little confused. "*Should* I be worried?"

"No," he says quickly, "No, of course not. Sorry, I'm an asshole. I just want to protect you as best I can, is all."

"If you want to protect me," I say, "Don't try so damn hard to keep me safe."

"That doesn't quite follow," he laughs.

"What I mean is, don't hold on too tight," I tell him, "That always spells trouble."

"Isn't that what Joni Mitchell told Graham Nash?" he asks.

"Look at you!" I exclaim, "Pulling out the Joni Mitchell trivia...Are you just trying to impress me?"

"If I can be honest," he whispers, "I actually have a secret music crush on Joni Mitchell. Always have. Don't you dare tell anyone, you got it?"

"Got it," I laugh, shaking off his bout of over-protectiveness. "Let's get home, shall we? I'm sure they're all waiting for us."

We start off through the back roads, sitting in silence. It isn't even awkward, just sitting with Trent without the distraction of conversation. I've never felt that with a man, before. Usually, silence just means that we've run out of things to talk about, but with Trent it's different.

Even without words, I feel like we're sharing something, just being here together. Our communication doesn't depend on words and phrases—our understanding of each other is far deeper than that.

I let my eyes wander over his body as we pull up to a red light.

He leans back casually in my passenger seat, one knee bent. His bright green eyes are gazing off into the middle distance, and his well-muscled body is perfectly balanced in its stillness. I still get taken off guard by how gorgeous he is, when I look at him long and hard like this.

But one thing has changed. I'm not worried anymore about matching his physical perfection. I'm not worried about what we might look like together, or who might have a problem with us. When we're together, he makes me feel like I'm his ideal woman, that there's no one else in the world he'd rather be with. I've never felt sexier in my life than I feel when I'm with him. His own beauty doesn't intimidate me anymore, because it isn't just his body that I'm in love with—it's his soul, too.

"Eyes on the road, you," he says, catching me staring at him. I ease my foot onto the pedal as the light turns green. It's a good thing these roads are so familiar to me, because I'm having a hard time concentrating on anything apart from how much I want Trent right now.

"You're not too hungry, are you?" I ask, my voice riding low in my register. My voice is always the first thing to betray my lust.

He looks over at me, intrigued by my tone. "That depends," he says, "On what kind of hunger we're talking about."

"I see," I murmur. "Well, if you're amenable to the idea...we could always take the scenic route home. I wouldn't mind showing you a little more of my hometown before we head out."

"Did you have a particular place in mind?" he asks, placing a hand firmly on my bare inner thigh. I draw in a deep breath, trying to keep my hands steady on the wheel.

"There's a lovely grove out in the woods," I breathe, writhing a little as his fingers work further and further up my leg. I can feel a deep, throbbing need growing between my legs even as I speak.

"That sounds great," he purrs, leaning toward me. As I flip on my turn signal, Trent lays a sweet kiss at the base of my neck, running his fingertips along the skin of my thigh. I need to be out from behind the wheel as soon as humanly possible, that much is for sure.

I reroute us as fast as I can, hurtling along the country roads until we reach a little dirt path leading off into the thick woods. I turn off into the forest, breathing deeply as Trent's fingers graze against the warm wetness just beyond the thin cotton of my panties. I've been back to this little corner of the woods with a couple of beaus in my day, but never with the sense of urgency that I have now.

"You're going to make me drive us into a tree," I moan, navigating the bumpy trail.

"You'd better pull over then," Trent growls, "Because I don't know how much longer I can keep from getting on top of you..."

I swerve off into a secluded clearing, throwing the car into park and switching off the engine. Darkness engulfs us as we rush into each other's arms, out in the middle of deep, dark woods. I scramble onto my knees in the driver's seat, wrapping my arms around Trent's shoulders. His fingers brush aside the wet panel of fabric that rests against my slit, and I moan as he begins to stroke me there. My thighs tremble as his fingers caress me, moving deeper and deeper until finally sliding up within me.

My breath is coming in short little bursts as I tumble into his lap, unable to keep upright as he begins to knead and flick my most sensitive flesh.

He knows exactly how to touch me, precisely how to get me off. I bring my mouth imploringly to his as he traces luscious circles around that sensitive little nub, urging me onward toward the latest staggering orgasm.

"I love making you feel good," he groans in my ear, rubbing me with dexterous, magnificent grace. I try to reply, but I can't manage anything but a low moan as that hot, familiar pressure builds up inside of me.

I grab onto him as I feel myself reaching the height of my pleasure. He knows that I'm close, that I'm just about to topple over the edge. Just before I come to the crest of that wave, he breaks off—lifting me up into his arms and into the back seat. I let out a groan of anticipation, of even more heightened need.

"I want to be there with you," he says, sitting back against the well-worn seat.

He doesn't have to say it twice.

I reach for his belt with an urgency I've never known before, ripping open the buckle and sliding his jeans down his firm thighs. He's already rock hard for me. I love that just touching me can do that to him.

Trent slips my panties down over my ass, and I wiggle free from the flimsy garment as fast as I can. I'm straddling him on the backseat, on top and savoring every moment.

He grabs onto my hips, looking up at me in the darkness. Even here, his eyes glow like two bright emerald orbs. Slowly, I lower myself down towards the hard length of his member. A groan rips from his throat as I let the tip of him rest against my wet slit. I hover there for a moment, letting him wait for it, just a little. I like taking control every once in a while, I'm coming to find. With my hands planted firmly on his shoulders, I lower myself just an inch, taking the bulging tip of him inside of me.

We breathe out together, relishing the feel of him sliding slowly into me. Inch by inch, I take him—sliding down onto his rock hard shaft. Finally, I find I can't wait anymore.

"Get a condom," I say breathlessly.

He doesn't waste time, and quickly wraps his manhood.

I press down onto him, gasping as I feel him slip up, deep inside my body. His fingers dig into the flesh of my hips as the sensation overwhelms him.

For a moment, we stay perfectly still, just basking in the feeling of meeting here, connecting in this most intimate of ways. But our desire can't be held at bay by wonder for very long.

As one, we move together, our bodies bucking wildly in the backseat of my car. I brace myself against the roof, bouncing up and down on the hard length of him. Further and further he drives up inside of me, spreading me open with each passing thrust.

I lean into him, hungry for as much of him as I can take. I want to feel every single inch of Trent as he drives ever further into me.

"Oh," I gasp, as he looses a hand and brings it back down between my legs. He starts to play with me again, rubbing and flicking me toward bliss.

The rest of my words get caught in my throat as I'm rendered speechless by thundering, unstoppable pleasure. I can feel him growing stiffer inside of me, even as I careen toward orgasm with every passing moment. I know that he's right on the brink with me, that he's about to lose it too.

I lower my eyes to his, wanting to share this moment with him. His handsome features are screwed up into a blissful, earnest mask. I muster up all the concentration I can manage and utter one word, my gaze locked with his.

"*Come.*"

His pummeling member pulses within me, just as I'm transported with him into pure ecstasy. We come together, our eyes closing in bliss as the shockwaves of sensation pass through us. My fingers dig into Trent's shoulders as I feel him filling me.

He bucks his hips as my own orgasm rattles through me, sweeping like wildfire over every single nerve. I slump against him, unable to even sit up straight, and he wraps his strong arms around my waist, holding me there. Our chests heave in unison, our breaths hot and heavy.

A choir of crickets serenades us from the forest as we slowly regain our senses. I peer at him in the darkened backseat, grinning from ear to ear.

"See what happens when you start pawing me?" I say, poking my finger playfully into his chest.

"Yeah," he says, "I'd better start pawing you more often."

My laugh echoes in the enclosed car as I roll off him, retrieving my panties from the floor. "I hope no one's worried about where we've gone off to," I say.

"They can deal with it," he says, straightening up. "We can't be held accountable for forces beyond our control."

"Beyond our control is right," I agree, clamoring back up into the driver's seat.

I guide my little sedan back onto the beaten path as Trent pulls himself together. I have to admit, this inexhaustible lust thing is working out just fine for me. But left to our own devices, I'm not sure how we'd ever get anything done.

Luckily, we'll have a touring schedule to keep us on track for the rest of the summer.

We sail back to my little Victorian home, all smiles. Night has fallen over Barton, and the fireflies are out in their full numbers.

As we climb out of the car and make our way back out to the yard, I can already hear raucous voices blending together in song and conversation. I open the back gate for Trent, and we come upon a most remarkable and unexpected sight: my family and Trent's band in the middle of what appears to be a modest bacchanal.

"You guys started the party without us?" I exclaim, taking in the scene.

There are plates piled high with all kinds of wholesome goodies—fat ears of corn, fluffy rolls, the works—spread out all over the picnic table. Our little fire pit is roaring heartily, illuminating the five faces gathering around it.

Kate is sandwiched by Rodney and Rodger, and the trio appears to be passing a bottle of merlot merrily between them.

Kenny and Mom sit across the way, arms thrown over each other's shoulders, in the middle of some drinking song or other. The assembled partiers look up as we approach, greeting us with happy cheers.

"Hope you don't mind that we got a move on!" Kate says, a little tipsy.

"Not at all," Trent grins, leading me toward the fire, "As long as there are some eats and half a bottle left, I'm a happy camper."

"Help yourself!" my Mom says, grinning happily, "It's not often that I get to party like a rock star, you know!"

"I'd say that the rock stars are partying like *you* tonight," I tease her, sitting down before the blaze. "This is quite the gathering, isn't it?"

"You can't tell anyone though," Rodney says firmly, "It would ruin our image. We're supposed to be out trashing hotels rooms every night, remember."

"Ah, screw your image," Kate says, punching him playfully on the shoulders, "Haters to the left! Right? Right?"

"That's right, Kate," I tell her, accepting the bottle of wine as it comes my way. Trent settles in next to me with a couple heaping plates of food, and we dig in, having worked up quite the appetite on the way over.

The conversation is easy, the wine plentiful, and the company surprisingly perfect. The night wears on with song and laughter, and I'm sure that I've never been this happy in my life. I don't feel as though I've come home again, exactly, because just about everything about my world has changed since I was here last. But sitting here, with my family, and Trent, and the band, I feel like I'm making some kind of tentative peace between my past and my future.

I'm weaving together the two worlds I've been straddling, finding new ways to seize my unknown future while holding my history near to my heart. It's a brand new sort of compromise, and maybe there will come a time where I have to choose between who I've been and who I want to be...but not tonight.

As the hours wear on, and heads begin to nod, we make our way back inside.

The boys collapse on couches and sleeping bags as Mom and Kate trudge upstairs. Trent practically carries me up to my old bedroom, chuckling a little as he takes in how very pink most of my childhood possessions are.

Gently, he lays me down on my familiar bed, snuggling in beside me. We barely fit on my slim little mattress, but it will do for the night. We'll see plenty of sprawling beds and king sized suites this summer, but for tonight we rest like regular people.

In my final moments before sleep, I wonder at the strange, magical turn my life has taken.

Most girls have posters of rock stars in their bedrooms—and here I am with the real thing. I have no way of knowing what lies in store for Trent and me. We could be headed for years of happiness, or a disastrous falling out in some far flung concert venue later this summer.

But whatever happens, I will always have these days to cherish. For the rest of my life, I'll have the memories of our wild courtship, our festival nights, our early mornings, for myself.

If this insane chance we're taking doesn't pan out, if it turns out that a hawk and dove just can't find their happiness together, I'll have no choice but to accept it.

But for tonight, and tomorrow night, and as many nights as fate is willing to grant me, I get to stay here in the moment with this amazing person I'm falling in love with.

And that's the stuff that the best love songs are made of.

THE END

About the Author

Amanda is a 24 year old graduate student studying computer science at a great Midwest University. Originally from Kansas, Amanda got her inspiration for the setting of Hawk & Dove from her own small hometown. She's a huge computer nerd, loves indie rock and bluegrass, and is a self-proclaimed bookworm. You can contact her at author@amandalawless.com

Printed in Great Britain
by Amazon.co.uk, Ltd.,
Marston Gate.